DARK FORCES
UNnatural
UNSelection

PASTILLE SHEEN

Grosvenor House
Publishing Limited

This book is published by
Grosvenor House Publishing Ltd
Link House
140 The Broadway, Tolworth, Surrey, KT6 7HT.
www.grosvenorhousepublishing.co.uk

This book is a work of fiction. Any resemblance to
people or events, past or present, is purely coincidental.

A CIP record for this book
is available from the British Library

ISBN 978-1-80381-095-9
eBook ISBN 978-1-80381-096-6

To all members of the human race,
past and present, dedicated to protecting,
improving, extending and saving life

Acknowledgements

I would like to thank Grosvenor House Publishing for their work in preparing the book for publication. However, my main thanks go to Martin Ouvry for his editing of the book. As with my first book, *Moral Decay*, Martin has improved Dark Forces immeasurably.

UNnatural Selection –
Compromised – Fear for others

Ed Thorncroft, Brindle Llanos and Jail Sleeks had been holed up in London's East End in a massive disused warehouse complex beside the River Thames since very early morning, discussing funding for new POLO operations and the group's political activities. It had been a productive but long day, and now, approaching 11 p.m., the three of them were getting ready to notify their head Guardian and bodyguard when Ed's phone rang. As Ed answered, both Brindle and Jail's phones started ringing too.

"Syrinx," (Ed's handle) "it's Honu" (Kai Losua). "Get out of the building NOW! Armed police are arriving into the area."

Ed, saying nothing, immediately hung up and looked at Jail and Brindle, recognising instantly that they already knew.

Concerned, his face flushing, Ed uttered, "What's going on? They can't be here for us?" But all three knew they were.

"Move, guys, move," shouted an ashen-faced Jail as fear shone through his eyes. Lunging forward, he grabbed Brindle and Ed, pulling them towards a staircase leading to a corridor with a door at the far end that exited the warehouse on the Thames side.

The warehouse was far longer than an aircraft hangar, and Jail hoped that leaving at the far end would give them cover from law enforcement officers entering at the front of the complex.

Upon exiting the building, they could see torch lights dancing around the sky, and blue lights flashing in the distance. Now running for all they were worth between the old warehouse buildings, a cacophony of sirens, yelling and intertwined voices were coming ever closer.

Brindle grabbed Ed and Jail. His piercing Arctic-blue eyes stood out amid the dim warehouse lights, and with fear etched into his face, he said, "Keep running. I'm armed – I'll hold them off."

Ed thrust his fists in the air, his expression screaming at Brindle while he whispered, "No, we go together."

Brindle momentarily buried his hands in his hair, then leaned forward, grabbing Ed. "We won't get away, Ed. You must realise that. There are too many of them. Go, man, go. The organisation won't survive if we're all caught."

Jail leaned in, his face almost touching Ed's. "Brindle's right, Ed, we have to go. We must go now!"

Slamming his fists on the ground, his body tense, and screaming inside, Ed murmured, "No." He was now nose to nose with Brindle. Brindle pulled back and placed his hand on Ed's shoulder, squeezing firmly. His face gave away his emotions: a stoical look took hold, and a crooked smile spoke of his deep sadness. As Brindle's sad smile waned, he took hold of Ed's other shoulder, squeezing briefly to acknowledge his friend's concern and loyalty. Then, drawing his weapon, Brindle took off in the direction whence they came.

Now scurrying towards the torch lights, he could see armed officers in the distance as he weaved his way between various obstacles scattered around the warehouse buildings.

Ed and Jail continued apace in the opposite direction, their progress hindered by the junk littering the warehouses. Then, approaching the corner of an adjoining building, shots rang out, startling the pair. Rounding the corner, Ed stopped abruptly, twisting his body 180 degrees to look back at what was happening. Peering around the corner, he could see a myriad of lights illuminating Brindle.

More shots were fired, causing Ed to take a sharp breath and his body to stiffen in fear. He watched in horror as Brindle was propelled backwards by the impact of a bullet, slumping to the ground between a batch of tyres. Horrified, Ed put his face in his hands, pushing himself up against the wall and screaming inside: *No, no, no.* Then Jail shouted in a low, muffled screech, "Ed, we don't have time to grieve. Move it, move it. Now."

Heavy-handedly, Jail pulled Ed towards him, and they took off, running parallel to the Thames. Torchlight illuminated them as they rounded the next bend, and a voice screamed out: "Stop! Armed police."

Fear halted them in their tracks so fast that Ed's body quarter-turned, toppling him onto his knees. Then, as Jail reached down to pull him up, more shots rang out. Ed and Jail flinched, and the light that had illuminated them went out. Both were confused

3

momentarily and hindered by blurred vision caused by the flashlights being shone directly into their eyes as a piercing shout was heard: "Move it, go, go, go!" The cry was from Kai, who'd taken down two officers directly in Ed and Jail's path, but now found herself in a firefight with an officer approaching from her right side.

Ed and Jail, exhaustion taking hold, were fast approaching a gap in the concourse, into which the Thames was flowing. It was impossible to gauge how vast the opening was in the dark, but they knew they had no choice but to try and clear it. Propelling themselves into the air, Ed vaulted the gap by a matter of millimetres; Jail almost made it, but his lower body slammed into the side of the wall. Ed grabbed him, pulling him to his feet, then dragging him along a disused loading dock. A few minutes later, and now on the other side of the pier, no lights in sight, Jail let out a muffled shout at Ed to stop.

"I can't go on, Ed." Jail grimaced, visibly exhausted and clearly in great pain. As Jail slumped to the floor, Ed noticed he was bleeding heavily. Ed turned his phone light on to get a better look at his injuries, holding his hand above the light in the hope of not giving their position away. Jail had dark bluish bruising to his stomach and chest and was bleeding from a large gash in his side.

"Go, Ed, go. You'll not get away while dragging me." As Ed went to speak, Jail stopped him. "Ed, don't go there. I know, really I do, but go, man. For the sake of POLO."

An emotional Ed stared at Jail, a brief but knowing stare – aware that he was likely not to see his friend again. He turned and started to run, looking back twice as his friend's outline disappeared into the darkness. Ed was aware that Brindle was either dead or seriously wounded. He also knew that even if Kai had not been shot, she would not have got away. And now a similar fate awaited Jail.

Ed approached the end of the warehouse area, where high wire fencing was in place to cordon off the warehouses, and a heavy padlock and chain secured the massive iron gates. Ed, now within 100 yards of the fence, caught sight of a light to his left. The light seemed to move slowly over the ground towards him and was now illuminating his body.

The words "Stop, armed police" billowed out so loud that Ed shuddered. Upon hearing the instruction to halt, he turned sharply to his right and started running towards the river as fast as possible, snaking between debris strewn across the ground. Then, as bullets whizzed by, Ed propelled himself into the dark, murky waters of the Thames.

Within seconds, Ed was fighting to stay above water as the strong undercurrent tugged at his body. Desperately trying to force his way to the surface, fear twisting in his gut, Ed managed to get his head above water long enough to take a large gulp of air before being pulled below again.

Battling hard to rise to the surface again, Ed, already exhausted, managed to breach with half his body, surfacing into a pile of flotsam, before again sinking below the surface, where the undercurrents latched onto him, dragging him deeper. Ed was now caught in a strong current, pulling him down the Thames at speed.

Acutely aware that he was consuming the last of his oxygen, Ed resisted his body's reflex urge to open his mouth for air, knowing there would be none. As the force of the current continued to drag him deeper, he momentarily succumbed, opening his mouth, only to have it fill with water. Fear became dominant over rational thought, and he continued to sink deeper into the dark, dirty water of the Thames.

Now choking, he was forced again to open his mouth, only filling his lungs with more of the polluted muddy, sewage-ridden water. The water gushed in, hastening his journey towards death. Ed continued to sink deeper into the abyss of the river he loved and ironically often kayaked on to relax and gather his thoughts.

As Ed's airway closed to prevent more water from entering his lungs, he held his breath involuntarily; in a minute or two at most, he would become unconscious. As he drifted towards that state, a vision of Leonora appeared in his mind. And then, as if turning the pages of an album, Ed could see faces rapidly flashing in front of him. Faces of those he'd saved since forming his illegal, life-saving operation. It was perhaps his mind's way of allowing him to pass peacefully.

Then, inexplicably, his body escaped the grasp of the undertow. Rising to the surface, Ed was dragged into one of the river's passive debris collectors, slamming into thick wire fencing and debris at the end of the receptacle.

"Ed, Ed, Ed!" Leonora shouted, ever louder. "Calm down, you're okay, you are dreaming."

Leonora was holding him tightly as he sat bolt upright in bed, sweat dripping from his forehead and running down his spine, eyes shut and gasping for air.

Ed, disorientated, opened his eyes, and looking directly into Leonora's storm-blue eyes, he shouted: "Run."

"Ed," Leonora responded, her voice noticeably louder again. "You're dreaming; it's okay."

Ed pulled her close to him. "I'm sorry I've let you down." He had not fully come round and was confused.

"Ed, don't be absurd. Focus, you're dreaming, you are okay, *we* are okay."

Ed, realising he had awoken from an awful nightmare, looked at Leonora and apologised again, this time for having woken her up so violently.

"My God, Ed, you were gasping for air when you sat up. You startled me, scared me, until I realised what was going on. In all our time together, you've never had such a bad dream. Is something playing on your mind, Ed?"

Ed's breathing was still laboured, evidenced by nasal flaring. He was sweating profusely, his heart rate was high, and an awful feeling of fear was still coursing through him.

"Not that I can think of, Leonora. Too much cheese before bed perhaps!" came the breathless but jokey response.

He kissed Leonora, saying he would take a shower to freshen up and calm himself down. As he made his way to the bathroom, his hands were trembling and his heart still racing. *That was too damn real*, was his thought.

Never before had Ed had such an experience, and he hadn't realised one could be so petrified by a nightmare. Quickly freshening up, he left the bathroom and went into the kitchen for a large glass of cold water. His mind was starting to focus. He knew the likely cause of the nightmare was the debrief with Brindle Llanos and Jail Sleeks a few days earlier. The brief covered what they had learnt about the terrorist attack in London that they believed was planned with Ed as the principal target. They'd also covered the death of a man in a restaurant at which Ed and Leonora were dining.

Although fully aware he'd had a nightmare, it got Ed thinking deeply about the risks to those around him, especially his bodyguards, and in particular Kai (Honu), his chief guard and ever-present chaperone. With little thought, Ed sent out a coded message to Honu, asking to meet her and suggesting a date a few days hence. He would set a location once they had an agreement on when.

Ed returned to the bedroom.

"Are you okay, Ed?" asked a worried-looking Leonora.

"Yes, thank you. I'm fine," he answered as he got back into bed.

"What was that dream about, Ed?"

Ed remembered all too vividly what the nightmare was about, but he couldn't tell Leonora. "Strangely, I can't recall all the detail. I know you and I were running, pursued by people who wanted to hurt us, and we both ended up in the Thames." *More lies*, Ed thought to himself.

"That explains your gasping for air, Ed."

"Yes, I think so. I don't want too many nightmares like that, and again, I'm sorry for having frightened you."

"Don't be silly, Ed. I'm just glad you snapped out of it quickly.

Although, I must say, when you sat bolt upright, you looked terrified."

Ed inched closer to Leonora and cuddled her, apologising again for having startled her, and they drifted back to sleep.

UNnatural Selection – Four days earlier

Ed, Jail and Brindle were together at the farm in Kent, hunkered down in one of the smaller cottages at the centre of the farmstead. Brindle had arranged the session to provide Ed with the latest information concerning a man's death in a restaurant where Ed had been dining. Further, they wanted to update him on the terrorist attack in which he found himself caught up, at the Pink Capitalism nightclub in London that he had opened for his friend Aurora Giordano.

You'll recall that Creak Nooks was head of POLO's bodyguard unit; he had been invited too but couldn't make the meeting. Creak had scheduled a trip to Scotland to visit Stephen Arnold, the bodyguard responsible for saving Hood's (Marcelle Carrick's) life after the big steal. Brindle, whom you'll recall headed up POLO's Guardians, opened the briefing.

"We proved that on at least one occasion, prostitutes had been paid to sleep with you, Ed. The rooms, one of which you would have gone to had you taken the bait, were made available to the working girls, and I'm pretty sure cameras were rigged in them. I've been working with contacts at MI5 who are sympathetic to our cause.

More and more, British Intelligence believes there is a secret organisation operating within LPAS. They've no hard proof, but a lot of robust circumstantial evidence. However, they cannot kick it upstairs until they have irrefutable evidence, for fear that it would be dismissed as a political attack on the LPAS organisation. I'll ask Jail to come back on this point in a minute or two.

"The man murdered in the restaurant was most likely killed by an assassin known only as Orpheus. Intelligence officers were aware that he had entered the UK a week or so before the man's murder."

Ed jumped in, miffed by Brindle's statement. "If it's not confirmed, what makes it 'most likely' in the eyes of the security service?"

"My contacts wouldn't say, Ed. However, they made it clear that Orpheus was strongly implicated in the killing." Brindle was making very clear his confidence in what his MI5 sources had told him.

"Okay, let's assume they are right. That still doesn't link the man's murder to me," was Ed's view.

"Oh, on the contrary, Ed, it does," said Jail, jumping in. "Orpheus doesn't work for criminals in the ordinary sense of the word. He only works for government agencies, and commands a high price for his work," Jail said confidently.

You'll recall that Jail Sleeks was now head of POLO operations, reporting to Ed, his original position as head of recruitment having gone to Covey Twinks.

"So what?" Ed pushed back.

"Nothing links the dead man to any organisations or activity that would warrant someone to contract

Orpheus to kill him. Everything about this man's life was ordinary – boring, in fact." So said Jail, hoping Ed would get his point.

"I bet his wife didn't think he was boring," was Ed's swift reply, in an annoyed tone.

"No, Ed, I am sure she didn't. I didn't mean to put the guy down. I'm just explaining that he is Mr Ordinary, and people like Orpheus don't get hired to kill people like him. So that leaves the logical conclusion that Orpheus killed him for another reason. And the only reason we can find in that restaurant is you."

"Jail, I find this difficult to get my head around. First and foremost, I'm a doctor, and only recently a campaigner and politician, albeit of an insignificant party. It's 2045, and yet we still have government bodies ordering assassinations? Maybe I'm naïve and have led too sheltered a life until POLO," was Ed's response, looking for confirmation of his view.

"Not wishing to offend, Ed, but yes, you are, and you have. Working in the shadows wasn't what you were at all mixed up in until POLO. And even now, you aren't involved in this murky world in the same way as many. That isn't the intent of POLO or your recent activity against the LPAS laws. But you're unfortunately a thorn in the side of someone with power, position, deadly contacts, and likely a dubious past."

Jail's confident assessment didn't help the way Ed was feeling.

"Okay, so why don't the intelligence services, police, anyone, arrest this fruitcake?" Ed wanted to know, still perplexed by it all.

"They would, Ed, with enough evidence. But not only is he astute and seldom makes mistakes, but he has many friends in senior positions. Maybe not in the UK, although I wouldn't rule it out. But certainly in many countries. People who will help him without hesitation." Jail's professional opinion mattered, and Ed knew it.

"I find this almost as depressing as the LPAS laws. So what of the terrorist attack?" Ed asked, not sure he wanted to know.

Jail again stepped up. "The funding sources for the terrorists who carried out the London nightclub attack were unusual for such a small, unknown group. Usually, such groups' funds arise from kidnappings, extortion, protection, robberies, drugs and the like. And for this group, you'd expect funding to come predominantly from drugs, robbery and protection money.

"My contacts won't get into the detail but have said they see it as a straightforward attack by Islamist extremists on the gay community.

However, they haven't ruled out the involvement of a rogue country, using them as a proxy to stir up hatred, hence the sophisticated funding, which they've so far traced back to a cultural organisation in the Middle East."

"I guess that means the attack was unlikely to have had me as the primary target," Ed said, somewhat relieved.

"Sorry, Ed, but for me this makes it way more likely that you were the target," Jail responded.

"Come again, Jail?"

"A funding anomaly isn't going to lead the security services to think an individual was the primary target, however well known. Why would they? They believe a sovereign nation could have funded the attack, although that's not their central belief; however, it would explain its sophistication. And if so, it would be political, which concerns them, and so there is an effort to try and trace the funding back to the source. Then again, I didn't get the feeling the security services had assigned many resources to this line of inquiry.

"For me, the sophistication used to fund these terrorists doesn't point to a sovereign state with a destabilising agenda. This group is way too small. Furthermore, I cannot see the logic in a country wishing to cause instability or put a certain group in the frame by attacking a gay nightclub. They would attack somewhere far more prominent. So it is more likely a shadowy organisation needing to cover its tracks in the same way as a sovereign nation would." So said Jail, now concerned about the anxious look on Ed's face.

An extremely worried-looking Ed responded.

"Okay, let me play back what I think you are saying. You both think that a dark and sinister organisation, operating illegally inside LPAS, murdered a man hoping that I would compromise myself to save him. Furthermore, you believe a terrorist attack was orchestrated – one which, had it been successful, would have killed and maimed a great many people – to kill me. Yet we can't find, let alone arrest, the assassin of the man in the restaurant. And can't prove diddly squat about a secret group operating within LPAS, let alone link them to the terror attack. Does that about sum it up, gentlemen?"

Jail and Brindle looked at each other, neither wanting to respond. "Yes, Ed," came Brindle's response, knowing they'd freaked Ed out.

"So, if you were me, what would you be thinking right now?" A nervous Ed awaited their answer.

"No, Ed, it doesn't mean you're screwed," said Jail, guessing where Ed was going with that statement and seeking to assure him that it didn't mean certain death.

"Okay, guys, we could go round and round on this. We are where we are, and we can't change it. I'll have to learn to cope with it," Ed responded at length.

"Ed, we can change it, and we will," an upbeat Jail replied. "I've rattled the intelligence community by telling my contacts I believe you were the target due to your high-profile work against the new laws, and through my belief that planning and funding likely came from this secret LPAS organisation. They were already deeply concerned at the prospect of a dangerous group operating within LPAS. I've added fuel to that fire. They've begun to share information with agencies in the US and other countries, and I'm confident they'll get what they need to act against this group. It'll just be a matter of time."

"Thanks, Jail," came the response from a dejected Ed. "I can deal with the prospect of going to prison for life if I'm compromised for the work I do to save lives, or being killed while trying to evade law enforcement. I do, however, find it most troubling that somewhere out there someone could be plotting to have me killed because of my stance on these obscene laws. I find that very difficult to get out of my head."

"We hear you, Ed," both Jail and Brindle responded. Jail then continued.

"It isn't a world you are used to, and frankly, when I was a member of MI5, I didn't face what you face now. Not knowing if another attempt on your life will happen, not knowing when, not knowing where, or by whom, looking at everyone with suspicion, checking–"

"For God's sake, Jail, shut up. I get it! You aren't helping me cope with this or making me feel any bloody better!"

"Apologies, Ed, I was thinking out loud."

"Please don't! The thought of a bullet in the back of my head is already messing with my mind. Okay, guys, let's wrap this up. I appreciate the update, even if I don't like it. Let's alert our folks and get on home. I need one or two brandies... Can you hide a bomb in a small bottle?"

"Ed, stop it," responded a frowning Jail. "I know it's hard. But don't let this take over. If you do, you'll be a nervous wreck within days."

"I'll let you both in on a secret. After this session, I *am* a nervous wreck. I'll be scared to open a cupboard, or lift the mattress, put a wash on, or do any number of normal things."

"If it's any consolation, Ed, I think it's unlikely they'll attempt to blow you up!" said Jail.

"Oh, thanks. That's a relief. I can focus on a bullet, knife, poison..."

"Easy for us, Ed, I know. But you have to come to terms with it and not let it rule your life," replied Brindle.

"Thanks, I'll try hard not to let it," Ed said with an edge of sarcasm in his voice.

UNnatural Selection – Preposterous

On the evening of his nightmare, Ed had sent a coded message to Kai, asking to meet. A very unusual thing for him to have done, and against protocol. He had since agreed on a date with Kai and arranged to meet for dinner at the farm in Kent run by Brindle. With the date set, Ed received a call from Creak.

"Hi, Ed. I was speaking with Kai, who said she was meeting with you on Friday. She's got no issue with it and is looking forward to it, but she alerted me as her boss and the fact that it is against protocol. Is this something I should be aware of? Either way, I'd like to attend, too."

"It's nothing, Creak, just something that happened a few nights ago that got me thinking. I should have let you know, although I don't see the need for you to be present. However, you are welcome to come along if you wish."

"Thanks, Ed, I'd like to. I'll see you up at the farm."

Ed didn't want to explain why he had asked to meet Kai, as he didn't want to get into what would likely become a heated debate with Creak. But having received his call, Ed could not avoid extending the offer to him.

Ed's drone landed at the farm in the early afternoon. He wanted to ensure he arrived well before Kai and Creak. Brindle popped in to see him from the main farmhouse, and they spent some time, while Ed was preparing dinner, talking about how to change the way Ed's Guardians worked, in light of the inner circle's belief that Ed was the primary target of the terrorist attack. While talking, Creak arrived and joined in the conversation. An hour or so later, Ed heard a copter landing and wandered outside to greet Kai.

As Kai exited the drone, she was busy removing her disguise. Ed knew what Kai really looked like, but only from a photo. While guarding him, she always wore a mask, although 'mask' was a poor description. It was far more sophisticated than that. The only time operatives were not in disguise was if it might compromise them, such as on an aeroplane, or entering a very secure location. Ed had never travelled with Kai or entered a secure site with her; in fact, he had never actually met her. However, disguised or not, Ed knew her well by her silhouette. She did a fantastic job of staying in the shadows; so much so, that Ed seldom saw her. But he'd seen her enough for her silhouette to be etched in his memory.

He approached her, kissing her twice, once on each cheek. He then guided her to the cottage. Inside, Kai greeted Creak, whom she knew personally, and Ed introduced her to Brindle, using his codename: Overwatch. Kai did not know Brindle, but was acutely aware of the Guardians, so figuring out his job wasn't too tricky.

"Well, that's our second breach of protocol, Ed," said Creak with a wink and a smile. In fact, they would both trust Kai with their lives, and she had already saved Ed's. Brindle made his excuses and left. Ed poured Kai a drink, topping up his own and Creak's before checking on dinner.

"He seems a nice man, Ed."

"He is, Kai."

"I'm surprised you let him choose such an obvious codename, though."

Ed spun around, making eye contact with Creak, who knew just how much angst Brindle's handle had caused Ed.

"Don't go there, Kai. Or we'll not hear the last of it from Ed this evening."

"Oops, sorry I said anything," a sheepish Kai responded.

"No, you're right to bring it up, Kai. I don't know why I let him keep such an inappropriate codename for someone in his job. We hadn't told you what he did, but it was so obvious you got it in a nanosecond!"

"See, Kai. See what you've started?" Kai kept quiet.

"Ed," said Kai, "Creak tells me that even he doesn't know why I received an invite to dinner. I'm not complaining; it's lovely to meet and talk to you. I must confess I've had butterflies in my stomach since I woke up."

"It's nothing major, Kai, we can discuss it after dinner." Ed paused. "I, too, have been a little nervous today, but I've very much been looking forward to meeting you in person. I know we shouldn't, but I'm glad we are – and by the way, a huge thank you for saving my life outside the Pink Capitalism." Then, briefly bowing his head, Ed went off-piste.

"Kai, I think of you whenever I drive past the nightclub. As I go by, I get nervous. Maybe it's the thought that my life could have ended right there. I remember struggling to get up after being propelled over the car. I only just managed to get onto my knees.

"When I saw the terrorist running at me with the machete, I knew that running would not have saved me. Oddly, I closed my eyes and waited – a foolish thing to have done, and not a response I would have expected. Sure, I knew running would not have helped, but I did not want to, even if I could have. I didn't want my life to end hacked to death from behind." Ed fell quiet for a few seconds to control his emotions. "Sorry, Kai, Creak. I didn't mean to go off in that direction."

"Don't be sorry, Ed," Kai responded. "It isn't surprising that it still haunts you. I am sure it will do for some time to come."

Creak agreed but had also been itching to jump in. "Ed, Kai saved your life because that's her job."

Kai nodded in agreement. "Creak is right, Ed. It is why I'm in POLO. So you don't need to thank me."

"A thank you may not be necessary for you, Kai. I get that. But it's necessary for me," said Ed, scowling at Creak for rudely interjecting.

Dinner out the way, all three retired to the lounge. At this point, Creak was getting a little fidgety waiting for Ed to detail why he'd asked Kai to dinner. It was out of character to have broken his protocols, so Creak knew it had to be very important.

Ed commenced. "A few nights ago, I had a bad dream, a nightmare.

This rare event led to what I can only describe as an epiphany. Reality hit home, and that's why I wanted to meet with you."

"I have bad dreams all the time, Ed. They don't lead to me wanting to break protocol and meet members that I know I shouldn't," Creak forthrightly expounded.

"Yes, Creak, I know, I've broken my protocols, no reminder needed, but there is a serious point to this meeting."

"And that is?"

Ed turned to Kai. "Kai, you are amazing at your job and make me feel safe. My confidence is hugely increased, knowing you have my back. I often find myself looking over my shoulder to see if I can spot you in a crowd. I seldom do, but I know you aren't far away. I want to instruct you on something that it would have been wrong of me to have done via an encrypted message."

Now Creak was sitting upright, almost on his toes, readying himself to get up, and feeling nervous. *Where's Ed going with this?* he wondered.

"I viewed the establishment of a bodyguard unit when first raised as a possibility by the fledgling inner circle as anathema. It conjured up visions of violence, and that wasn't why I founded the organisation. I soon realised, however, that it would be essential to keep our senior people safe, a belief since proven – twice. Even given this fact, though, I still worry. I know the conflict in me is the cause of my concern. It's about saving lives versus breaking the law, and what we must do to achieve our ends." Ed paused, looking at Kai and then Creak.

"Kai, if anything ever happens that threatens me, and you know that responding would put you in mortal danger, don't. I don't want your life swapped for mine."

Creak was furious. Jumping up from the chair, he yelled at Ed. "What the fuck is this about, Ed? Kai's your damn bodyguard. What do you think she's there to do? Your ask is ridiculous of a bodyguard, and more so if brought on by a bloody dream!"

"The reason I ask isn't relevant, Creak. I don't want Kai giving up her life for mine."

"Ed, drop it," yelled an incensed Creak. "It's no wonder you didn't let me know what you had in mind."

Ed, trying not to get angry with Creak, as he knew he had no right to be, stood up, but as he was about to speak, Kai thrust her hand up vertically in front of his face to stop him.

"Ed, that was rude of me, sorry. You are speaking from the heart, as a man not used to needing protection. A caring and compassionate man. I think I died in your dream, didn't I? And it has made you look more closely at the job I do for you."

"I can see the conflict in your eyes, Ed. But you've muddled the risks of my role with what you do: saving lives. Well, my job is to save lives too. Taking a life is a last resort. And I'd not be a very effective bodyguard if I thought of my safety first, would I? And besides, you would be the target. Not me." Kai paused briefly before continuing.

"Ed, Creak is right. I'm sorry, but your ask is not realistic. Even if I agreed, my instincts would take over in any given situation. I appreciate working for someone who cares so much, but I'm afraid I have to disagree. I will do my job, whatever the outcome."

"The dream triggered my feelings about this, yes. And I don't know if you died in it." Ed paused momentarily to compose himself. Thinking of the dream had brought back vivid images of Brindle's shooting, Kai getting into a gun battle, leaving Jail injured on the docks, and the memory of drowning in the Thames. All of which at the time felt real.

"This isn't merely about a nightmare, Kai. The dream was just a trigger for what was already playing out in my mind. In all likelihood, I've become the target of some dangerous people. Looking after me is now many more times riskier than before, and that troubles me deeply."

Kai leant forward and hugged Ed, telling him, "I was one of the youngest officers in the secret service, and we didn't just guard the President and his family. We did much more dangerous work. When I left the service, as you know, I started my own protection company, KAIGuard. A safe conduit, now, for recruiting bodyguards into POLO. I suspect, however, Ed, you don't know that I worked in some very politically volatile countries, for politicians who had many enemies. My team and I had many close calls." Kai paused before continuing:

"I gave up most of my day-to-day involvement in my company when Creak asked me to join POLO, as I saw it as a worthy cause. Helping to fight against an immoral set of laws by keeping safe those who are saving lives. So I could not have been happier when Creak told me

I'd have the big job – guarding you. I've always loved my work, protecting people, and more so now that I'm working for a critical life-saving organisation.

"This gives me a far greater sense of purpose. My role adds significant meaning to my life. So, Ed, please don't worry about me. If I wasn't working to keep you safe, I'd likely be in a far more dangerous situation, keeping someone safe who had many more enemies. We each have skills to further the cause of POLO and we must use them the best we can."

Creak stepped up a gear. "And before you even think about it, Ed, no, you are not operating without bodyguards."

"I wasn't going to suggest that, Creak," was Ed's response. "Okay, I'm not going to stop being troubled by this, but I accept that I need protection, and I have to respect Kai's position – reluctantly."

"Good," said Creak, with a sigh of relief that was echoed by Kai. "Let's get these glasses filled up and talk about something more uplifting."

The three of them continued talking, enjoying each other's company well into the early hours of the morning. At 2:40 a.m., Ed put in a call for three drones to get them back to London.

The drones arrived, and as they said their goodbyes, Kai leant forward and kissed Ed on the forehead, saying nothing, then walked off to her ride home.

As Kai's drone took off, Creak leaned in close to Ed. "Ed, Kai is a highly trained and exceptionally talented professional. She will do what is necessary if trouble kicks off. But I think meeting you, listening to you, spending time with you will, if it's possible, make her redouble her effort to ensure your safety."

"Rub it in, Creak, rub it in. I made a mistake and I recognise that. But I'm very troubled by what we've learned. That poor man in the restaurant; and the fact that these people working in the darkest recesses were willing to kill and maim hundreds to end my life," Ed commented, fear pooling in his stomach.

Creak bear-hugged him and said, "You're a good man, Charlie Brown."

"You're the second person to say that to me, Creak. Maybe I should have made Charlie B. my handle?"

"Nah, it doesn't have quite the same allure as Syrinx!" was Creak's view.

"I didn't choose my handle for allure!" Ed snapped back.

With that, they boarded their drones back to London, with Ed still troubled but accepting that it was a stupid ask and something he should have thought through more thoroughly before voicing it. He now felt a tad silly for having done so, but he'd enjoyed meeting Kai, whom he had bonded with quickly.

UNnatural Selection - Kenya

Ed was holding a session with inner-circle members, planning his upcoming trip to Kenya. In Kenya, he would address parliament, and chair sessions on the LPAS – Life Preservation Assistance Suspension – laws. And he would have a private dinner with President Vincent Njuki.

Kenyan officials were interested in seeing changes to LPAS legislation, and hence were eager to hear what Ed had to say. It would give parliamentarians a chance to probe his views and alternative ideas. Brindle, Jail and Creak had the job of ensuring Ed's safety while out of the country. Now close to agreeing on what was required, Ed took the floor.

"So, we've bodyguards supported by Tradesfolk and a few Guardians running communications. When Kai cannot stay close while I'm with the parliamentarians or the President, I'll be protected by Kenya's Presidential Escort Unit – the PEU. I think that's just about it for now, right?"

"Almost, Ed, almost. We still need to figure out how to get shorts in Kenya," Creak responded, wanting to ensure Ed didn't close out too soon.

Ed, believing they'd finished, and about to move on to ask if anyone had other topics, thought Creak's attempt at humour had fallen very flat. "For one, it isn't a jolly. But if you're serious, which I doubt, tell them to pack them," he rather grumpily snapped back.

Now, as if watching a tennis match, Creak, Brindle, Jail and Ashlin, whom you'll recall was head of POLO's Collectors, began looking to and fro at each other, before bursting into laughter, followed within 10 or so seconds by Gig (George Clemons, head of Trades). Ed, bewildered by the laughter, asked why it was so funny, but none of them could speak. Finally, after about 30 seconds, Ed, becoming irritated, asked again why his response had caused them to laugh.

Jail attempted to answer but couldn't control his laughter. Brindle, however, managed to gain enough self-control to respond.

"Ed, when Creak says *shorts*, he means handguns!" Then Brindle again burst into laughter.

Ed was now a tad embarrassed, asking how was he supposed to know that? To which Jail's response was, "Ashlin knew."

"Don't use me like a whip," said Ashlin, jumping in quickly. "I only know because I heard the term used in a documentary some years ago."

"Ed, I had no clue either," George put in. However, George was laughing along with the others. Not because he understood why they were laughing, but because, as is often the case when others spontaneously burst into laughter, it's infectious. Though not for Ed!

"Okay, guys, you've had your fun. Can you get a hold of yourselves so we can finish?" an exasperated Ed responded with a mirthless smile on his face. He didn't particularly enjoy being the butt of the joke. "I think I'll be safe in Kenya, and most of the time, Kai won't be able to be nearby. Can't Kai and her team stay unarmed? Isn't it much more of a risk having visitors to a country wandering around carrying weapons?"

"It is, Ed, but no, Kai can't be unarmed." Jail's response was instant and firm. "You are right, in that most of the time the PEU will cover you, but we need to ensure that when they are not watching over you, you have sufficient protection and that Kai and her folks have the tools they need to engage anyone, should it be required."

They'd agreed that Kai plus one other bodyguard would make the trip. Several of Gig's Tradespeople would also make the trip to provide logistical services to the team. A few Tradesfolk had been in Kenya for a while, getting prepared for when Ed arrived. In addition, several Guardians would look after all communications and track all POLO operatives in Kenya using a sophisticated tracking system, with transmitters built into jewellery: bracelets, necklaces, watches and the like.

Kimberly Marleah (Kimmy, to her friends), head of medical, having replaced Jennifer Skull after Jennifer's untimely death, would also be in the country to provide medical assistance if needed. Kimmy's day job was consultant thoracic surgeon at the hospital where Ed worked.

"I think I can deal with the shorts, Creak," said Jail, still trying hard not to laugh, although the evidence was all over his face. "I have a few contacts that have relationships in Kenya. I believe I can arrange to have a couple of handguns made available once Kai is on the ground. Leave it with me; I'll let you know if I draw a blank."

With the POLO side of the equation sorted, the team discussed the logistics of the meetings with parliamentarians and the President and how they could best gain their support at the UN for changes to LPAS laws. A few more hours passed, and Ed stood up.

"Okay, good work, people. I'm happy we have a plan that works. I'm still unsure about having armed personnel, but I'll bow to your better judgement."

"Good, Ed. Kai will often not be able to keep sight of you, given the people whose company you will be keeping. But at such times you will be protected by the country's protection officers. However, when at the hotel and away from senior officials, you will still need Kai around. Especially given our suspicions surrounding a dark side of LPAS," was Jail's forceful assertion.

With that, the meeting ended, and small talk commenced while they awaited their leave times.

Ed arrived at Heathrow for his flight to Nairobi. Advances in airframe and engine design had brought significant improvements in safety, comfort and environmental impact. Large commercial hydrogen-fuelled aircraft, introduced in 2038, and new commercial supersonic jets came back into service in 2031. Now they were built almost entirely of carbon composites, making them lighter and far more fuel-efficient. In addition, the reduced weight meant that planes required much less thrust for the aircraft to go supersonic, allowing designers to drop afterburners.

However, the big breakthrough was airframe design that dissipated the shock wave caused by supersonic flight, muffling the boom to a gentle thud for those on the ground. Senior executives, business owners, politicians and the like wanted to get from one place to another faster. Thus, a market existed, and supersonic travel was now available on many major routes.

Ed was today flying supersonic as his schedule was tight. Usually, he'd have travelled subsonic, as he enjoyed relaxing with a few glasses of wine and a good book. However, he only had three days in Kenya and wanted to maximise face time with parliamentarians. Flying supersonic meant that his flight time would be a little over three hours.

Arriving in Kenya, Ed was fast-tracked through border control and customs and taken to a waiting government car for his journey to the Nairobi Serena Hotel. He checked in and unpacked, but his mind was racing, repeatedly going over his plans for the three days and hoping he would generate the support required to get Kenya in his corner. With his mind too active to sleep, he decided to go down to the lobby bar for a nightcap.

In the bar, slowly sipping what looked like tonic water, was Kai Losua, in disguise as per protocol. Which meant the person with her had to be Fallon Rose-Eton, codename Senyera, who Ed knew was Kai's back-up.

Looking at Senyera, Ed noticed his lapel pin badge, and grew annoyed. Something he would later take up with Kai.

Kai had hired Fallon into her security company, moving him to POLO once she had complete confidence in him. Kai's company was now, more often than not, used to recruit bodyguards into POLO. With offices in the UK, USA and Europe, there was no shortage of qualified bodyguards. Fallon had spent his early years in Ireland, moving to England in his mid-thirties after leaving the Irish police service. He met Kai when he applied to her company for a job.

Ed had never met Senyera, but he could pick out Kai's silhouette within seconds, as she had become his second shadow. Ordering a large cognac, Ed took a seat at the bar and started to think about walking through Mount Street Gardens, a place he often went to relax, and a place he could transport his mind to when not in London and achieve the same relaxing effect as if he were. Not so long ago, he could imagine kayaking on the Thames to achieve the same soothing effect. His nightmare had, however, put paid to that.

As Ed sat at the bar, a beautiful lady sat down beside him, ordered a

Moscow Mule and asked if they had a copper mug to put it in; the answer was no, and she started up a conversation with Ed.

"Here on business?" she said, with the most breathtaking of smiles.

"Yes," came Ed's terse response. The lady piped up again, ignoring

Ed's unmistakable message that he had no interest in a conversation.

"Me too. I travel a great deal, but I've never really got used to the loneliness of travelling by myself."

Ed engaged, not wishing to continue to be offish. "I've travelled a fair bit. Immerse yourself in a good book; it'll help. Especially if you want to avoid people talking to you on a plane."

"You don't have a book now, and I've tried that. It isn't a substitute for good conversation... But do you wish you were on a plane now?"

"No, and I'm sorry, that remark wasn't meant as it sounded. It is just what I do when I am on a plane and the person next to me shows signs of being a non-stop talker. I'm Edward Thorncroft, but please call me Ed."

"I'm Olivia, but call me Nawt."

"As in zero?" Ed inquired.

"Yes, but spelt NAWT."

"Oh, not 'not', if you get me?"

"Yes – I mean, no. Not an alternative for 'not'. Aargh. You're the first person who's made my nickname so complex!" Olivia screaked.

"Sorry! Please go on." Ed hadn't meant to be a stickler.

"A friend thought it a good nickname because both my names began with O, and he thought spelling it that way looked nicer when messaging. So it didn't take long before everyone started to use it in text messages, and it stuck," Olivia elaborated.

"It's often the case, Olivia, that nicknames stem from loosely or unrelated things or one-off comments, but then stick and grow on us. Nicknames fascinate me. And sorry, I didn't mean to be pernickety."

"I didn't think you were, Ed... Are you talking from experience, by the way?"

"No, I don't have a nickname, but quite a few friends do. And your family name?"

"Olsson," responded Olivia.

"With a double S?"

"Yes."

"Swedish then?" Ed probed.

"Yes – not difficult, hey?" she responded with that same beaming smile that Ed thought could melt icebergs.

He thought her friendly, low-key approach to him was down to earth and was somewhat intrigued by her. He also felt the small talk had been a little more interesting than the usual weather and sports conversations. Ed had a weakness for strong, forward ladies, which was one of the big things that had attracted him to Leonora. He decided to chat some more, which also helped calm his mind.

Ed and Olivia talked for around an hour before Ed apologised, saying he had to get some sleep as he had an early start in the morning. Olivia swiped her business card onto the screen of her phone and tapped it against his.

"There you go, Ed. You've got my card. If you are ever short of a dinner companion, call me." Interestingly, that was more or less what Leonora had said when he first met her at the hospital gala dinner.

It turned out that Olivia lived in London. Ed felt a little guilty as he left the bar, as he hadn't offered her his card and hadn't responded to Olivia's dinner offer. As he walked towards the door, he gestured to Kai, who got up and followed him out to the lobby and got in the lift with him. As the doors shut, Ed swiped Olivia's card onto his screen and tapped Kai's phone.

"Kai, have Creak check this lady out for me."

"Interested in her, Ed?" said Kai, with a mischievous look on her face.

"No, no, not in that way. I'm interested to see if she is who she says."

"Okay, Ed, I'll transmit a copy of the card to Creak and get back to you with whatever he uncovers."

"Great, thanks – and as you still seem full of beans, why don't you and Senyera keep close to her? See if she meets anyone and if she is resident at the hotel. But be careful she doesn't suss you out."

"Oh, Ed, what would I do without such astounding advice on how to stay in the shadows!" Kai laughed.

"Sorry, Kai, that was ridiculous, but I mean–"

Kai cut him off, shaking her head and rolling her eyes. "Yes, Ed, I know. You meant 'be careful'; thank you, but please stop worrying about me. I think you'll find it is supposed to be the other way around!"

"Oh, and Kai, tell Fallon to take off his lapel badge," Ed demanded, showing signs of being a little flustered.

"Sorry, Ed. I thought the yellow and red stripes were colourful. So what's the problem?" Kai wanted to know.

"It is the flag of Catalonia."

"So?" replied Kai, still none the wiser.

"The flag is the Senyera!"

Now she got it and was more pissed than Ed. Wearing a badge openly that had the same name as your handle was unwise, to say the least. And Kai was going to make this abundantly clear to Fallon.

"I'm sorry, Ed. I will deal with him. I can't believe he'd be that idiotic."

With that, the lift doors opened on Ed's floor, and he exited; Kai stayed in the lift to return to Fallon in the bar. A return that Fallon wasn't going to enjoy.

Ed entered his room, took off his clothes and got into a dressing gown before scanning his clothing for bugs or trackers... All clear.

He then retired to bed, hoping to get a good few hours' sleep.

Meanwhile, Kai spoke with Fallon, who apologised, agreeing that it had been a mistake but pointing out that his great-great-grandfather was born in Barcelona before the family moved to Eire on his mother's side. And the family still felt a connection to Catalonia, which only last year had achieved independence from Spain.

"I get it, Fallon. Wear it, but wear it discreetly."

Fallon apologised again, removed it from his jacket and placed it on his shirt pocket, under his coat.

Twenty minutes later, as Olivia left the bar, Kai indicated to Fallon that he should follow her, while Kai stayed to finish her tonic. Kai had planned to do the surveillance but was still a little irked with Fallon.

At 7 a.m., a car drew up outside the hotel to collect Ed. He was to attend a breakfast meeting in parliament (*Bunge la Kenya*, in Swahili). Kenya operated under a bicameral system, made up of the Senate and the National Assembly. Ed would be meeting with senior members of both houses.

Breakfast meeting over, Ed felt it had gone well. He would now hold a round of one-on-one sessions before lunch, after which, he would address both houses.

Just before 2:30 p.m., the Assembly Chair got to her feet, and, standing in front of the lectern, started to introduce Ed. After a few minutes and what Ed thought was a lovely introduction, the Chair called him to the floor to rapturous applause. He opened with the usual niceties and a few jokes (that didn't work particularly well) before getting into his hortatory speech, which would last around 45 minutes. Nearing the end, Ed closed with:

"Faced with the frailties and limits of the human body, we embarked on a path of discovery to find solutions that have allowed the human race to flourish and lead much healthier and longer lives. Is this tried and tested approach not the one we should have trod in searching for solutions to population growth and protecting our home, planet Earth?

Should not a law so devasting to the lives of millions have had approval from the populace and not merely those chosen to govern us?

Unfortunately, history has shown all too often that decisions with the potential to wreak havoc, made by the few, have not ended well. We have unfortunately entered an era of social destruction."

Thunderous applause, coupled with a standing ovation, was the response to Ed's speech. Many were shaking Ed's hand as he left the stage.

On his way to the exit, a large group blocked his path, mobbing him.

Some wanted to shake his hand, others wishing to continue the conversation. Guards eventually stepped in to free him from their clutches. He did, after all, have an important dinner to attend.

UNnatural Selection – Sagana State Lodge

Leaving parliament, Ed stepped into a waiting government car for the short drive to a helipad. A military helicopter was waiting to take him to Sagana State Lodge for a private dinner with the President. The lodge, located in Kiganjo Town in the foothills of Mount Kenya, was around two and a half hours out of Nairobi by car, but a short helicopter flight.

Sagana State Lodge had become to the President of Kenya the equivalent to Chequers to the British prime minister, or Camp David to POTUS. Built as a royal residence, the Duchess of Edinburgh, later Queen Elizabeth II, learned in 1952 that her father, King George VI, had died and that she had succeeded to the throne as queen, while at the lodge.

Ed was thrilled to be having dinner there, given its colonial history, and would add it to his list of ice-breakers when meeting new people. Landing just 50 yards from the building, the President, looking casual, greeted him.

Ed had a relationship with the President. They had met on three previous occasions and had hit it off during their first meeting. They frequently corresponded via a secure messaging application and talked once a month by phone. Their friendship was Ed's prime driver for making Kenya his first 'official' trip to a country to discuss LPAS alternatives and garner support for the law to be watered down.

Ed already had several countries on board after many sessions held at secret locations in the UK and at the United Nations in New York. But this was his first public outing to drum up support. So selecting a country where he already had tacit support and a strong relationship with the head of government had seemed wise.

Ed and the President sat down to dinner, having spent an hour or so beforehand catching up on personal matters. Starter served, President Njuki commented, "Well, Ed, I hope you are enjoying your time in Kenya and that the trip is proving fruitful?"

"I believe it has been so far, Mr President."

"Come, come, Ed, dispense with formality when we are alone."

"Sorry, Vincent."

Ed continued. "I know we share a similar view on LPAS, and it is clear that many politicians in Kenya do too. And should you decide to openly support the small coalition that I've been fortunate enough to pull together, it will mean that seniors within WHO and at least seven countries will push for vaccine removal from LPAS control. I see that as a massive step forward. I know that this doesn't mean it will happen. But now, having many countries talking about it, and the WHO pressing hard, gives me much hope that other countries will follow our lead."

"Ed, I know you think I should go all out against these laws. But doing so won't change anything. Instead, I should work with you to slowly change the opinions of others. If I come out and advocate repealing the act, they will marginalise me, and that will not serve the cause."

"I know, Vincent, I know. I appreciate what you are doing, and I do not expect you to go further. I agree it would be counter-productive. But open support on vaccine changes would be a big boost."

"Ed, let's finish dinner. We can then retire to the lounge and talk more about your plans. And I have some important information to share with you."

Dinner over, President Njuki and Ed retired to the lounge, and the President poured them an exceptionally large brandy.

"Too many of those, Vincent, and I'll not be talking at all!"

As Vincent handed Ed his brandy, he said, "Ed, how did we get here?"

Ed wasn't expecting Vincent to ask such a question, given his extensive knowledge of population growth, LPAS and other solutions. But he surmised that the President wanted to hear him give his honest, raw view.

"The short, or the slightly longer version, Vincent?" Ed responded.

"Both!"

"We were far too late to act, making both the problem and the remedy far worse. Our approach to fixing the issue wasn't joint up, and we allowed the looney and extreme activists to set the narrative aided by media doom- mongers!" was Ed's short answer as to why LPAS became law.

"Vincent, it's similar to climate change, where we also had a very late start. Our approach was wrong, and the world wasted billions on inadequate and costly solutions, coupled with a lack of global commitment, resulting in a poorly mapped out global pathway to resolve the problem. The approach has caused unnecessary hardship for millions, not to mention numerous deaths. Politicians didn't target their spending wisely, and many countries didn't genuinely commit. However, all politicians wanted to assure their voters, their people, that they'd fix it!

"Overpopulation is no different and is still a large part of the climate issue. But it is fixable, through technology, education, lifting the world's poor out of poverty, empowerment of women – it's no more complex than that. Yes, it will take time and money, the correct economic policies, and much more. But nothing we aren't able to achieve. And we will be in a better place in the end, a far better place than the dark times many realise the world is now heading into."

"LPAS was a knee-jerk reaction from politicians who'd acted decades too late," Ed went on. "They then gave in to the doom-mongers and wanted to show strength! No doubt in the belief it would earn re-election points. But, submitting to the most extreme views, the noisemaking few caused panic. We needed to act. And act we did.

"Telling people repeatedly over many years that the end is nigh, slowly creating fear in the majority, seems to work. When you then boldly put forward a solution, the majority don't query it. They are just happy to see you act."

"Steady, Ed. I'm a politician too! I wish I hadn't asked you!"

"I didn't say all politicians, Vincent, and I certainly didn't mean politicians like yourself, who get it. And sorry, I tend to get on my soapbox when asked such direct questions on LPAS."

"I'm not sure I have the knowledge you have, Ed, but it was always clear to me that LPAS was a step too far, and like you, I know LPAS will not fix the issue but will change society in a way we should fear. It is a change that will be very difficult to reverse. It affects developed countries most, as their ability to fully deploy technology and medical advances has consistently outstripped ours. So the pain is more acute there.

Nonetheless, it is hurting all countries the world over.

"For me, it conflicts with Ubuntu, a Nguni Bantu term representing a philosophy of shared humanity and the essential need for community in society. That, LPAS is rapidly stripping away. I know, Ed, that the damage to society is one of your biggest concerns."

President Njuki had not come to power until August 2042, two and a half years after LPAS passed into law, and would be facing re-election in August of 2047, a little under two years from now, with no assurance of being re-elected. He knew, therefore, that his support for Ed, while president and at his most influential, could be short-lived. Vincent then changed the conversational tack.

"Ed, my security folks briefed me a few days before your arrival in Kenya, and I was concerned by some of what they told me."

"Go on, Mr President – sorry, Vincent – I'm listening," Ed responded as he leant forward in his chair.

"My National Intelligence Service put forward a brief before your arrival, advising that they felt you were being watched closely by LPAS."

"Okay, Vincent, trust me, that's not news to me. I've suspected for some time that they've been watching me on and off." Ed was aware of when he was under surveillance, through his Guardians.

"Ed, when I say LPAS, I do not mean the LPAS you know, the LPAS you are fighting, the LPAS in control of a set of laws that you and I agree are immoral. That is a group that, however we might disagree with them, nonetheless operate within the law.

"No, Ed, I mean a sinister side of the organisation. A side that my intelligence service and services in several other countries suspect is working outside the law. A group we suspect of blackmail, coercion and possibly much worse."

"No agency has direct proof, but many agencies are now discussing this openly, including the British and Americans. So my people are convinced this shadowy group exists within LPAS, and we are deeply concerned about their reason for being."

"I appreciate you briefing me, Vincent. I assure you I will take all possible precautions."

"Please do, Ed. Unfortunately, there is information that I cannot share with you, but I am fearful for you. I do not want to wake up one morning to find something bad has happened to you." Pausing, Vincent then continued.

"Ed, I fear these people are deeply troubled by your success, and my people suspect they will work hard to limit the damage you might cause.

You have awakened the world's conscience. People worldwide are now looking much closer at LPAS and the damage and suffering it is causing. You have many followers, and demonstrations against these laws are becoming larger and more common. And everyone knows that is in large part because of you."

Vincent switched topics again, not wishing to plague Ed with too much grim news.

"But enough of this worrying talk. Let me fill your glass. We still have much to discuss, including your lovely girlfriend, by whom I can tell you are smitten. And who would not be? She is fun to be around, and, I think, the smartest lady I've ever met. I bet she gives you a run for your money, Ed?"

"It isn't a run, Vincent. I'm at walking pace compared to her intelligence."

"So, have you asked her?" Vincent wanted to know.

"I think, Vincent, you are interested to know if I have asked her to marry me?"

"Yes, Ed – have you?"

No one had asked Ed directly before, and Ed hadn't thought of popping the question because of his secret life. He could think of nothing he wanted more than to have LPAS repealed, and he wanted that for the benefit of everyone. Selfishly, however, what he would like more would be to marry Leonora and lead an ordinary life. However, it was a difficult question to answer, as he could not tell Vincent why he had not asked Leonora to marry him.

"Vincent, I'm captivated by Leonora. I love her more than any words could convey, but the Arabic word *tuqburni* says it best, as it conveys a desire to die before the person you love so as never to have to live without them. In answer to your question: for now, we are happy as we are, so I guess I haven't thought about asking."

"You express strong love indeed, Ed. A love evident to me on those few occasions I've spent time with you both. Have you told Leonora this? Have you broached the subject with her to see how she feels?"

"I tell her all the time that I love her; but no, I haven't talked about marriage."

"Okay, Ed, I'm prying a little too much. I apologise."

"Vincent, I don't mind," Ed pronounced, now in deep thought about the topic of marriage.

At around 5 a.m., Vincent suggested they retire. "Ed, if you are to be fit to engage in meaningful conversation over lunch tomorrow, we should turn in."

"I agree, Vincent. It has been the most enjoyable of evenings. I've realised how much I've missed engaging with you in person."

As they reached the top of the stairs, Vincent back-slapped Ed. "You are a good man, Ed. *Lala salama*, dear friend." Meaning 'sleep well' or 'safely' in Swahili.

"You too, Vincent. I am looking forward to our next catch- up."

"As am I, Ed. As am I," Vincent responded as he headed down the hallway to his room.

Ed got into bed, taking some time to get off to sleep. He was thinking about what Vincent had said about LPAS, but more so, marriage. Could it be that Leonora was disappointed that he hadn't asked? Would it be on her mind? Should he bring up the subject?

He had not previously had these thoughts, so immersed was he in both – in fact, all three – of his jobs.

In just a few hours, his friend had hit Ed with two wake-up calls on his safety and his relationship. So, naturally, he needed to think about both, although his safety had already been very much on his mind.

Ed drifted off to sleep around 6:15 a.m. Fortunately, he did not need to be anywhere until 3 p.m., when he would be meeting several politicians for lunch, this time at the Carnivore restaurant in Langata, just outside Nairobi. The President would not be joining him, but a helicopter had been made available to fly him directly to the restaurant. The President had also advised him that two of his presidential guards from his escort unit would stay with him until he boarded his flight home. A clear message to Ed about his friend's concern for his safety.

Ed knew Vincent was not someone who worried unnecessarily. So the fact he had assigned two of his elite guards to protect him was something that concerned him. As a result, Ed had advised Kai to stand down. Instead, Kai and Fallon would utilise the time following Olivia. So far, they'd turned up nothing untoward on Nawt.

A little after 2 p.m., with Ed about to board the helicopter for his short flight to the Carnivore, the President hugged him and said he could not wait for his trip to London to again catch up in person. As Ed boarded the helicopter, Vincent handed him a sizeable stiff-backed envelope, of the kind used to protect photographs. As he gave Ed the envelope, Vincent said, "*Mungu akulinde*," Swahili for 'God protect you'.

With a raised voice, almost a shout, to counter the noise of the rotor system, Ed thanked him and quipped, "If it's a photo of you, Vincent, I'll be sure to hang it in the hallway of my apartment."

"It does indeed contain photos, Ed, but I don't think you will be hanging them on your wall!" Vincent shot back.

As the President stepped back, the door closed and the helicopter lifted off, with Ed waving to his friend from the small side window. Now climbing into the sky, Ed opened the envelope. Inside were a few pictures of people Ed did not know, and all appeared against a Nairobi backdrop. Inside, a note from Vincent: "Telephoto gifts from my security team," signed *Rafiki yako* (your friend).

The President had admitted to having information that he could not share with Ed, but it was apparent he wanted Ed to take his warning seriously. Ed placed the photos back in the envelope. He would give them to Kai when the opportunity allowed for any of the three spooks, Creak, Brindle and Jail, to do a little digging with their contacts on who these people were.

UNnatural Selection – Carnivore – Leaving Kenya

In what seemed no time at all, Ed's helicopter was landing just yards from the Carnivore, and he exited the chopper with his newly assigned presidential bodyguards.

The house speaker greeted Ed, ushering him into the restaurant and to a closed-off section, with more security personnel hovering around, strategically placed to ensure everyone's safety.

Ed had visited the restaurant many times during his previous trips to Kenya while working for medical charities. An open-air restaurant, capable of seating over 300 diners, with adjoining space for concerts – the Simba saloon nightclub – it could house more than 2,000. Ed loved the atmosphere at the restaurant, and the smell of meat cooking on the vast charcoal pits at the restaurant's entrance was detectable from a fair distance away.

Before Ed could sit down, a waiter presented him the house cocktail, the Dawa (meaning 'magic potion' or 'medicine'). He was then immediately encircled by politicians who wanted time to talk about his work on pushing for reform on the LPAS laws.

After much friendly, engaging and at times humorous discussion, Ed looked down at his watch. It was a little after 9 p.m. already. Time had flown by, with Ed engrossed in conversation with many politicians who expressed what Ed perceived as solid support for his ideas.

Ed, flanked by his bodyguards, left the restaurant and walked to a waiting car for his trip back to the hotel. Arriving back at the Serena Hotel, he went up to his room, showered, changed and went down to the bar. Before leaving his room, he sent a message to Kai, asking her to visit his room and collect the envelope he had left on the bed, advising her to get the three spooks to use their contacts to see if they could identify any of the faces in the photos. Ed sat down at a small round table, with one guard staying at the doorway to the bar and the other taking a seat at a table next to Ed's.

Ed leant forward, tilting his chair towards the guard, and whispered, "I'll be perfectly safe in the hotel. Why not get off and spend some time with your families?"

"Sorry, sir, we can't. It is our job to ensure that nothing happens to you in Kenya. You will have to put up with us until you board your flight home tomorrow evening," was the response from the guard.

Ed accepted his guard's position. Then, sitting back in his chair, he ordered a large glass of tonic water and started to read the agenda for the next day's meetings.

A few minutes later, his guard stood up abruptly, moving in front of him. As Ed looked up, he saw Olivia Olsson, the lady he had met in the bar the night before last.

"It is okay; she's a friend," Ed said to the guard, who already had his hand inside his jacket.

"Well, I guess you're not your average businessman?" said Olivia, with that adorably big smile that had drawn him into conversation with her when they first met.

"Every time I've switched on the news the last two days, I've seen your face on it," Olivia continued.

"I'm sorry you've had to suffer that," Ed quipped.

"And you now have a minder, I see," Olivia said, staring at the guard.

"Two, actually," said Ed with a smirk on his face. "Overkill, I know. But nice that someone is worried about me."

"Oh, I thought the guard on the door was for all our benefit," responded Olivia, again smiling. "May I?"

"Sorry, how rude of me. Please, sit down. What are you drinking?"

Ed ordered a drink for Olivia and tonic water for himself.

"I apologise for having not recognised you the other evening. I don't watch too much TV. But when travelling, I have the news channel on in my room. I had read a couple of your early articles but didn't connect them when you said your name. However, I recall one from *Time Magazine* when you gave your initial thoughts on the societal damage LPAS caused. I wouldn't go as far as saying I'm a fan, but I agree, generally, with your views on LPAS, and it is good that someone is bringing alternatives to the table and highlighting the suffering, deaths and social damage these laws cause."

Ed's mind flashed back to the terror attack when Nawt mentioned the issue of *Time Magazine*, for this was what the first terrorist had used to get close to him, pretending he wanted Ed to sign it. Ed snapped out of it and replied: "Well, thank you, Olivia. I'll take that as an 'almost endorsement'."

The two continued to talk for a couple of hours. Ed was still a little suspicious of the woman but enjoyed her company. A little after midnight, Olivia said she had an early flight back to London, shook Ed's hand, saying she had very much enjoyed talking to him, and hoped they could meet up in London. With that, she left the bar.

Ed, as before, didn't respond to her offer to meet up. He too had enjoyed their conversations, and liked her, but not in a romantic way. She was bubbly, quick-witted and knowledgeable. He wanted to believe their meeting was coincidental and that she just wanted some company to pass the time, but as yet, who she was and what her intentions were wasn't entirely clear.

Ed, having finished a full day of meetings, was now at the airport.

The flight time was three and a half hours, departing at 5 p.m. They were scheduled to land at 6:25 and Ed hoped to be back at his apartment by 8 p.m. He'd planned to call Leonora when he landed to see if it was okay to pop over and see her. What with the trip and a busy schedule beforehand, he hadn't seen her for over 10 days.

The two bodyguards in the lounge would stay with him until he boarded his flight. Also in the lounge was

Kai, although not in disguise. Her ownership of KAIGuard gave her cover enough, especially given that it was so well known. As Ed scanned the lounge, he saw a face that wasn't familiar until two days ago. It now was, as it was one of the faces in the photos that President Njuki had handed him.

Ed briefly looked over to Kai, who discreetly indicated that she too had clocked the face in the lounge. At this point, neither of them knew who he was or why he had been keeping tabs on Ed. Hopefully, one of the three spooks would come up with the answer. For now, however, neither Ed nor Kai was too worried. An attempt on Ed's life during the flight home was highly improbable.

Now boarded, the doors closed, and the plane pushed back from the stand. Ed drifted off to sleep, only to be woken by a slight jolt as they took off. Within 30 minutes, they were at cruising altitude, 58,000 feet, and the drinks trolley was making its way through the cabin.

Ed was feeling relaxed and going over the last few days in his head. But then he was disturbed by someone tripping beside his chair, one arm hitting Ed's table, the other the back of the chair in front of Ed. As Ed's glass tilted, the person caught it before it toppled over.

"My apologies for being so clumsy. I lost my footing." With that, the man steadied Ed's glass. As Ed looked directly up at him, he tried hard not to react, as the man that had just bumped into his chair was one of the people in the photos, the man he and Kai had clocked in the lounge.

"No trouble," replied Ed. With that, the man continued down the aisle to the bathroom. Within a minute, the man was returning from the restroom, smiling at Ed as he passed by and mouthing sorry as he did.

Ed looked down at his glass, and immediately his mind flashed back to dinner at one of his favourite restaurants in Chelsea, when a man had collapsed. He and Leonora had only just finished their starters when the man hit the floor, clutching his chest. It subsequently turned out he'd had a drug dropped into his beer, inducing a heart attack that killed him.

Ed zoned out, wondering if he should drink his wine. He was brought out of his trance by a paper ball landing beside his glass. As he looked up, Kai was walking towards the bathroom.

Picking up the paper ball, he unscrunched it.

"Don't drink or eat anything on this flight", Kai had written. But, even before Kai's timely advice, Ed had been thinking the very same thing.

Ed pulled a sick bag from the front pocket of his chair and poured a third of his wine into the bag, folding it over many times and placing it in his jacket pocket. As he did, he became aware that the passenger in the seat beside him was looking over at him. Ed turned and faced her, whispering, "It's a good wine. I thought I'd save some for when I get home!" The lady smiled faintly, then looked back out of the window. No need for a book to stop this lady talking!

Ed did not wish to give anything away. He'd left roughly two thirds of the wine in the glass and feigned sleep before dinner commenced to avoid having to decline dinner.

He continued to fake sleep as the seatbelt signs came on and the captain announced that they were starting their descent into London. Ten minutes later, Ed was 'woken' by one of the stewards.

"Sorry to wake you, sir. I was checking that your belt was secure as we'll be landing in 15 minutes."

UNnatural Selection – Everyone's luck runs out

Having decided to go directly to Leonora's, Ed called her upon clearing customs and was now in a taxi heading to her apartment. But he felt very stressed, nonetheless. Thankfully, almost all toilets in public places were unisex, making it easier for Ed to hand over the sick bag containing the wine to Kai. Before leaving the airport, Ed had entered one of the cubicles, Kai had entered the one next to his, and Ed had slid the sick bag under the gap. There was no need for them to speak: Kai knew what needed to happen with the contents of the bag.

Ed arrived at Leonora's apartment, and, entering, gave her a massive hug and kissed her for so long that she almost turned blue.

"Wow, Ed, that was some greeting!"

"I've missed you. I'm going to take a quick shower. I could do with a drink."

Ed had felt a little odd after leaving the airport. Stepping into the shower, the sensations of tingling and numbness became more apparent in his arms. However, he'd had the feeling in his hands and legs for an hour or so. Ed recognised it as paraesthesia, brought on by anxiety. Or at least Ed hoped that was the cause, as paraesthesia could also be caused by a mini-stroke or several other not-so-nice things. Could poison cause it? he wondered. Say a poison that was attacking his nervous system?

Stop it, Ed, he told himself. *I must calm down. I didn't drink the wine or eat anything, and he didn't touch me. It can't be poison.* Now showered, he put on a pair of shorts and a T-shirt and went back into the lounge, where Leonora had curled up on the sofa, a large glass of brandy on the side.

"So, Ed, I can't wait to hear about your trip. I wish I could have gone with you, but as you know, I couldn't get out of the charity work I'd signed up for. So do tell, how was it?"

Ed wanted so much to update Leonora on what he perceived to have been a very successful trip. But the anxiety was dragging him down, so he didn't feel much like having a long conversation that would not be as enthusiastic as it should be.

"Leonora, I've so much to tell you, but it's late, and I thought we'd retire?"

"After that kiss, Ed, I'm not sure I could handle an early night!" Leonora said, succumbing to the giggles.

Ed didn't mean he wanted to retire early for that reason. He had it in mind to sleep, but he understood why Leonora thought otherwise. He wasn't at all sure he was up for it, and more so now, given Leonora's response, suggesting she thought it would be special. But he certainly wasn't up for a long conversation about Kenya either.

Ed woke around 6:30 a.m., threw on a pair of shorts and went into the kitchen to make coffee and toast. As he put the breakfast on a tray, Leonora appeared by his side, kissing him and saying, "Ed, we should have more long breaks from each other."

"Has my 10-day absence made you realise you need a break more often?"

"You know that's not what I meant, Ed. But the sex was off the scale last night. So I'm just saying, time apart agrees with us! That is, of course, assuming you haven't been taking lessons elsewhere?"

Ed's face filled with disapproval. Pulling Leonora close, he told her that, no, he'd not been sleeping with anyone else. Pulling back slightly, he looked deep into her eyes. "Leonora..."

Then silence. He'd almost said, "Will you marry me?" stopping himself just as the words were about to roll off his tongue. He knew that would have been a mistake. True, it was a conversation he wanted to have, and he was acutely aware that leaving it too long could risk damaging their relationship. But blurting it out would have been a mistake.

"Ed, hello? Come back; you've vanished off to Planet Thorncroft."

Ed snapped out of his trance. "Sorry, Leonora, I was going to say I still cannot believe how fortunate I am to have got together with you. There would be a gaping hole in my life if you were not part of it."

"Ed, stop it. Your life would not have holes, gaping or otherwise. Even if we split up, you'd get over it. You are too strong a man, too focused to let anything drag you down for too long."

"Let's agree to disagree, Leonora."

"Ed, you usually get silly when something has got on top of you, not when you've just returned from a successful trip. Was it a turbulent flight home, or did I actually guess right on your lessons?"

"Stop it, Leonora. I don't need lessons!" Ed boasted. "And the flight was uneventful."

He was thinking to himself the flight was anything but uneventful, but not in the way Leonora had in mind. On the plus side, sex had the unexpected side-effect of zapping all his nervous energy, allowing him to drop off to sleep without returning to his fears. And given that he was still alive, he was optimistic that the man on the plane had not poisoned him.

Ed called an emergency meeting, inviting Creak, Brindle, Jail and Kai.

Ed now treated Kai as a de facto inner-circle member, inviting her more often than not when he was present. A week had passed since his return to England, and he wanted to discuss the photos and the incident on the plane.

"Good timing, Ed," said Jail. "I was going to call you yesterday, but knowing we were meeting today, I felt it could wait and would be better face to face."

"Okay, Jail, so I assume you've had something back from your contacts on the photos?" Ed pushed, waiting anxiously for an answer.

"Yes. They've identified two of the three people in the photos. The older man and the woman. The third, younger man, they've had no luck with yet." The third, as yet unidentified, man was the man in the lounge and on the plane – the man who'd bumped into Ed's chair.

"The older man and the woman work for LPAS in Europe and are based in France and the Netherlands. Neither has a very senior role, but both have previously worked in Pro-Watch and may well still be working for them."

Jail continued. "So it could be they were working for LPAS on surveillance legitimately. Or it could be unofficial surveillance, working for the dark side of the organisation. Right now, I've no easy way of finding out, as we do not have people on the inside, which you and I have discussed we need."

"And the wine?" Ed wanted to know, showing a little more anxiety.

"Negative. We've had the wine tested six ways from Sunday: nothing. It contained nothing more deadly than antioxidants." Jail looked disappointed. If they had known that the wine had been poisoned, they'd have known who administered it, and they had a photo of him.

"I don't get it," said Ed, now in deep thought. "There is no way he accidentally bumped into my chair. He didn't place a bug or tracker on me; it was the first thing I checked when I entered the toilet cubicle at the airport. So why knock into me? Why take the risk of drawing attention to himself?"

Creak and Kai looked at each other as concern crept into both their faces. Brindle caught sight of their reaction.

"Kai, Creak, what's up?" Brindle wanted to know.

"He wanted to see if anyone had your back, Ed," was Kai's view.

"I guess that's possible, Kai," Ed thought.

"No, Ed, it's fact," replied Creak.

"You can't know that, Creak," said Ed, now more worried, given that he knew Creak wasn't prone to wild guesses.

"I can, and I do," Creak instantly shot back.

"Creak, you're making me twitchy. Explain," Ed insisted.

"Kai and I didn't think very much of what I'm about to tell you until just now when we looked at each other – it was apparent we'd had the same thought. Three days ago, a robbery took place at Kai's house. Jewellery and money were taken, and paint was sprayed on the wall in the hallway and up the stairs. Kai and I discussed it, Kai filed a police report, and we put it down to kids – but not now. I believe this was a professional looking for information."

"If so professional, why not get in and get out without a trace? No need to fake a theft and vandalise the property, right?" was Ed's take.

"Wrong, Ed. He still might have left a clue, something to alert Kai that someone had been in the house. And that would have led to far greater concern on Kai's part. Steal a few items, cause some damage, and it all appears like street kids doing their thing."

"Kai, was there nothing that made you question the break-in, beyond it simply being kids?" Ed asked.

"Maybe I should have thought more about it, but no, as Creak said,

I put it down to the local thieves. I did dust the place, given the police showed no interest in doing so. No prints, no sign of anything being disturbed, other than the missing jewellery, money and the paint on the walls."

The team talked a little more about the robbery, and Ed agreed with Creak that a team would go into Kai's house to check for any devices and perform a complete sweep to see if they could come up with anything.

Kai had use of a safe house, a tiny apartment a couple of streets from her home, in which she kept her gun, ammunition and disguise kits most of the time. These items were in a safe with a tamper alarm hidden behind a false cupboard wall. If tampered with, Kai would have been alerted, and thankfully that hadn't happened. Ed further agreed that a team would be assigned to watch Kai's home to see if anyone was watching it in turn.

Ed started to shake his head. "Kai, I'm sorry for this mess."

"Ed, don't be. And before you suggest it, no, I am not standing down as your bodyguard."

"I don't think it's an option not to, Kai. It's too dangerous for you to continue. We need to get you off the grid for a while. We need to move you to a safe house," was Ed's firm belief.

"No, Ed, we don't. Kai is right. She needs to continue, and we need to assign a team of Guardians to her, and a bodyguard. If he has a mind to follow Kai, we'll nail the bastard!" said Creak, in as firm a tone as Ed's insistence that Kai stepped back.

"Sounds like we are using Kai as bait; we aren't doing that," said a visibly angry Ed.

"Oh, we are, Ed," Creak pushed back. "It is the only way to protect her. By now, we can be sure this guy knows who Kai is and that she owns her own security company, and in some ways that's fortunate for us. He will think you've hired personal protection. So he may well follow her, but even this guy is unlikely to think Kai will have a team of watchers or personal protection of her own," Creak concluded.

"I don't like this, Creak; it's too dangerous. Just hearing you say it out loud fills me with dread. This guy's a professional and a killer, maybe. We are not putting Kai in that position," Ed forcefully objected.

"We are, Ed," said Kai, cutting off Creak as he was about to respond. "I'm a professional too, Ed, and I'm not hiding from this bastard. I want this guy stopped; whatever he's doing, it's bound to be bad. This is the best way to lure him out."

Ed didn't like it one bit, but it was clear he was outvoted.

"Ed," said Creak. "It may well be that he has what he was looking for at Kai's. If he's going after you, he knows he will have to deal with Kai. If she disappears off the scene, the game will be up. And if he is making plans to cause you trouble, or worse, he will change his plans. It's the only option we have."

Ed reluctantly agreed.

"Kai, don't even consider getting killed, or you'll have me to deal with!" he put in, his voice quivering. He wasn't trying to be funny; it was his way of letting Kai know just how scared and concerned he was. Kai understood but was perplexed. Ed had lost sight of the fact that she wasn't the target. He was! But such was the man, and it was why everyone who knew him would trust him with their life.

"Ed, we will do everything possible to ensure that doesn't happen," Creak chipped in.

"Okay, folks, I don't know about all of you, but I need some down time from all this," said Kai, giving Ed a wink and a cheeky smile. Creak agreed, got up and asked them all what takeaway they'd like him to order.

Food out of the way, the group sat down to ensure everyone understood the changes that would be needed. It only took a few hours of planning to complete everything. Ed then called Gig to arrange transport.

The first eVTOL to land was for Creak. As his ride disappeared over the treetops, two more drones came into view, landing either side of the helipad. Brindle and Jail said goodbye to Kai and Ed and started walking back up to the main house. Jail was staying over at the main farmhouse to discuss other operational changes with Brindle. Before boarding her ride, Kai told Ed everything would be fine, and he shouldn't worry so much. As her drone rose above the treetops, Ed walked towards his. As he did, he reflected that those who had it in for him had now made several attempts to take him out of the picture but had so far failed – leaving him with a dreadful thought.

Everyone's luck runs out eventually... Ed just hoped that if it had to be, it would be his luck, not Kai's.

UNnatural Selection –
We all make mistakes

Kai had been going about her job of guarding Ed while various Guardians and her bodyguard ensured that she stayed safe. She had brought back Stephen Arnold to watch her back. Stephen had been off grid up in Scotland since the big steal in which he saved Hood's life. An ex-marine marksman who was a member of the British Special Boat Squadron, Stephen had also worked briefly for GCHQ and MI5 after leaving the armed services. Kai could think of no one else she wanted at her back.

Over the past couple of weeks, Guardians had taken shots of several people they believed were keeping tabs on Ed, but no one had been following Kai. Late Saturday evening, Ed was with Leonora, and Kai had assigned another bodyguard to stay close to him. POLO now had an apartment in the same block as Leonora, allowing them to remain close to Ed when he was at her place, which was often. Kai had been out on a late-night shopping trip buying Christmas gifts, after which she'd initially planned a night out in London. But, feeling tired, she had cancelled with her friends, having decided to turn in early. It had been a busy week of work and pleasure, and she was feeling flaked out.

A little over a month had passed since the team's return from Kenya, and almost as long since the break-in at her home, which now had an extensive covert alarm system, including silent alarm fittings, motion detection and a listen-in switch activated by infra-red sensors. If triggered, whatever was going on in the house could be overheard by a POLO operating centre set up by Creak. Since the break-in, he was fitting all senior and high-profile operatives' homes with sophisticated new alarm systems.

Around 22:30, Kai retired, falling asleep quickly, but at 2 a.m., she woke. She was thirsty and went downstairs for some water. As she walked past her lounge, a sense of unease washed over her. Her gun would usually be at her safe apartment, but she'd kept it with her at home due to current concerns. It was upstairs in a holster attached behind the headboard...

Kai continued to the kitchen, grabbing a large knife from the block. As she turned to walk back up the hallway to check everything was okay, she realised a man was standing behind her. With no time to respond – *whack!* – he hit her with a carotid strike, rendering her unconscious almost instantly. Kai was utterly defenceless.

Her attacker knelt beside her, laid out a cloth and pulled a plastic case from his jacket, laying it on the fabric. Opening it revealed a syringe and a vial filled with liquid. Lifting the vial, he pushed the needle into the rubber stopper and started to fill the syringe. As he did so, he was alerted by a slight noise from behind, immediately jumping up and turning as Stephen confronted him. As he lunged at Stephen with the syringe, Stephen knocked it from his hand, and a desperate struggle broke out.

Stephen pushed the stranger back. He toppled over, having tripped over Kai's inert form. He fell to the floor, pulling Stephen down with him. As they struggled, he pulled a knife and tried to stab Stephen in his face and upper body. Grabbing the blade, Stephen severely cut his hand but managed to hit the man several times in the face, forcing him to loosen his grip on the knife, which Stephen discarded behind him. Using it would have been preferable, but he had hold of the blade end and could not have turned it without risk.

The men were now in a mortal fight and as Stephen got up onto his knees, he continued to lash out with his fists. Blood sprayed around the kitchen, mainly from the cut to Stephen's hand. Now both were back up on their feet, the fight continued, with the assassin grabbing a large saucepan, hitting Stephen across the face before Stephen could respond with blows to the attacker's body. Then, holding the man by his hair at the neck, he smashed his head into the tap and dragged his body along the preparation area, with pans, crockery and cutlery crashing around the kitchen. Again falling to the floor, both men rolled among the smashed kitchenware, sustaining further injuries.

As Stephen managed to get up, he reached up for a rolling pin attached to the wall, lunging at the man several times. Then, as he stepped away and the would-be killer toppled back, Stephen hit him with the pin square on the chin, knocking him back hard against the wall and momentarily dazing him, allowing Stephen to line up a hard blow to his head, followed by two more, taking the man down hard. Stephen leant forward to hit him again before realising he was out cold.

Stephen dropped to his knees, breathing heavily, blood pouring from his hand and several minor cuts.

Stephen stood up and rinsed his hand in the sink, which made no difference, given the wound was so deep and the blood was oozing out so fast. Cutting a tea towel down the middle, he tied it around his hand to staunch the flow. Then he looked down at the intruder.

Stephen thought it could just as well have been him lying on the floor unconscious. The man before him, whoever he was, was well trained, and the fight could have gone either way. Stephen cleaned up best he could before raiding Kai's cupboards.

He found kitchen string and proceeded to double it and tie the assassin's hands and feet. Once secure, he lifted him out of the kitchen and headed to the hallway, opening the door to the cellar and carrying him down the stairs, having first considered throwing him down. Stephen checked again to ensure that the man was tied securely before searching him and taking a phone, wallet, keys and a gun strapped to his leg. Finding the weapon sent a shiver through him. He knew, had he managed to reach that, it would have been a different outcome.

Stephen knelt beside the unconscious man for the next few minutes to get his breath back and compose himself before making his way back up the stairs and into the kitchen. He checked Kai's radial pulse; thankfully, and surprisingly, it was strong, with a steady rhythm. Picking her up, he carried her into the living room, placing her on the sofa, before returning to the kitchen to look for the vial and syringe. He made a call to Creak while looking through Kai's medical box. Having spoken with Creak, he rushed upstairs, searching Kai's bathrooms and returning to the kitchen for a bowl, spoon, some warm water, a cloth and towel, and then going back to the living room.

He cleaned up as best he could a nasty gash on the side of Kai's head. He then placed a few teaspoons of Epsom salts he had found in Kai's medical box into the bowl and poured some essential oils he had found in the bathroom on top, mixing it all before waving it under Kai's nose.

Within a minute or two, Kai came round on the sofa, and Stephen sat by her side. As she tried to sit up, she felt a little giddy and laid her head back down. A stabbing pain ran from her right ear across the top of her head.

"Don't get up, Kai. You have a doozy of a cut on your head. I've stopped the bleeding, but you don't look your best. Do you remember anything?"

Groggy, Kai responded. "Very little. I became uncomfortable as I walked past the lounge. I continued to the kitchen, grabbed a knife, and as I turned, someone was standing there, but I can't remember reacting."

"It's clear from the blood on the kitchen cabinet that you hit your head on the way down. But that wasn't what took you out so quickly that you could not respond. I think, as you turned, you took a blow to your carotid sinus; game over," was Stephen's view.

"I'm confused, Stephen. Just what the hell happened?" said Kai, unable to pull it all together in her mind, in pain and feeling nauseous.

Stephen swiped his phone and turned the screen to Kai. "He happened."

Stephen played a short video of the man tied up in a dimly lit room. Kai recognised it instantly as her basement.

"Who is he?"

"I don't know, but when I arrived, he was preparing to inject you. Creak is on his way over. I was hoping you'd recognise him?"

"No, I can't say I do," Kai responded. "And how was I so lucky as to have you skulking around in the dead of night? I didn't think I was being covered overnight at home now I have a state-of-the-art secret squirrel security system in place. But boy am I happy you were around."

"Ed changed the rules soon after you set them! He assigned Tan – real name Tim Lawton – to watch over you during the day and told me I was to stay with you through the night. Ed was very insistent you had cover 24/7, and just as insistent that I take the night shift."

"Ed's a good judge of people," Kai said with some relief.

"I'll take that as a compliment," said Stephen with a smile.

"We may not know who he is, but he's damn good. Your kitchen's a bloody bomb site, in every sense of the word. He almost got the better of me. He's well trained." As Stephen said this, Kai noticed the cuts and bruises on Stephen's face and arms and registered the bright red tea towel wrapped around his hand.

"Geez, man, I'm sorry, how did I not notice? You look a mess!"

"Don't worry, Kai. He doesn't look too good either."

"You need to get that hand seen to, Stephen."

"I will, but the blood flow has slowed."

"Very restrained, Stephen. I'm surprised you didn't just shoot him."

"Kai, Creak would not have been happy had I killed him, losing our only chance of getting information on the bill payer. But secondly, I'm not packing my gun."

"Well, had the new state-of-the-art security system worked, it wouldn't have been a problem, would it?" Kai said abruptly, still a little dizzy and having to focus so as not to vomit.

"There's a reason for that, Kai."

"Oh, what's that?"

"It only works if you arm it!" Stephen quickly responded, staring at her incredulously.

"Oh, damn it, you're right. I'm not used to having alarm systems," she said, thinking that somehow mitigated her colossal error.

"Kai," Stephen responded with a fearful look on his face. "You are so lucky to be here, and I'm not bigging myself up. You can't afford to make schoolboy errors; you know that. I think you are just too fearless for your own good. When that stuff–" Stephen pointed to the syringe on the coffee table "–is analysed, I think it will be heroin – diamorphine – they find. We used to carry it on missions. And it often smelled vinegary. Just like that stuff."

It now hit Kai hard. This man was going to kill her, no question. Kai was a tough lady, but she struggled to stop a few tears rolling down her face. Hugging her, Stephen told her to let it out. But she was too strong to break down in the company of another bodyguard.

"I'm okay, Stephen, but this should never have happened." Kai spluttered a little as a few tears hit her top lip and ran into the crease as she spoke. "What a stupid mistake to have made, and one that had it not been for you..." Kai paused at that thought, and anger, not at her would-be killer, but at herself, coursed through her body.

"We all screw up, Kai. Just imagine how he feels right now!"

"I don't think 'thank you' cuts it, Stephen, but – *mahalo*," Kai said, smiling at him.

"Did you just swear at me, Kai!"

"No, Stephen, *mahalo* means 'thank you' in Hawaiian." Kai's place of birth.

"No *mahalo* needed, Kai. I'm just so pleased I was around."

"Not as pleased as I am, Stephen."

"Well, on the bright side, you got him to come out into the open."

"I don't think so. That's not the man on the plane. I said earlier, I don't recognise him."

This comment worried Stephen. How many of them were there?

After about fifty-minutes, Creak arrived, and one of Kimberly's people was with him. There were also two other men. Neither Kai nor Stephen knew either of them, and Creak didn't introduce them.

"Honu–" Creak wouldn't use her real name in front of others "–this lady is going to check you over once she's helped these two gentlemen. After that, she will take you to one of our safe medical houses for a proper examination."

"I've got a headache and feel a little sick and dizzy, no more. I'll be fine," Kai responded.

"It wasn't a request; you're going," Creak said bluntly. "Seal–" Stephen's handle "–you need to go too and get those cuts seen too. That hand looks nasty."

"Yes, boss." Stephen knew better than to push back.

"Where's our guest?" said an angry-looking Creak, looking directly at Stephen.

"In the cellar, basement, whatever it's called!"

With that, the two men who'd arrived with Creak disappeared down the stairs with the nurse, reappearing five or so minutes later with Kai's attacker tucked between them, still out cold. They exited the house, climbed into a waiting van and drove away.

"What's going on with him?" Kai said, looking up at Creak as the nurse started to check her over.

"Don't ask, Honu." So came the sinister response from Creak.

"I don't recognise him," said Kai. "He's not the guy on the plane."

"Oh, I think he is, Honu. I think he took a chance on the plane. Fake passport and a disguise. But I recognise that face from a grainy still taken from a freeze-frame video some time ago."

"Do you know him from your previous life?" Kai inquired.

"No. Thankfully, I didn't have to deal with psychos at Special

Branch."

"Psychos, Sepia?" (Creak's codename) Stephen asked.

"If he's who I think he is, he's a dangerous man. And I think I'm right… But enough. Forget he was ever here; understood?"

Kai and Stephen nodded.

Creak arrived at a derelict warehouse in London's East End, one of a handful of sites owned by POLO. The site, secured with nine-foot steel fencing, had posters up saying a new drone pad was coming soon. Gig had plans to build a few private landing pads in the East End as part of Ed's broader plans for POLO expansion. Albeit Gig Transport was a legitimate business. Inside were the two gentlemen that Creak had arrived at Kai's house with and chained to a steel bar on the wall was Kai's would-be killer.

"Brave man," Creak said, visibly shaking with anger.

"Cut the crap," replied the man chained to the wall. "You got lucky.

You work for a security company that's not even that big in the UK, and you got lucky. If you think you're scaring me, think again. You can keep up this pretence of a hard and dangerous man for as long as you like, hoping I'll start to feel that something terrible is going to happen and start blabbing. It'll be a waste of time. Your actions have already compromised the case against me. I'll be out in no time, and I'll disappear as quickly as I appeared. So fuck off."

Creak looked at his two guys. "Leave us. Watch the outside." Creak's folks left, and he pulled up a box beside the chained man.

"I'm not playing a game, Orpheus." Creak paused, wanting to see any sign of a response to the use of the name. Nothing.

Creak continued.

"You've made a lot of money working for powerful and important people. You've got a great many friends in high places, and I suspect many would work hard to get you out of a tight spot." Creak paused again; still nothing.

"I agree with part of your assessment. I'm sure if I handed you over to the police, you'd manage to get off. And if that didn't work, I'm sure someone would get you out. Let's face it. You know way too much not to be helped." Pausing again, this time for longer, but still there was no response.

"I'm not looking to scare you, beat or torture you. I wouldn't waste my time. Hell, I don't even want to talk to scum like you. However, you are going to give me information on who hired you for this job. And here's why."

"Giving me the details will dent your pride, your sense of professionalism, and be a breach of your contract, but you'll get over it. And I know you're not the kind of man who would be looking to come after me for having got you to hand over information on who's paying the bill. There is no profit in that; so, once I have the information, you're free to go."

Creak stood up. "Can you hear that? Listen carefully; it's the sound of fast-flowing water. Let me show you."

He went over to a heavy iron grate on the floor. Creak, 6ft 2in, thick-set, and someone who worked out daily, struggled to lift it with the hooked metal bar designed to open it. Beneath his feet, you could now see and hear more clearly a torrent of running water. Shouting slightly, as Creak was standing right beside the four-by-four-foot open hatch, he continued:

"This huge pipe runs the length of these warehouses, and the water in it eventually enters the Thames. From this location, it takes around seven minutes, then it enters from a pipe at the bottom of the Thames where the current is strong. If someone fell into this hole, I'd hate to think how horrible that would be. I guess that's why these covers are so damned heavy and normally bolted in place with three heavy padlocks. I mean, even if you could hold your breath for seven minutes, there would be no guarantee you'd reach the surface upon entering the Thames, given the strength of the currents."

Creak pushed the trap door down, which let out a loud crack as it closed, making Orpheus flinch.

"Right now, you look too beat up. You must have tried hard to get the better of my friend. But he's good, isn't he? So, for now, you're safe.

And that gives you a little time to think about my ask.

"When your cuts and bruises have healed, I'll be back. There'll be no more talk from me then. And no more deafening silence from you. When you next see me, you will start talking, give me what I need to ensure the safety of my friends, and be on your way. If you do not, I will drop you into that hole without uttering a single word. Of that you can be damn sure."

Ed was at the farmhouse in Kent with Creak, Jail, Brindle and Kimberly. It had been five days since the attempt on Kai's life, and Stephen's, for that matter.

"Okay, do we have anything?" Ed, clearly shaken by events, wanted to know.

"As you all know now, the substance in the syringe was heroin. Had it been injected, the amount in the syringe would have killed Kai within a minute," Kimberly noted.

"I don't need you to tell me that, Kimberly, I'm well aware, thank you," Ed responded angrily.

"Okay; sorry, Ed. Bloody hell, you asked for an update, so I'm updating you," Kimberly snapped back.

"Sorry, Kimberly, that was out of order. I'm on edge. I wasn't clear. I was asking if we have anything from the man who attacked Kai."

Crunching an apple, Creak responded: "Don't know, Ed, haven't spoken to him," then shrugged his shoulders.

"Oh, you haven't spoken to him? Great. Then what the fuck are we doing? We've kidnapped a nutter, but we haven't spoken to him. So what was the point of not handing him over to the police?" Ed's anxious demeanour was turning to anger.

Now Creak kicked off, standing up and laughing. "Like that would have worked out, Ed. He'd have been out quicker than they could have booked him in. And then the questions would start. And how do you think that would have panned out? The police would have been all over us, not Orpheus."

"Great, so what's the plan? Beat him, kill him – what's the plan?"

"Ed, for God's sake, calm down. I know what I'm doing. This man won't talk unless he thinks the game is up. We aren't going to beat him up or torture him, but without his information, we aren't letting him go either," replied Creak, leaning in towards Ed.

Before Ed could answer, Jail piped up. "Ed, we know you don't like this side of the business, but Creak knows what he's doing. He is also right on the point of letting him go without him giving up what we need, the name of the money man. And handing him over to the police won't work either. It would damage us more than him. So he'll walk, or someone will top him because of what he knows.

"If, however, he gives us the information, we can let him go. His type isn't vengeful. He's a professional hitman and will have no reason to warn his current masters once he has outed them. That would be way too risky and could end his career, if not his life. So he gets to live. Letting him stew on that for a while is the best hope we have that he will give them up. If he doesn't, so be it."

"So be it? What, we just off him?" Ed asked in frustration.

"Yes, Ed. We off him. Unless you have a better idea – and when I say better, I mean safer. One that keeps us and the organisation secure. Well, have you?" replied a now bad-tempered Jail.

Ed sat on the arm of the chair between Creak and Jail. "Let's rewind, folks. I'm sorry, I guess I somewhat set the tone. You're right; I do hate all this. I can't articulate how much I hate all this. So not talking to him is part of your 'stewing plan'?"

"I've had a chat with him, Ed," Creak responded. "He knows that when I turn up next, he either talks or drowns."

"Drowns, Creak?"

"I can burden you if you wish, Ed. But there is no need for you to hear all the detail right now."

"If there's a God, it is clear where I'm going when I die." This was Ed's way of saying he didn't need the detail.

Brindle piped up. "Ed, good people do bad things too, but for good reasons."

"Is that meant to make me feel better? Because it doesn't. You can tell yourself that if you wish, but it doesn't work for me. I stomach it because we are saving lives, and that's the moral thing to do. It is forced on us by an immoral set of laws. But that fact does not make the bad things we do moral."

No one responded. He was right, and they all had to live with the bad things they'd done.

"Okay, when do you plan to close this out, Creak?" Ed wanted to know.

"His cuts and bruises are healing nicely, so I'd say around five more days."

"I think I get that, Creak," Ed responded, while a chill shot down his spine. "Okay, thanks for the updates, and sorry I'm being grumpy. I'm working from one of the small cottages today, if that's okay, Brindle?"

"Okay, Ed, I'll have some food brought in for you."

Ed went over and settled in one of the smaller cottages; he started to work, opening his laptop. But he couldn't focus. He knew that this wasn't the same as when his group had killed a serving police officer. This man was a professional killer who intended to kill Kai, and then him, just for money. So why was it playing on his mind? It was because they should have turned the guy over to the police but hadn't. And now they had made plans for his possible murder, should he keep quiet – premeditated murder. At the same time, Ed knew letting him go without leverage would be a huge mistake.

"A penny for your thoughts?" said Brindle, who'd been standing in the open doorway for a minute or two, watching Ed, who looked extremely worried.

"That's a dated saying, Brindle."

"I know, Ed. I got it from my grandmother."

"My dark thoughts aren't good for the soul, Brindle."

"A problem shared is a problem halved."

"That's just as old."

"I know. I got it from my great-grandmother."

Ed laughed, then Brindle did too. "Thanks, Brindle. I needed a distraction. I have a constant internal battle with all this. I know it's right, but then I know it is also wrong. I tell myself we do what we do to save lives. And then I ask myself, is taking a life justified to save a life? To be honest, Brindle, I'm in a constant state of turmoil."

"I hear you, Ed. I wish I could help, but the way you feel is because of the person you are. And I wouldn't want to change that."

UNnatural Selection –
Mounting concern

The assassin, believed to be Orpheus, was finishing the food put before him by one of his minders, who was waiting to take away his utensils: a wooden knife, fork and tin plate.

"When are you morons going to give up on this macho bullshit? You and I both know that you aren't going to kill me. You're professional bodyguards, not murderers. You were just pissed that I almost topped one of your own – two, actually," he continued with a smile that pissed off his minder. Orpheus had spoken for the first time since Creak left the building, which was now nine days ago.

"No good talking to me; I'm not the decision-maker. That's someone else's job."

"So you're not going to play the tough killer role like your boss?" the assassin asked.

"Nope. But if I were you, I wouldn't sit there all smug, thinking he's bluffing. I've known him for a long time; he doesn't bluff," the minder put in.

As the minder took away the utensils, Stephen Arnold walked in.

"I was wondering when you'd show up to try and scare me," said the assassin with a cocky grin on his face.

Stephen walked up close, grabbed a box and sat about six feet away.

"We haven't beaten you; we've not been talking with you other than when you first arrived. Does it seem to you like we're the kind of people who want to scare you into giving up the bill payer?"

No response, so Stephen continued.

"Between you and me, I want nothing more than for you to stay silent. Now, my boss dislikes you as much as the rest of us. But he does want you to give it up. Aside from all the bad things my boss has done in his life, he still has a heart. He'd much prefer the information than to have to kill you." Stephen paused again, then pulled his box closer and, looking directly into the assassin's eyes, continued.

"I want you to be clear just how it's going to play out. First, we're going to put you to sleep, just like we did when we brought you here. Then, while you are sleeping, we'll strip you, shave you, wash you up, put on some nice aftershave, and put you in an expensive suit that we've already purchased for you. Then we pour a reasonable amount of excellent cognac down your shirt and jacket, a splash on your trousers, and wake you up."

Stephen stopped momentarily, still staring intensely into the assassin's eyes, before continuing.

"We'll hold you down, put a funnel in your mouth, and give you the rest of the bottle. We'll then open the grate and throw you down the hole." Stephen again paused briefly before continuing.

"See, mister brave, macho killer, we aren't all bad. You'll be so pissed you won't care about the fact you're drowning and will be dead within a few minutes. And when your body eventually pops up somewhere way down the Thames, they'll log you as just another drunk who fell in – or maybe you had problems and topped yourself. Whichever way it goes, I don't care. I'll be glad we whacked a low-life who earns his money killing good people."

"My boss, he'll be a little upset. But you should know this: if you're not talking the moment he walks back through that door, no amount of talking will change his mind once he starts that process; none." Pausing one last time, while holding eye contact the entire time, Stephen went on.

"I'm hoping that you think you're so smart that you've figured this all out. Because I'm going to be looking you in the eyes one last time as I heave you down that hole." With that, he got up and left the warehouse.

Orpheus was now starting to think about the possibility that he had called it wrong. Several times over the past nine days he'd doubted his perspective, especially as he hadn't been beaten or interrogated. Hell, no one was evening talking to him. Orpheus had fixed his eyes on Stephen's the entire time he was talking, and this had almost convinced him that the man before him was telling the truth and that in no more than a few days' time, his life was going to end.

Three days after Stephen's talk with Orpheus, just before 22:30, Creak, Stephen, Kimberly and Kai entered the warehouse. All had on disguises except Kai, as Orpheus knew her face anyway.

Kimberly sat on a box well away from Orpheus, opened a small medical bag and started to prepare an injection. Creak pulled a litre bottle of cognac from a holdall and placed it on a box beside him. The two minders had already started to fill an enormous plastic container over the back of the warehouse with water.

Orpheus was now feeling fearful. Even so, he was still pushing himself to believe this was just a group of bodyguards trying to scare him into giving up the money man. He was hanging on to this still being a game of chicken that he was going to win.

Not a word said, Kimberly looked at Creak. Creak nodded and, pointing at both the minders, gestured back to Orpheus. As the minders and Kimberly moved towards Orpheus, he finally cracked.

"Okay, okay, you fucking madman, you win, you win."

Kimberly and the minders continued towards him; Creak still hadn't spoken.

"Logan Miller… Logan Miller's the money man. Leave now, fucking leave, don't kill me. I've given you what you wanted."

He was sobbing loudly, like a young child who'd been scolded and sent to their bedroom. Through his tears, he continued to beg Creak not to kill him, firing expletives off so fast that he was making little sense.

Creak finally spoke. "You left it sixty-seconds too late," he said in a soft but sinister voice.

Sobbing, making it difficult to be understood, Orpheus screamed out: "You promised me! You said you'd let me live if I gave you the money man. You promised, you fucking promised! I've got young kids, two kids, girls, don't do this. Please don't kill me; they need me." His face red, covered in sweat, snot and tears, Orpheus made eye contact with Creak. "Please, please, don't do this," he begged, sobbing all the while.

"The killer begs. You are indeed the lowest of the human race, and a coward. God knows how many lives you've taken to fund your lavish lifestyle. Yet here you are, begging me to spare yours." Creak's face gave away his disgust at the man before him.

Stephen winked at him, causing him significantly more distress, flashing back to the chat Stephen had with him a few days earlier and now realising he was looking forward to gazing into his eyes as he threw him down the pipe.

Creak stared at him for a few seconds, then continued. "I told you that if you were not talking when I walked in, it would be too late. And you weren't talking. So I've broken no promises."

As the assassin's minders grabbed him, Kimberly knelt a few feet away, syringe in hand. As Orpheus saw her flick the needle, he gave out a blood-curdling scream, flaying about in fear, the adrenalin flowing through his body giving him almost superhuman strength, making it difficult to contain him. As Kimberley got close, he shouted for all he was worth at Creak not to kill him, begging for his life for the sake of his wife and children. Creak, still staring into his eyes, said nothing.

"Sepia," – Creak's handle – shouted Kai. "Give him a chance. Give him a chance for me."

Creak looked up at her, momentarily transfixed by her eyes, which looked a little sad. He looked back at

Orpheus, then back to Kai. The assassin had fallen silent but was still sobbing and staring intently at Kai before averting his gaze to Creak. Creak remained silent; the seconds now seemed like minutes as they ticked away: 1, 2, 5, 10, 20, 30. Then, finally, Creak blinked, dropped his head momentarily and looked back at Orpheus.

"You are never going to know the fortune bestowed on you by Kai's words. Your crying, begging, talk of your wife and children, none of it would have saved you. I don't make idle threats. But you're still not out of the woods, not even because of Kai."

"I've some questions for you, and if you answer them immediately, I'll spare your sad, pathetic life. Not because I don't want to kill you. Oh, I want to so bad. But Kai has given you one last roll of the dice. You've played the big man once tonight. I don't recommend you do so again – so answer without hesitation."

"Thank you, I understand, and thank you, Kai." Orpheus continued: "It wasn't personal. It's just a job." Even that ridiculous last statement didn't send Kai off on one. She just looked down at him in pity.

Creak spoke again. "Are you the assassin known as Orpheus?"

"Yes."

"Who is Logan Miller?"

"He's a deputy director of LPAS based in New York at the UN building."

"Is there a secret organisation within LPAS?"

"I don't know; maybe, but I'm not privy to that information."

"What was your contract?"

"To terminate Edward Thorncroft, but it had to look like an accident, a mugging, or maybe suicide."

"Why target Kai?"

"I researched her when she dropped a note to Thorncroft on the plane. Good pedigree, so I couldn't take a chance on her screwing up my plans."

Creak shuddered at the cold heart of the person in front of him. Then, leaning down, he picked up a paper pad and threw it and a pen at their captive. "Write down your real name, where you live, and the names of your wife and children."

Orpheus looked into Creak's eyes. Utter fear was now streaming through his body, but he knew that to refuse would mean certain death. As he started to scribble, he begged Creak not to hurt his family.

"I'm not a monster like you. This information is merely insurance for my friends. If I even suspect you've talked or I hear your name come up in the intelligence community as being active, I'll find you. After today, you've retired."

Orpheus pushed the notepad back towards Creak, and Creak asked one of his folks to take it and check it out.

"If what you have written checks out, I'll release you. It'll likely take us a while to confirm. Once we have, we'll drop you somewhere in town. But don't take too long to leave the country."

Orpheus went to speak, but Creak shut him down. "Don't. Not another word or I'll struggle to contain my desire to throw you down that hole."

The four of them made their way to a safe house in London where Ed would meet them. As they left the warehouse, Creak messaged Ed, letting him know they would be at the house within the hour. Ed arrived at the house in Mayfair just after midnight.

"Should I ask how it went?" Ed asked apprehensively.

"He decided to retire."

Ed's mouth dropped open before Creak could explain.

"No, Ed, we didn't kill him," Creak continued. "But I don't expect he'll be taking on any new work."

"How can you be so sure he won't come after us? After all, we've let him go, yes?" Ed responded.

"We've not let him go yet. We've some facts to check out. But I suspect they'll check out fine. In the end, I don't think his mind was in any state to play games," responded a confident Creak.

Ed asked Creak to lay out all that had happened to help him understand Creak's confidence. Twenty minutes later, Creak concluded his walk-through, and Ed commented.

"I shouldn't have doubted your methods, Creak. We've got good information from this, which, I agree with you, should stop him from working in the future. And we now have a lead on the darker side of LPAS, so maybe we can shut them down too."

"Jail or I will share what we have, or at least all we can, with our contacts in the intelligence community, Ed, but don't expect overnight miracles. It will take a lot of surveillance on Logan to figure out who his fellow dark actors are before any intelligence service moves on them. When Logan realises that Orpheus has gone off grid, he'll shut down any activity he's involved in for the darker side of LPAS, just as we do when we sense trouble. He'll go back to being a regular director for LPAS."

Creak's statement disheartened Ed, but he knew he was right.

"It's been a challenging few weeks, and I've still not shaken off my anxiety about what happened to you, Kai. So I can't imagine what you're feeling right now. I'm just so thankful for the way it's turned out." Ed paused, then continued.

"Creak, nice ruse, having Kai jump in with a reprieve. It got him singing like a canary," Ed quipped.

"It wasn't a ruse, Ed. I didn't ask Kai to jump in."

Shocked, Ed looked over to Kai for her response.

"I wanted to give him the chance that I know he would not have given me," Kai said in a low, caring tone. "It is what sets us apart from people like Orpheus."

"Yes, Kai, you're right. It does," Ed concurred, thinking that he needed to take on board what Kai had just said. That might help him rationalise the bad things they did.

"Creak, what would you have done had he refused to talk?"

"He'd have been swimming with the fishes, Ed."

Ed gulped. "I'm so pleased you are on my side, Creak!"

UNnatural Selection – New York

Ed commenced a long-planned trip to the United Nations. He would be meeting UN seniors, members of the World Health Organisation, a few representatives of various countries, and, surprisingly, the global head of LPAS had invited him to a private lunch.

It was January 2046, and New York was bitterly cold. Ed had visited New York numerous times over the past few years, but he'd forgotten just how mind-numbingly cold it could be. A taste of the weather as he was waiting in the taxi line at JFK put paid to that.

His protection officer wasn't happy that Ed hadn't accepted the offer of a car to collect him.

Stepping into a taxi, the officer turned to Ed. "Mr Thorncroft.

Protecting you isn't going to be easy if you insist on public transport and the like."

"I don't plan to change how I live. That would be giving in to whoever wishes me harm," Ed responded.

"Dying will be giving in too!" the officer shot back.

Ed shrugged but didn't respond to this rather obvious point highlighting Ed's stubbornness in leading his life in a somewhat foolhardy manner.

His visit to New York made him irritable and uncomfortable when it should have had the opposite effect. US Secret Service agents were assigned to keep him safe, working alongside British Special Branch. SB was now known as CTC (Counter-Terrorism Command) after an internal merge but was still referenced as Special Branch in Ed's circles due to Creak's history with the unit.

UK officials acted a few weeks after Ed's folks shared their information with the security services. Ed was contacted and advised that officers would be looking after him for the foreseeable future, as the intelligence they had received indicated that his life could be at risk. Not that Ed didn't already know that. But after his team had so effectively dealt with Orpheus, Ed was feeling far more relaxed, almost forgetting that those who had hired him were still at large.

Guardians and his bodyguards had been pulled and would not re-engage until Ed's government minders stepped down, and that would not likely be for some time. The presence of his new minders also meant he would be unable to play an active role in POLO. He would, however, engage with the team using secure communications, and a briefing file would keep him up to speed on critical operational matters.

Ed knew it was for the best, and Creak had already warned him not to refuse help from the security services. Special Branch was a large, highly trained group of professionals. Ed, however, still felt safer with Kai at his back, even though she would often have to keep her distance.

This first disagreement with his British guard would, Ed was sure, be the first of many. The secret service, who'd turned up at the airport, also showed their annoyance at Ed's choice of travel, now having to follow his taxi.

Ed was making his way through the halls of the UN, discreetly making sure to look at everyone around him in the hope of spotting Logan Miller. Not wise, though, as Ed could ill afford to react, intentionally or otherwise, should they pass each other. Ed already knew what he looked like after reading his UN profile but was curious and wanted to see him in the flesh.

By sheer coincidence, a few rooms up from Ed's meeting were Benjamin Brown and James Brown (no relation), critical people within the secret LPAS organisation. Benjamin, you may recall, headed up this clandestine group. Absent was Logan Miller. As Creak had predicted, Logan's failure to make contact with Orpheus meant he'd dropped out of anything to do with the criminal organisation within LPAS.

"I've spoken with Logan, Benjamin. He briefed me last night on the continued break in contact with our mutual friend," James Brown said at the start of their meeting.

"We should be concerned about this development. As you know, our mutual friend was in Nairobi and London, working on our problem, which still exists, but our friend has seemingly dropped off the planet," Benjamin responded.

"One of the security agencies could have detained him, Benjamin," James speculated.

"Possibly, but for what? And if so, they can't legally detain him for this long; they'd have to charge him with something, and we would then know," said a confident Benjamin.

"Ben, extraordinary rendition has been in practice since the late 1980s. Do we think it isn't going on now? Come on. If a security agency felt they had reason to pick him up, we would not know until he popped back up in public, likely at court," said James, giving his opinion on the security services.

"You could be right. Maybe our friend has upset someone he's contracted with," mused Benjamin.

"We aren't going to know until someone lets him stick his head up. So until then, Logan's out of the picture. He's the only person known to our mutual friend," said James firmly.

"And what if he doesn't pop back up?" fretted Benjamin.

"Then Logan will have to resign his position with us," James posited. His view was that allowing him to restart work on covert operations would be too big a risk.

"He's made a few mistakes, James. But he's the best we have operationally. He's achieved a lot for our cause. We'd be light without his particular set of skills, and especially his contacts," Benjamin pushed back.

"Your call ultimately, Benjamin. But if our friend doesn't resurface, I'd leave Logan out in the boondocks for some considerable time."

"I hear you, James. I'll not be looking to bring him home too soon if we hear nothing. Don't fret," said Benjamin, looking to reassure James that he was not going to take any unnecessary risks.

"Talking of our problem, Benjamin, I passed him in the lobby this morning," James informed his colleague.

"I knew he was here, even before I saw him myself. The visitors' register listed his visit some time ago. I had, however, rather hoped the visit wouldn't take place due to, well, shall we say, a tragic accident... But unfortunately that didn't happen. I also noticed that he has government protection." So said Benjamin, who'd been wondering all morning why Ed now had protection.

"Yes, I saw them with him. He's a high-profile figure now; perhaps the UK government felt obliged to afford him protection," James responded, not attaching too much importance to it.

"Maybe, James, maybe." Benjamin, however, wasn't entirely convinced.

"It'll make it much more difficult to get to him, if not impossible," James put in.

"Yes, I know. Our problem just became a little more complex."

Benjamin was annoyed at this development, coming on top of losing contact with someone tasked with making this most troublesome fellow go away.

Ed completed a full day of meetings, but his day wasn't over. He would meet later with Gabriel Meyer, the UN secretary-general, for a private dinner at a restaurant in Greenwich Village, where Meyer had an apartment. It had been almost six years since LPAS passed into law, and you'll recall that Meyer was the secretary-general then and announced the UN's decision to enact the new laws. Meyer was now into his second term as secretary-general.

Ed's work against LPAS was getting plenty of attention, and Meyer, genuinely interested in his views, had asked to meet him for dinner. Ed arrived first, flanked by a Special Branch officer and two secret service agents. The American agents stayed outside the restaurant, having first checked it out, with the British agent taking a seat at the bar. Ed was shown to his table, ordered a gin and tonic, and browsed the menu while he awaited Gabriel Meyer's arrival. Thirty or so minutes later, Gabriel walked in.

"Apologies, Edward. Stuck in a late-running meeting, and then, as it often is in New York, the traffic was horrendous."

"No problem," Ed responded, standing up to shake his hand.

The pair talked so much over dinner it was surprising either of them managed to eat anything. To Ed's surprise, Gabriel seemed sympathetic to his cause and agreed with many of his views. "I must say, Gabriel, I was expecting a much more difficult conversation with you this evening," he confessed.

"Ed, I was never a big supporter of LPAS, rather the mouthpiece for the United Nations once it had made its mind up," Gabriel responded with an embarrassed smile.

"I recall Switzerland voting against LPAS, Gabriel, and judging by your face as you approached the lectern all those years ago, I assumed this had rather upset you?"

"No, Ed, it made me feel awkward, but I was pleased that my country felt this was a step too far," Gabriel continued. "Ed, I want to help you, which presents me with a conundrum. While I am secretary-general,

I cannot do so openly. But if I were not in this post, I would be of far less use to you. If you push for the right changes, not too fast, not too bold, I will work in the background to help drum up support."

Gabriel's statement stunned Ed; it was beyond anything he'd expected. "I'm taken aback, Gabriel. But I am truly grateful and exceptionally pleased to have someone so senior at the UN prepared to provide support – I understand, off the record." Ed's smile was wide.

"Ed, I've not too much time remaining as secretary-general, so time is of the essence," Gabriel responded thoughtfully.

"Oh, okay, I wasn't aware you were planning to stand down."

"Not planning, Ed, but my second term will be up in a few years,"

Gabriel responded.

"Not going for a third, then?" Ed inquired.

"Technically, there is no limit to the number of five-year terms a secretary-general can serve. However, in United Nations history, no one has ever served more than two, and I think it unlikely that this would get support from the members, even if I wanted to. So I still have a few years, but getting changes to LPAS of the kind you are looking for is likely to happen at a glacial pace."

Gabriel, looking directly into Ed's eyes, wanted to ensure Ed understood.

Ed understood all too well, but support from the Secretary-General was a significant break. The two of them continued to talk for another hour before Ed advised Gabriel that he needed to leave, having an early start in the morning. As they left the restaurant, Gabriel reaffirmed his commitment to support Ed covertly, if presented with changes he felt he could muster broad support for from other UN members.

The morning after his dinner with Gabriel Meyer, Ed was up early and already on his second cup of coffee in an office in the United Nations building. It was 6:35 a.m. In a few hours, he would be eating lunch with the global head of LPAS, 'El Diablo', as Ed always referred to him in private.

Timur – pronounced Teemor – Oblonsky had been the head of LPAS globally since its inception. A native of Russia, he had a reputation for getting his way. Unsurprisingly, Timur meant 'iron man'. Ed was well briefed by his people on Timur and was also given a short brief by Gabriel Meyer over dinner. He wasn't too concerned about meeting him. He wasn't expecting a breakthrough or a meeting of minds. Instead, Ed expected Timur to attempt to intimidate him. And for that, Timur had Tweedledee and Tweedledum, as Ed had named them.

Vladimir and Sergei Kazakov, identical twin brothers, were referred to even at the United Nations as Timur's 'enforcers'. Not just identical twins, they always styled their hair the same and always wore identical clothes.

Although they often seemed at odds with each other, in reality they were almost always in agreement. They played the 'at odds' card to draw in their target, a take on the good cop/bad cop routine, with one of them looking to befriend a mark before undermining them.

Ed already had a large file on the twins and had read a lot about them, so this tactic would not work on him. Just before 1 p.m., Ed started his short journey to the concierge suites. A private room had been booked for lunch. Ed arrived, was greeted by the concierge manager, and was escorted to the room.

Inside were Timur and, as Ed had suspected, Tweedledee and Tweedledum, Vladimir and Sergei.

"Good afternoon, Mr Thorncroft. I'm delighted to meet you at last," said Timur Oblonsky, sporting a mischievous grin.

Lying bastard, Ed thought to himself before responding. "Likewise, Timur, but I didn't get the message to bring my bodyguards along too."

"Come, come, Mr Thorncroft, you know these aren't my bodyguards. They are senior LPAS managers who wanted to meet you."

I bet they did, Ed thought.

Oblonsky pointed at each in turn. "Vladimir Kazakov runs LPAS throughout Europe, Middle East and Africa, and Sergei Kazakov runs North and South America."

Ed quipped, "Okay, lunch for four it is, then!"

Service began with an *amuse bouche*, with staff explaining what they were, pouring water, and asking if they preferred red or white wine to start. Now onto the main course, the conversation had so far been polite small talk, rather dull, Ed was thinking, and then Timur asked the first real question.

"Edward."

Ed stopped him.

"Ed, call me Ed. I find myself looking around for my mother when I hear Edward."

"Ed it is," Timur agreed.

"You are causing a stir, waves around the world, Ed, with talk of how damaging LPAS laws are to life and society and how easy it would be to take another path to avoid the apocalypse. You've attracted a fair following, and I understand that some of my UN colleagues have started to follow your tune. I hadn't imagined you as a supporter of Armageddon." Timur was goading him.

"I think the idiom you were looking for is 'follow my lead'," Ed replied. A cheap shot, but he wanted to embarrass Timur.

Ed continued. "I wish it were true, Timur. But unfortunately, this is not the case. My goal is to repeal the law. And right now I'm not even close to the level of support required to modify or reduce its influence, and no one at the UN has fully committed." He briefly paused. "To have done nothing, in fact, would have hastened Armageddon, so we chose the slower path to the same outcome. Killing millions in the hope of saving billions isn't going to work," Ed fired back.

"So you want to give a few million more people a few more years before the entire human race falls?" Vladimir shot back.

As Ed opened his mouth to respond, Sergei Kazakov piped up. "Vladimir, it isn't that simple. Ed is looking for the same thing we are. He wants to save our race and our planet. However, he has a different view on how to do it, and we should hear him out."

Ed's immediate thought was that it hadn't taken the Tweedles long to get into character.

"I appreciate the support, Sergei, but if you saw it that way, you wouldn't be a senior or working for LPAS at all, would you?" Ed pushed back, ignoring Vladimir's previous point.

Ed's last comment was rooted in the fact that LPAS was an ideology.

Ed's view of any ideology was simple, and he would say it often: "You can enter the house of an ideology with an inquiring mind, but you can't keep it and stay." Leonora was a testament to that fact.

"Not at all, Ed. I have a job to do, ensuring compliance with laws agreed to by almost every world leader, and I'd be happy to support changes that can achieve the same goal – a healthy planet that can sustain the human race and all other life forms. A return, if you will, to the equilibrium we, at least to start with, unwittingly destroyed," was Sergei's follow-up.

Timur jumped back in. "Ed, had there been alternatives, do you not think the leaders of the world would have selected them?"

"There is no short answer to that question. But no, I don't.

Alternatives were there, but they were not easy. They would, will, be far slower in reducing the population and would come at a far higher financial cost – initially. In the long run, however, they would be far more beneficial and would not erode and degenerate our society as LPAS is doing." Ed paused, trying to contain his growing anger; letting go would not be valuable.

"The four of us are not going to agree; you've all bought into LPAS, and have well-paid jobs, providing you with great lifestyles. Oh, and yes, that thing we aren't supposed to air in public: a get out of jail card for you and your closest friends and family in the event you get sick or are involved in an accident." Ed paused, scanning their faces, wondering whether the Devil or one of his demons would respond.

"Ed, this rumour about treating senior LPAS members differently from the general public is nonsense. It has been put out there by those looking to cause trouble. It is simply not true, and you should not go around repeating such garbage. It will get you in trouble." So Timur posited, with a hint of malice.

Ed jumped up from his chair. "Gentlemen, the only appetite I had when I walked in was for honesty, and there isn't much of that at this table." With that, he threw his napkin on the chair and left the room.

As Ed started down the corridor, Sergei Kazakov tapped him on the shoulder.

"Ed, I feel your frustration on the LPAS laws. But it might surprise you to hear me say that I agree there are alternatives. We should stay in touch; I think we could help each other."

Ed knew this was complete horseshit. His aim was simple: get information and see if Timur could use it against him to counter his plans or discredit him. However, Ed wasn't about to let on to one of the Tweedles.

"Thank you, Sergei. It's good to know there are some folk at LPAS who are prepared to listen and embrace other solutions."

"I'm listening to you, Ed. I will set up a regular call between us to discuss things in more detail," Sergei responded, a beaming smile on his face, as much as to say, *"I'm your friend, trust me."*

Ed thanked him again and continued down the corridor, thinking that you'd have to be dim to fall for this guy's fake friendship. But it might just be possible to turn the tables. And if not, he wasn't going to give Sergei anything of value anyway, so it was worth playing along, for now at least.

Sergei returned to the room. "I think I can get close to him," he said confidently.

"I'm not so sure, Sergei. He's astute, and we should not underestimate him," was Vladimir's view.

Timur was fuming, foaming at the mouth almost. Then, thumping the table, he screamed at the brothers.

"Who the hell does this jumped-up Englishman think he is, taking my hospitality and calling me a liar. He thinks he's important because he has a few political groupies and a following of people who don't know any better. We will soon see who's more important. I want dirt on this guy. I want him off the air. He must have skeletons in his closet we can use against him – find them."

The Kazakov brothers had their orders and knew this wasn't something they could fail on.

Late that evening, Jail Sleeks rang Ed to catch up on how his trip to the UN was going. It was 10 p.m. in

New York, and Jail was burning the midnight oil, finalising some changes that he wanted to implement within POLO, so he thought he'd try and catch Ed before Ed, and he himself for that matter, turned in for the day. Ed's phone rang.

"Hi, Ed speaking."

"Hi, Ed. It's Jail. Do you have time to talk?"

"Sure, go ahead."

"I was hoping *you* would go ahead. I was calling to see how your trip is going."

"Oh, sorry, okay." Ed started to outline the meetings he'd had and his views on their success. He made it clear to Jail that he didn't see the wind of change yet, but felt it was coming, and he found that uplifting. After 30 or so minutes, Ed ended the update by advising that he was very uncomfortable having government agents with him and hoped this would soon change.

"Ed, I hear you, but you need to accept that they are far more likely to save your life, should an attempt be made on it, than Kai and her team. The limitations our bodyguards have to work under put you and others who have bodyguards within POLO at greater risk. There are too many times when they cannot provide close protection," was Jail's honest assessment.

"I get it, but I'd prefer that risk over having government agents so close. If I'm honest, I'll not allow government protection to continue for too long." So responded Ed, depressed at the thought of having these folk around for months on end.

"Okay, Ed, we can talk a little more on this when you return," Jail responded before continuing.

"It sounds like your meeting with Timur went well, Ed! Did you not think it wise to take it easy on him?

You were never going to be best friends, but we have enough to worry about without having this guy pissed at you too."

It was a clear rebuke from Jail that he felt Ed's outburst was both wrong and dangerous.

"Okay, agreed, I should have played it differently. It wasn't going too bad until Timur lied about the 'special protection' LPAS seniors and their families have. I couldn't ignore such a blatant lie. He's aware I know the truth, but he felt he'd get away with denying it. He felt I'd keep quiet."

"Well, he either called that wrong, Ed, or he wanted to provoke you.

Either way, it's done now," said Jail. "I have a couple of updates for you if you have more time?"

"Go ahead."

Jail updated Ed on Orpheus, advising that all the information Orpheus gave them, including the location and names of his wife and children, checked out. Hence, good to their word, they had released him. He had also passed Logan Miller's name to British Intelligence, hoping to help them more quickly close down the dangerous organisation working within LPAS.

"Didn't the intelligence folk wonder how you came by such a significant piece of information?" Ed inquired.

"Unquestionably, Ed. They pushed hard on the source, which, of course, I couldn't give up even had I wanted to."

"Quite, Jail. I don't think telling your contacts we kidnapped a hitman and told him we'd kill him if he didn't talk would go down too well."

Jail continued. "Aside from not getting the source, it was clear that this provided them with a significant breakthrough, but that doesn't mean it won't take a long time to gather appropriate evidence. It will be a waiting game. They will be waiting for Logan to re-engage."

"I'm clear on that, but it's a significant piece of intelligence, and all down to Creak's strategy in dealing with Orpheus," was Ed's positive comeback.

"Yep. While at Special Branch, Creak honed the art of eliciting information from those determined not to give any up. He didn't often come up empty-handed."

Ed fell silent for a few seconds, causing Jail to ask, "Are you still there, Ed?"

"Sorry, yes, but I was wondering... What are Orpheus's family like?" Ed's curiosity stemmed from his inability to understand why anyone would want to kill people for a living, however well paid it was. It was the antithesis of what he did.

Jail outlined that it was Stephen and a small team who checked out the facts Orpheus provided. Stephen flew to Aruba, where Orpheus had said he lived, reporting that he did have two daughters: Celeste and Bijou. And, in Stephen's words, "a beautiful wife, Amelia", whom Stephen had talked to, pretending to be interested in renting a yacht.

Stephen told Jail and Creak that he was taken aback by just how lovely a person she was, given what her husband did for a living.

Jail further updated Ed that Orpheus's real name was Tygo Janssen: born in Amsterdam, married his French wife in his early twenties, and moved to Noord, Aruba.

They owned a luxury villa complex and several yachts that they rented out to affluent individuals looking for a luxury break away from prying eyes. Orpheus's wife ran the guest part of the business, and Tygo took care of all other aspects.

"It took us longer than we expected to get everything verified, Ed. Orpheus was a bit of a wreck when Creak walked in some four-plus weeks after his last little chat, telling him we were releasing him. Creak also reminded him that he'd retired and should never again enter the UK.

"Talking with Creak, I'm confident Orpheus knows how close he came to death and will now live out his life with his family and dirty money," Jail said, completing his update.

Still unable to comprehend such a profession, Ed piped up, "Do you think his wife knows what he does?"

"I couldn't say for sure, Ed, but I think it unlikely. He commissions yachts, works with international holiday agencies, buys real estate abroad. So I think it likely she believes him to be a successful businessman. And one could argue that he is!"

"How does he manage to keep this wicked part of his life secret?"

Jail responded: "You do!"

Ed snapped out of thinking about Orpheus. "God! How bloody stupid was that thought. I hadn't meant to say it out loud, Jail."

"Sorry, Ed, that came out wrong. Your secret life isn't comparable with his."

"That's okay, Jail; I know it isn't. It's just that…" Ed paused. "It's just wrong for my relationship to be like it is."

"Ed, we are all doing things we would not if LPAS wasn't a reality. You have to accept it: what you do will inevitably harden you. But that doesn't make you a bad person. Geez! My life in the army and working for military intelligence changed me in many ways that I'd have preferred it hadn't."

"I have hardened up, Jail. I recall the early years. Your nickname for me was *Gooey*!"

"Who told you that, Ed?" said Jail sheepishly.

"Spies in the camp, Jail, spies in the camp!"

Jail, red-faced, had not realised that Ed was aware of how he often referred to Ed in private. If he found out who'd snitched, he'd throttle them!

With that revelation, Ed thanked him for all the information, and they ended their call. Jail was embarrassed, and Ed was feeling guilty, but far less so than he would once have been.

UNnatural Selection – Routine theft

Jail had authorised a plan for a sizeable theft, a plan presented by Hood (Marcelle Carrick – head of the Stealers). Regular drug thefts were essential to ensure a good supply of drugs that would help save lives. But recently, POLO had had a few failed operations that had diminished their stocks. In addition, Kimmy asked Hood if she could obtain up-to-date surgical booms, monitors and integration systems to replace the ageing equipment at secret medical locations. In the years POLO had been operational, they had only managed to obtain older operating-room equipment, and modern equipment would help save lives.

Hood had put together a plan to hijack two lorries they knew were to deliver six new state-of-the-art surgical booms, complete with monitors and integration systems, to be used to kit out operating rooms at a hospital in Leeds, Yorkshire. And a large shipment of drugs was coming in on the same ship from Europe, heading to a warehouse in Southampton. POLO had managed to get operatives in almost every major hospital around the UK, and many large drug warehouses, providing critical intelligence on equipment and drug movements. Some months prior, the information on these shipments had been presented to

Hood, giving her ample time to build a plan to intercept the delivery coming in from Germany.

The plan was simple enough. Stop the trucks and intercept the drivers' call for assistance so that POLO operatives could help. Then, move the lorries to a safe area, empty the cargo, replace it with boxes of stones of the same weight, and re-seal the doors. By the time the drivers realised what had happened, it would be too late.

One of Gig's – George Clemons's – engineers, working with Jesse Omaha's technology team, had designed and built a sophisticated miniaturised device that would be attached to the side wall of a tyre. The device was small and would sit comfortably in the palm of your hand, even a tiny hand. Made of titanium, it operated in three stages, driven by a software chip activated when attached.

When pushed against the tyre wall, sensors would deploy tiny barbs to attach the device, an action that, once completed, would trigger a small explosion. This would force a hollow tube into the tyre, containing a mole device with a drill-like mechanism that would burrow into the tyre wall to extend the hollow spike into the tyre while simultaneously forcing the end cap out – allowing the tyre to deflate without rupturing. With this stage complete, the housing mechanism would fall off. They called their device a stinger bot. They would use four devices to ensure that the lorries stopped.

Operatives would attach the devices when the trucks stopped at lights, and POLO would be manipulating the lights at pre-selected locations. It would then take around seven to nine minutes for the tyres to fully deflate, forcing the drivers to pull over and seek assistance. Which POLO planned to provide.

They'd tested the device many times, and it worked well. The only real difference between it and a conventional police stinger was its size, sophistication, and the fact you had to attach it physically. Hence, the vehicle had to be stationary.

Delivery day had arrived, and the port was being monitored by POLO operatives waiting for the trucks to disembark the ship. As the first lorry exited via the ramp, operatives clocked it, placing it under surveillance. As an additional precaution, an operator fired a tiny tracking device onto the truck. The truck team watched as it drove up Jubilee Way, heading towards the A2, a major road leading to Brenley Corner, where the lorry would merge onto the main motorway. It was at this point that POLO members would start to follow. A second team would do the same when the second truck exited the ship.

About an hour and a half into the first truck's journey, operatives would stop it at a designated set of traffic lights as it waited to turn onto the A1023. The stinger bots would then be attached to the tyres. A warehouse near Brentwood had been rented and kitted out as a lorry repair centre.

Once the truck was attached to a breakdown vehicle, the lorry would be towed to the repair shop, and, unbeknownst to the driver, for offloading the cargo. The warehouse was a mere 15-minute drive from where they expected the lorry to pull over, assuming they'd done their homework correctly. A similar process would be playing out for truck number two, the truck carrying the drug shipment.

Jail Sleeks had asked Creak Nooks to run the show. Creak had been part of the planning team with Brindle Llanos and George Clemons and was much better at directing and controlling such operations than Jail himself.

All POLO vehicles had trackers, as did all operatives, along with vehicle and personal cameras, so the command centre could keep a close eye on events in real time. In the control room with Creak were Kimmy and Covey. Neither had experienced a significant steal before, so Creak invited them along to watch.

Although Gig's Tradespeople were on hand to take out power in specific areas, there were no plans to do so. Creak didn't believe it to be necessary for this job, given that, if all went to plan, the drivers would not be aware that their cargos had gone missing until they arrived in Leeds and Southampton. And by that time, POLO would have safely delivered the goods to their final destinations in several smaller trucks.

Around 10 minutes from the traffic lights where operatives would stop the first truck, the second part of the operation kicked in, with a car positioning itself in front of the lorry and four vehicles behind. They did not want other drivers to see operatives place the stinger bots on the tyres.

POLO had hacked into the traffic light control system and now had control. When the lorry arrived at Dover, they had zeroed in on the driver's mobile phone using specialised software and could now intercept any call he made. Those at the operations centre who would handle the driver's calls spoke German.

As the lead car approached the traffic lights, the team switched them to red. As traffic ground to a halt, operations members crossed the road behind the lorry and placed the stinger bots firmly on the sides of the tyres. Lights now green, the lead car, lorry and support vehicles turned onto the A1023. Two heavy recovery vehicles were parked up not too far from the expected breakdown point to ensure they didn't take too long to get to him after his call for assistance.

Soon the driver noticed the steering getting a little heavy, and manoeuvring the truck became more cumbersome. There was a bus pull-in point around 100 yards ahead, and he decided to stop there to check out what the problem was. Discovering that he had two deflating tyres, he could hardly believe his bad luck. He returned to his cab to pull out the list of numbers for breakdown services he could use. Having done so, he started to make a call.

One of Creak's folks who was operating the intercept shouted out to him: "He's calling a German number. What action should I take?"

"Kill the call," Creak replied. The driver's phone briefly went dead before regaining a signal. "He's trying the same number again, Sepia" (Creak's handle).

"Kill it, and keep killing it every time he tries calling back to Germany." The driver tried several times before giving up.

"He's calling a UK number now, Sepia."

"Which number?" Creak snapped back, not happy with having to follow up on such a fundamental point.

"A local breakdown service. Damn it! They've picked up."

"Kill it now, and when he tries again, intercept it."

Now, with bad timing, the second team engaged with Creak.

"Sepia, the second lorry has stopped, and the driver is calling a local breakdown service; we are intercepting now."

Creak was much happier with team two, which was much more proactive than his first team. "Good, run it as you see fit. Let me know if you need me." So said Creak before switching back to speak with team one.

The driver of truck one, the vehicle carrying the operating-room equipment, had called the breakdown number again, and this time POLO had intercepted the call. The driver gave his company name, truck type and membership code, and provided rough details about his location.

"No need for location details, sir. I've already marked your position from your phone's GPS signal."

"Great service," said the trucker.

"We'll get a vehicle and mechanic out to you within the hour, sir." So responded the POLO operator who'd intercepted his phone call.

"Okay, thank you," replied the driver before hanging up.

"Okay, folks, let's get a truck to him in 25 minutes or less. Let's not be too eager, as that might make him a little suspicious. If he attempts to make further calls, kill them," Creak instructed.

POLO operatives arrived in a heavy recovery vehicle at truck one's location, chatting briefly with the driver before inspecting the tyres.

"No good me trying to fix this roadside, sir. It'll take way too long," said the POLO mechanic.

"Won't it take longer towing me away to fix it?" questioned the driver.

"No, sir, we have a large depot close by, with specialised equipment. We'll have you on your way in just over an hour."

"Okay, that sounds good." The driver sounded happy with what he saw as a quick turnaround.

When they arrived at the lorry repair centre, the driver was shown to a waiting area away from the lorry, to allow them to unload it unseen and load it back up with boxes full of rocks.

The driver was given coffee and asked if he wanted something to eat.

"No, I am good, thank you. Can I use your phone? I need to let my company know what is happening."

"We don't have fixed lines on the premises, sir. Can you use your mobile?"

"I can try, but it keeps going dead."

"Yes, sir, we've been having problems in the area all morning. I think they are performing some maintenance on the cell towers, and the work is mainly affecting international calls."

"Oh, okay, never mind, then. I will call back to base later."

That was good, the POLO operator thought. Meanwhile, phone monitoring continued.

Back at the truck, Gig's Tradespeople were busy unloading the medical equipment from the lorry while other operators were working on the tyres. At the same time, they weighed the equipment removed from the truck, as the boxes of rocks to be loaded had to have the same weight. When the driver started the engine, he would be alerted if a change had occurred.

Creak now asked for an update from the truck two team.

"Truck still at roadside, Sepia. Our breakdown truck will be with the lorry shortly, and then we'll move it to the repair station."

"Okay," said Creak. "You are running a little slow, guys, pick up the pace. I don't want you completing too long after truck one."

"I hear you, Sepia."

As the call with Creak ended, the breakdown truck arrived at the location of truck two. Speaking with the driver, they encountered their first problem.

"No, no, I don't want to be towed in." The driver was adamant.

"Sir, we can't fix both tyres roadside. We need to get you to a safe location and one with the right equipment. It isn't too far, about 10 minutes away."

"I don't care; fix it here, or I'll go to someone else to do it."

"I've told you, sir, I can't. So go somewhere else." With that, the POLO operative started back to the breakdown truck. He'd taken a gamble, knowing that if the driver didn't ask him to come back, he'd have to leave. And that was how it played out.

The POLO operative placed a call to his command unit, who patched in Creak. "I've had to leave the truck on the road, Sepia. The bloody driver is refusing to have the truck towed. He wants a roadside fix."

"Have you told your control team?"

"Yes, Sepia, they are waiting to intercept his calls."

"Good. Intercept, get a new team out and tell the idiot the same thing.

Or tell him on the phone if he says he isn't having it towed."

Intercepting the driver's next call, it was clear that he still wasn't going to have the truck towed. The POLO operative advised the driver that he'd have his people assess the situation when they arrived, but he could not guarantee that the lorry would not require a tool shop repair.

"No, don't come out unless it is roadside," the driver responded.

Updating Creak again, the control room operator raised his hands, as much as to say, "Hey, Creak, what should we do?"

"Okay, just let him keep going through the list, and don't make the mistake of having the same operator talk to him!"

"Thanks, Sepia. We aren't that stupid!"

"Just making sure," Creak said. "Just keep giving him the same story, and make sure you are blocking all his calls to international numbers."

"We are, Sepia."

Meanwhile, the POLO member who'd provided the truck one driver with coffee and had the conversation with him about the phone call looked up from the desk just as the door to the small office closed. The driver had left the waiting area, heading back in the direction of the truck repair area.

Using his communications system, he broadcasted out, "The driver's heading towards the truck."

The guys who were unloading moved what they had on the forklift and shut up the back doors – no time, however, to re-seal the doors. As the driver rounded the corner, one of Gig's Tradespeople walked towards him. "Sorry, sir, you can't hang around this area. Health and safety, I'm afraid."

"Health and safety, my arse," the driver pushed back.

"It may well be nonsense to you, sir, but it's the rules, so please return to the waiting area."

"I need my phone. I left it in the cab," the driver responded.

"I'll get that for you, sir," replied the operative as he walked back towards the truck, jumping up into the cab a moment later. "Here you go, sir. Now, if you don't mind, please return to the safe waiting area."

The driver returned to the waiting area, and Creak then broadcasted over the system: "Whichever one of you is supposed to be watching him, do your job!" Creak wasn't happy.

Having returned to the waiting room, the driver tried numerous times to call back to his company, without luck.

"You are right; the service here is terrible," said the driver to the man on the desk.

"Yes, sir, I told you, we have cell problems in the area. Best you wait until you are on your way. More coffee, sir?"

"Yes, thank you, that would be nice."

Creak again called out for an update from the team looking after truck two.

"No change, Sepia. The bloody fool is just sitting in the cab. He isn't even making any calls!"

The situation was now beginning to alarm Creak. Having POLO operatives work on this truck for too long after the first truck left with fresh tyres would put them at risk if truck one's driver became suspicious and checked his cargo or performed a random check. The trucks, hence shipments, were from different companies, but that wouldn't stop an all-drivers broadcast going out for companies to check on their drivers should the truck one steal be noticed. Any driver not responding would have their location checked, and the police would be asked to investigate. Creak knew that, if not resolved quickly, he would have to terminate the steal on truck two, and with it the loss of hundreds of thousands of pounds' worth of drugs.

"Okay, let's change tack," he said.

"Okay, Sepia, what do you want to do?"

"Give him some grief."

"Come again, Sepia?"

"Get some of the Tradesfolk we have on standby for power outages to give him some hassle."

"About what, Sepia?"

"I don't bloody know, think of something. Just make the driver a little jumpy, for God's sake."

The control room acknowledged and put in a call to the Trades folk in the area. Within 20 minutes, a couple of them arrived near the lorry parked at the side of the road. Seeing a group of lads in the park nearby, one of them had an idea.

Creak messaged the lead Tradesperson responsible for getting the equipment off truck one and the boxes of stones onto it for an update.

"Just about there, Sepia. About 10 more minutes and we will be ready to re-seal the lorry."

"Okay," Creak responded, "but get moving. We've issues with truck two and I want you guys well out of it soon."

The lorries had electronic seals connected to the door opening mechanism; breaking the seal off and then replacing it was easy. Unfortunately, though, reprogramming the seal was troublesome. If not done correctly, the moment the driver started the engine, he would be alerted that the seal had been tampered with or removed.

One of Jesse's technologists had been busy reprogramming the seal while the lorry was being unloaded and reloaded. She'd had a problem initially breaking the security code but had now done so. In a few more minutes, her work would be complete, and the Tradesfolk could then reattach it to the lorry doors. The Tradespeople replacing the tyres had finished their work around 10 minutes before Creak had called for an update.

Medical equipment off and boxes of rocks loaded, finally the doors were closed up, and Jesse's operator placed the seal back on the truck. Fingers crossed that her encryption re-configuration had been successful.

The operative behind the desk approached the driver.

"If you'd like to read the report, sir, and if you are happy, sign and date it. Your truck is ready."

The driver looked over the report, which said two tyres had been replaced, signed the paperwork and handed it back. The operative handed him a copy, thanked him for his patience, gave him back the keys and wished him a nice day.

"Thank you – a speedy and efficient service. I will recommend that my company makes you their number-one go-to breakdown assistance company in the UK."

"Thank you, sir," said the operative, all the time thinking: *He won't be saying that in a few hours!*

As the driver got into the cab, seven operatives were looking up at him, fingers crossed behind their backs. Then, as the driver started the engine, there was a collective intake of breath, which they all held momentarily, before the driver waved, mouthing *thank you*, and pulled away.

As the lorry exited the premises, Rochelle Mylice, the technician responsible for dealing with the electronic encrypted seal, turned to the others. "I can't believe you doubted me!"

"We didn't," the head man on the ground responded.

"You mendacious bastard!" came Rochelle's rude reply.

"Charming, Rochelle," he replied as he turned to a colleague to ask what 'mendacious' meant.

"You all had your fingers crossed behind your backs!" Rochelle followed up.

"We did that to wind you up, Rochelle. We had every confidence in you. And as much as I'd like to debate it with you, we have to get this place cleared out within the hour. So chop, chop, folks. Let's get moving. Sepia is pushing. He has problems with truck two, so let's not give him cause to get annoyed with us!"

The team started packing the medical equipment into vans and getting them off to their storage locations. At the same time, they boxed up and loaded the equipment they had used to repair the truck. Once all the equipment and vans had left, a small team sanitised the premises before closing the warehouse. The on-the-ground lead then sent a message to Creak: "I know you're watching and listening. But just wanted to say: Job done!"

Meanwhile, the driver of truck two was getting a little twitchy. In fact, he'd even tried to call the police, but his phone kept going dead.

Speaking with the lads in the park was one of POLO's Tradesfolk, who'd arrived with instructions to make the driver a little jumpy. He had paid the lads to give the driver some abuse – which this particular group would have been happy to do without payment.

The lads began jumping up on the cab's steps, tapping on the windows, calling him names, and then one of them broke off his wing mirror. The driver jumped down from the cab to chase them off; at which point, one of the lads climbed in the cab, locking the doors. The driver rushed back, screaming at the kid to unlock the cab. He tried his phone again, and again it failed.

Now for the second part of the plan. The original breakdown truck driver drove up and pulled over, telling the deliveryman that he had noticed the locals were giving him grief. Of course, the lads were already aware, meanwhile, that they should expect this, so the lad in the cab now jumped out of the far door and legged it with the others.

"You okay, mate?" the breakdown driver said.

"I'm fine, just stupid kids."

"That's true, but those stupid kids are likely letting the more insane thugs in the area know that you've broken down and are easy pickings. I'd call the police if I were you."

With that, the POLO operative started walking back to his cab.

"Hang on, can you still fix the truck?" the driver responded.

"We've had that conversation, mate. The answer is still no, not roadside. Call the police; I'm sure you'll be fine."

"No, wait. If you've still got time, tow it in. No point taking a risk, is there?"

"Okay, let me check with the folks to see if they can do it."

The breakdown driver appeared to make the call, said they could still fix the truck, and hooked it up.

Within 20 minutes, truck two had arrived at the repair centre and the driver was taken to a waiting area before the command centre updated Creak.

"Okay, Sepia. We've started to repair truck two and unload the drugs."

"Great," said Creak. "Any more grief from the driver?"

"No, Sepia. I think the driver was very pleased to see the breakdown truck driver again."

"That's good; you can fill me in later on how you got him off the dime."

About 90 minutes after truck two arrived at the repair centre, the driver was on his way to deliver his consignment of drugs to Southampton. Although in fact he'd be delivering boxes of rocks!

Creak reflected on the simplicity of the plan, and its success, even given their near failure to steal the drugs due to a very cautious driver. He felt that they should obtain more equipment and drugs in this way; it seemed to him pretty straightforward and carried far less risk than other methods.

With that thought, he left the operations centre, pleased but also a little stressed about the day's outcome.

UNnatural Selection – Personal, political, psephology and back

Ed was enjoying a quiet weekend with Leonora. This weekend preceded a day of meetings he would attend at parliament. A day of meetings with MPs at the Houses of Parliament, coupled with being the main speaker and witness at a meeting of the House of Lords' special inquiry committee on LPAS. The MP sessions would be in small groups, but reporters would be present. Then he would be grilled for three or four hours during the special inquiry.

Ed had requested the sessions many months earlier, and the persistence of his lobbyists had facilitated them. Once agreed, the Chair of the lords' special inquiry committee on LPAS thought it would be good to hold a committee session on the same day, inviting Ed along to give his views and be questioned by the committee members.

It was six years since the passing of the law known as Life Preservation Assistance Suspension, dubbed 'Human Return to Natural Selection' by the law's architect, Cornelius Assante. A law that, critically, restricted life-saving intervention of any kind.

Ed appeared to be reading a book but was in deep thought about what to expect in parliament on Monday, and more precisely, at the House of Lords' special inquiry.

"Can I coax out of you what it is that's making you frown, Ed?" Leonora said, having noticed he hadn't turned a page in more than 10 minutes.

"I'm concerned that MPs will be reluctant to say what they believe in an open session for fear of reprisal. The behemoth that is LPAS has power and reach beyond what anyone could have imagined when this global monster was first set up."

Leonora cringed, still finding such harsh criticism of the organisation, in which not so long ago, she was a senior manager, difficult.

"Throughout history, groups have looked to suppress the views of those who disagree with them. It has worked, to a greater or lesser extent. This ploy – or method, if you will – is too often practised by groups that know criticism will end their hold over many of their followers and reduce the flow of new recruits. Those who know that scrutiny will weaken their arguments will aggressively look to stifle free speech. I suspect that those on the lords' special inquiry committee who have negative views on LPAS will not air them, at best. At worst, they will come down in support of LPAS, believing it will protect them. I believe they have far less to lose than MPs. Nonetheless, I think they will be concerned and watch what they say."

"Ed, your view of government is too often overly negative. When it comes to the MPs, you are likely somewhat correct, but they are not all mouse-like! As for the lords, they have little to lose in being open and frank." A rare rebuke from Leonora, this, on Ed's view of those in government.

"Ed, it is no wonder you're frowning. You can only put forward the case against, as you have done so forcefully, so eloquently, in gatherings all over the world. You've come a long way, but you knew it wasn't going to be easy or quick. You have an invite. That's a big deal. Not so long ago, neither house would have been brave enough to have invited you."

Ed knew that Leonora did have a valid point. Not so long ago, he would not have got near to anyone in government.

"You're right, Leonora. It's too easy to focus on obstacles and what we *haven't* achieved, when our focus must be on what we've already accomplished, and our next challenge."

"That's the spirit, Ed. And I wouldn't worry too much about politicians being honest. My father had a quote he would repeat often: 'The odds of meeting a politician who doesn't lie are as long as sleeping with a virgin prostitute'!"

Ed laughed, which was what Leonora had hoped to achieve, snapping him out of his troubling thoughts. But he still followed up by making it clear that, whether MP or lord, LPAS was now a powerhouse that worried most people in positions of power and influence. Ed then felt it wise to get off the subject.

"I'd have liked to have met your father, Leonora. We would have got along well, I believe."

"I still miss him, Ed. Even after so many years, I often feel the pain of his passing. When he was in a room, everyone knew he was there. He had a natural presence and innate ability to draw people in and hold them. He was very knowledgeable, thoughtful, and had a great sense of humour. He told stories that you knew were almost certainly apocryphal, but it didn't matter. Although mostly untrue, the stories were interesting and would give you a genuine insight into the person or subject he spoke of, and people would hang on his every word." Leonora fell silent, and Ed got up and sat beside her.

"Leonora, there is much of your father in you, I think. So much of what you've said about him, I see in you."

"Thank you, Ed. His ability to pull people into his way of thinking was, in my mother's view, what got him killed. She has always believed he was making good progress in whatever he was doing in South America. And that concerned those in opposition. Mother believes that British Intelligence knows the truth about his death and that it was not accidental."

"His death must have been difficult enough for you and your mother. I suspect, though, that believing there was more to it but not knowing must leave a pain almost as bad as his death."

"It does, Ed, and it leaves me with a fear for the future. A fear that you will become too influential, too great an adversary to LPAS, and that something bad will happen to you." Leonora started to well up.

"Hey, don't be sad. I'm not in the same league as your father. And I'm not in the same line of business. I'll be fine. No one is coming after me." Another lie escaped his lips. Leonora had no clue that the terror attack was in fact an attempt on his life.

"If that were true, Ed, the British government would not have seen fit to provide you with close protection."

"That's simply a precautionary over-reaction by the government, worried that if something did happen, the public would blame them; no more than that, Leonora."

"I don't think it is, Ed. And I don't think you believe that either."

Ed hugged her tighter, kissing her on the head. He wanted to reassure her that there wasn't a parallel with what happened to her father. He was, however, well aware that if bad actors had murdered her father, Leonora's view was right on the money.

In moments like this, he wanted so much to tell her who he was, tell her about his POLO life. But instead, as always, deceit stepped in where the truth should be. This plagued Ed, causing him to dislike himself more as time passed. His heart wanted him to walk away from it all, as Leonora had once suggested. Her suggestion, however, was to step away from his job, which she felt was damaging him – as it was. Seeing people die needlessly causes him immense pain and stress, every bit as bad as the stress his illegal work caused. He longed for a life with Leonora without the lies, the anxiety, and the fear that he would end up in prison or murdered to shut him up.

The strength of feeling Ed felt to save lives and end these heinous laws against life were winning the battle that raged inside him. But all the while he hoped he would have the strength to continue until the collective leaders of the world saw sense and revoked a set of immoral laws that never should have seen the light of day.

Ed lifted Leonora's head and looked intently into her eyes, kissing her and sliding his body and Leonora onto the floor as he started to unbutton her blouse. Leonora, giggling as Ed ran his hand gently along her side, tilted his head up and smiled.

She pointed out that it was the middle of the day, the curtains were open, and only the net blinds were closed, providing little cover from prying eyes from the overlooking apartments.

"I know, Leonora. But to close them would kill the moment; your call?"

She pulled his head back down, kissing him.

"So that answered that question."

Monday, mid-morning, Ed was greeted by Sir William McMasters, the chair of the LPAS committee, as he arrived at parliament. William would escort Ed to his first MP session and collect him after lunch for the special inquiry committee into LPAS.

The day started well, with approving nods and gestures from several MPs (although, as Ed had suspected, most kept quiet, and only a handful took a swipe at LPAS openly). Overall, Ed felt the sessions had gone well. But that was not the case in the special committee meeting. Members of the committee, many of them prominent supporters of LPAS, a few not so much, and some that Ed knew did not support the laws, were present. In particular, one lord was thundering at him, firing off question after question, without waiting for Ed to complete his answer before firing off another.

"STOP!" Ed shouted, silencing the lord who had been hammering at him for the last 20 minutes or so, having cut Ed off for the fifth time while he was still attempting to answer his previous question.

"It seems to me that some of you do not wish to listen to what I have to say. I've seldom been in a meeting with such a rude crowd. You hadn't listened to the concerns of many citizens before supporting this godawful law. And it is clear to me that you have no intention of doing so now." Ed paused, and the Chairman spoke up.

"I'm sorry, Mr Thorncroft. I ask my colleagues again not to interrupt. You are right; it is rude. We asked you here to listen to you, and listen we must."

Ed thanked the Chairman, and the Chairman asked Frederick Holder, the lord whom Ed had abruptly shut down, if he had finished his questioning, to which he replied yes. Then the next question came in from another member of the panel.

"It is obvious that the law is working, Ed. So why would governments the world over risk a return to resource wars and, likely, far worse?" Abigail Williams asked.

"Morality, decency, compassion... I could go on – but I think my point is clear. In my job as a doctor, if I made a mistake that cost someone their life, the hospital trust would hold an inquiry. An inquiry after which I could easily be struck off. Harsh, maybe, as we all make mistakes. But when dealing with lives, we can't afford to. You can pass a set of laws that allow people to die in their millions, and that's okay? It's okay, why? Because you legislated it? Because you felt you had no choice if the world was to avoid a nuclear holocaust? Neither is a good reason."

That comment provoked an audible gasp from many on the panel. "Oh, please. Hold the fake outrage; I've only just started."

"Point of order, Edward; your suggestion that members' gasps are for effect isn't the accepted language, and I trust you will withdraw it?"

Ed didn't want to, convinced that was all it was, but he withdrew the comment and continued.

"Legislating something doesn't make you right, it right, or make it essential. The legislation doesn't absolve you. It doesn't provide a protective barrier behind which to hide for having got it so wrong. We've seen many an example of legislation being wholly inappropriate."

"Saving the world and those who inhabit it is paramount, as is the *way* we do it. You had a chance to do the right thing many years before passing LPAS into law. And even as you did so, you could have chosen a different path. A slower and more costly approach, I grant you, but nonetheless, a path that would have worked, without the needless slaughter of human lives in their millions the world over."

Frederick Holder interrupted. "I object most strongly to your use of the word 'slaughter' concerning the act. LPAS law is not *slaughtering* anyone. The LPAS laws allow nature to take its course."

Ed stood up and started to clap. "My God, you have drunk the Kool-Aid. Having failed to act sooner, you now look to justify the laws by suggesting you had no other choice, and that allowing people to die in their millions isn't murder. And of course, technically, it isn't.

But I cannot think of another way to describe allowing a death that needn't happen.

"LPAS is morally repugnant, and you know it. However, there are alternatives, such as those outlined in my paper 'Thriving Without LPAS – a way forward'. Yes, it will be slower and more expensive, financially. But far less costly in lives. And as human beings, that should be the far more important path for us all to tread.

"I'm not suggesting we abandon these laws on day one, although that is what I would prefer. Instead, I advocate that we start to unwind them as we ramp up work in other areas to support the planet and its occupants. Population growth alone hasn't led us here. Human numbers broke the camel's back. We've abused our planet in many ways. Finding equilibrium with Earth and all things on it isn't as difficult as some might have us believe. After all, we humans are resourceful."

Ed stopped, taken aback by the fact he hadn't been interrupted for the first time since entering the room. He waited for the comeback but was greeted by silence until the Chairman stepped up.

"Are there any other questions for Mr Thorncroft?" A few shook their heads, but otherwise, more silence. "Mr Thorncroft, we thank you for attending today's special committee meeting on LPAS law. You have given us much to think about, and I, for one, believe you have put forward some strong arguments."

Ed left with the Chairman, who had invited him for a drink at the House of Lords bar.

"Ed," said Sir William McMasters. "You held your own in there today. I think you had many of the members re-thinking their support for the LPAS laws."

"It didn't feel that way, Sir William."

"Ed, please, call me Bill. And don't mind Fred – Frederick Holder. He's a die-hard LPAS man. But trust me, the other 14 committee members listened, and many, normally vocal in defence of LPAS, were quiet. And for me that is telling."

"I have confidence in your assessment, Bill. We've known each other a while now; I know you tell it as you see it," said Ed.

"Ed, I've supported LPAS since it passed. Okay, not as vigorously as some, but I saw it as a necessary evil, and most of my colleagues and I fully supported the legislation. Listening to you over the past months, however, I've started to waver considerably. I now believe you are right, and we need to change tack."

"Thank you, Bill; I am pleased to hear that. If a permanent member such as the United Kingdom were on board, that would give our campaign a massive boost. Although I know that isn't going to happen any time soon."

"Keep pushing, Ed. You are making a great deal of progress with MPs and lords alike. Maybe more than you know. Keep going; your efforts will pay off. And you may get UK support at the big table.

Especially on your push to exclude vaccines."

With that, William ordered another round, and they sat talking about cricket, the only sport Sir William had any interest in discussing.

An hour passed and Sir William said he needed to leave, as he was meeting the Secretary of State for the Environment.

"Do you have a car waiting for you?" Sir William asked.

"No, Bill. I'll hail a cab."

"Okay, Ed. I'll escort you out. It's been nice having you visit today, and please, take note: you *are* making progress. Don't let the likes of Frederick Holder get you down."

"I won't, Bill. And again, thank you for setting up the session and for your support."

Ed was today meeting with a psephologist whom Jail had lined up. "Jail, tell me again what this lady is going to do for us," asked Ed, still unsure what to expect.

"She is going to explain the analysis she has been working on in key countries regarding voter trends, election results, et cetera," Jail responded, even though he had thought he had already been unequivocal with Ed during their previous conversation.

"Okay, and this will help me how?" Ed wanted to know.

"I didn't say it would help you, Ed. But it will give you a far greater understanding of how LPAS is playing into voter choice at elections in several large countries."

"Right, then, I guess I'll be attending. I hope your psephologist doesn't send me to sleep. I had to look up what she did! I'd never heard of one! So I now know it's a fancy name for an analyst of voting patterns."

"Ed, you have people in your political group doing similar work. They just aren't as good as Amelie. As for the name being a 'fancy' name for an analyst, that's like saying 'neurosurgeon' is a fancy name for a doctor."

"Anyway, I've agreed to meet her. No need to get on your high horse, Jail."

The meeting was at Amelie Charbon's office in London, not too far from Ed's apartment. He was shown to a conference room and was told Amelie would be with him shortly. "Coffee, sir?" asked the lady who had shown Ed in.

"No, but thank you," he replied.

While waiting, he continued to wonder if this was worth the effort.

He doubted it would be, but he hadn't wanted to upset Jail, who'd put some effort into the arrangement.

"Experts, experts, experts," Ed mumbled under his breath. His view was that many so-called experts never got it right, which was why the world was in such a bloody mess.

A few minutes later, Amelie entered the room. *Wow*, Ed thought. The wow was twofold: Amelie was beautiful and looked around 20 years old.

Ed got up.

"Hi, I'm Edward Thorncroft, but please call me Ed."

Amelie drew a large breath, thinking that Ed was rather good-looking.

"Pleased to meet you, Ed. Sorry if I startled you as I walked in."

"Oh, did I look startled? Sorry. It was just that you are younger than I imagined."

"I often get that comment; I put it down to good living. And you are just as I expected!"

Ed knew that was a straightforward put down due to his comment. "I apologise, Amelie. That was rude of me."

"Apology accepted. Shall we get down to business?"

The two of them sat down, and Amelie started to go over the election analysis she'd been working on over the past two years. Finally, after around three hours, she concluded, and Ed responded.

"I was dismissive of my people's insistence that I attend a session with you. But your analysis provides robust affirmative data on what's driving voters with regard to LPAS, and it is evident many are starting to vote for parties who wish to see LPAS powers cut back."

When Ed said, "my people," as far as Amelie was concerned, he meant those who worked in his political organisation. But Jail had arranged this session on a friend's advice, using an intermediary. The information he had received was that she was well respected in her field and had focused a lot of time and effort on how the world's perception of LPAS was shifting, especially as such information was now routinely available on the web.

Information published illegally, that was. Anyone caught sharing it would be given lengthy custodial sentences.

"Thank you, Ed. I'll take it as a compliment that someone so *young* could receive such praise!"

"I apologise again, Amelie. It was a thoughtless, ageist comment." Ed felt that this was a lady who brooked no nonsense – and then had another thought.

"Come and work for me, Amelie. I have several analysts on the team but no lead. I'd like you to head the group."

"I wasn't expecting a job offer," she replied, but said no more.

"Think about it. Here's my card. Call me and let me know. No rush, but you would be an asset to the programme."

Ed thanked Amelie again and left, deciding to walk home to give himself time to think a little more about the analysis Amelie had presented. He was also wondering what her age was, although he didn't know why that was bugging him. He placed a call to Jail and updated him.

"Okay, Ed. So you found it useful!"

"Yes, Jail, I found it very informative. Thank you for setting it up."

"Any follow-ups, Ed?"

"No, I didn't ask any questions that she didn't answer while I was with her. Oh, but I did offer her a job!"

"She impressed you so much that you offered her work on the spot?"

"That's about right, Jail."

"Did she say yes?"

"She didn't say yes or no. She accepted my card and that was it."

"I appreciate you calling to thank me, Ed."

"I didn't call so much to thank you as brief you." Ed didn't want all this to go to Jail's head.

Just as he was about to hang up the phone, he asked: "How old did you say Amelie is, Jail?"

"I didn't, Ed, but she's 35, I believe. Why do you ask?"

"No particular reason."

"You put your foot in it, didn't you, Ed?"

"Maybe… but I think we are good."

With that, Ed closed the call, thinking, *why wasn't I blessed with such good genes!*

After arriving at his apartment, Ed showered, changed and took a taxi to Leonora's. She greeted him in the hallway, and, within less than a minute, Ed, in an upbeat mood and feeling amorous, was all over her like a rash.

Pushing him backwards, Leonora said abruptly: "Ed, have you been taking something?"

"No, why do you say that?"

"For one, your octopus arms have returned, and you're grinning like a Cheshire cat."

"I'm not sure that's a compliment, Leonora."

"Sorry, Ed, it wasn't meant to be."

"Oh, I get it. Rough day at work, and it's my fault," said Ed, wondering why he was getting grief.

"No, I'm not giving you a hard time because of a rough day at work, but I wouldn't mind a hello, or a little conversation, before we hit the floor and shag!"

That snapped Ed right out of his playful mood.

"Leonora, that's a little unfair, and not the language you use. What's wrong? Maybe I should go out and come back in?"

"Maybe you should, Ed," she replied tersely.

Ed left the apartment, immediately knocking on the door again and walking in, calling out to Leonora. "Hi, are you home, Leonora?" All of which somewhat confused his Special Branch minder, who was outside the door!

Leonora popped her head around the corner of the hallway, and in a low, sad voice, responded, "You know I am, Ed, don't be silly."

"How would I know that? I've only just arrived."

"*Yes*, Ed, I'm home."

"Oh, good, and how was your day today?"

"It's been fine, Ed."

"That's good, Leonora. So, with the small talk out the way, should we, you know, bump uglies?"

Leonora burst into brief laughter, ran at Ed, threw her arms around him, and hung tightly around his neck.

"Hey, what's up? What's upset you so? Was it something that happened today, Leonora?" Ed said quietly, now nose to nose with her.

"Not so much a bad day, Ed. More a bad few months, and I guess it has just caught up with me. I'm sorry I was rude."

"No worries, Leonora. Do you want to talk about it?"

"It's the children's home where I'm working three days a week. I love working with the kids, but so many of them have gone."

"You miss them. That's okay."

"Not gone away, Ed, died."

"Oh, I'm sorry, that's sad."

A couple of tears dropped onto Leonora's face, splashing down Ed's shirt. He pulled a tissue from his pocket, looked at Leonora, and wiped her eyes.

"Don't stop fighting these laws, Ed. We can't live in a world like this. We can't continue to let people die needlessly. My God, children dying who needn't... it's just heartbreaking."

That comment had Ed momentarily drifting back to Jennifer, but he snapped out of it quickly, focusing again on what Leonora was saying.

"Three of the children at the care home have died in the last two months. As if it isn't bad enough that they had lost their parents. I had to leave early today; I couldn't stop sobbing. I used to explain these laws to people, justify them. I didn't understand why people could not see the need for them. I can't do that now. And I find it difficult to forgive myself for having supported them." Leonora fell silent.

"What caused their deaths, Leonora, if you can talk about it?"

"Thomas, 12, died seven weeks ago of a bacterial infection. He'd been ill for a couple of months, and it was heartbreaking to watch him deteriorate, in so much pain. He suffered so much before he died. Going blind a few weeks earlier was one of many issues, before he finally succumbed. I'd put on a brave face in his room, hold his hand and talk to him. Then I'd fall apart when I left his bedside.

"Anita, just six years old – Ed, just six – died of an infection after a bad fall off a slide in the garden a few weeks earlier. I begged the home's nurse to get her some antibiotics. I couldn't bear to see another child die as Thomas had, and for something so easily remedied. I know she wanted to help, but she said she had no access to them. She made calls, but no one listened."

Ed again drifted momentarily, thinking about what Jennifer had been going through, watching children die on the cancer ward, before she'd decided to work on saving as many as she could, outside of the protection that POLO offered.

"And then there was Sylvia, who was eight. Her stunning green eyes would twinkle as the light hit them. She had beautiful long silky hair halfway down her back that I would plait for her. She was an angel, my favourite of all the children. I know I shouldn't have favourites, but she was, Ed. I loved reading with her. She had a lovely personality, and her amazing little-girl laugh was heartwarming. So bright for such a young age too. She lost both her parents last year in a road accident. She died earlier today after an allergic reaction to a bee sting."

Leonora lost it again, crying uncontrollably. Ed pulled her closer to him, trying hard to comfort her.

"Ed, a *bee sting*. We let this little girl die from a reaction to a bee sting. It's too much to bear." Leonora was still sobbing, and Ed was struggling not to cry too while holding her tight. She continued.

"The world is now as dark as if we were not here. And if this is our remedy, our solution, perhaps we should not be." She paused momentarily.

"I don't know why I am telling you this, Ed. You've consistently told everyone who would listen that these laws are wrong. And you see needless death on a scale that I know would destroy me. Humans have evolved to protect life when possible. Children's deaths are perhaps the hardest to take of all. I can't describe the pain I felt when each of them died. And when Sylvia died this morning, I couldn't breathe. One of the nurses had to force me to take a breath."

What Leonora had just described was indeed what Ed went through every week, indeed every day. He was all too aware of the pain and anger it unleashed inside. And aware also of the damage it could cause over time.

"Leonora, you don't need to do the work you're doing. It will damage you, as it has me. I can't stop what

I'm doing. As few of those I now save are, it is still worth the anguish I go through. But you must stop. I don't want you going through what I go through every day. So quit and join me full time opposing the law.

"I wanted you to join when you left LPAS after the terror attack, but I didn't want to pressure you. Join me now. You can make more of a difference working with me."

Ed grabbed a handful of tissues from the box on the table and cleaned up Leonora's face, which was an awful mix of smudged make-up and tears. Kissing her on the forehead, he then held eye contact, awaiting a response.

"Okay, Ed, I will." As she burst into a half laugh, half cry, she added: "You might regret asking me to be around you more often, though."

"Leonora, I've many regrets. But you being around me more often won't be another."

"It'll take me some months, Ed. I can't leave the charities in the lurch, but I promise I'll join you as soon as I can."

"Take all the time you need, Leonora. The work I'm doing isn't going to end, unfortunately, anytime soon."

UNnatural Selection –
Medical house

A cardiothoracic surgeon working for POLO was part way through performing a robot-assisted aortic valve repair on an otherwise fit and healthy patient experiencing frequent chest pains and shortness of breath, including when not exercising. The patient had been in the care of a POLO cardiologist, but his condition had worsened during the last few months, to the point that surgery was the only option.

The patient was brought to the safe medical house a few days before the operation for preparation and planning, for what would be minimally invasive surgery, as opposed to open-heart, which was now extremely rare, given the significant improvements in medical robotics.

Although, any operations were rare now due to the LPAS laws. This one would not be happening had it not been for Ed's organisation.

Treatment house locations were known only to those who needed to know. Therefore, patients would either be blindfolded or anaesthetised. If blindfolded, the Collectors would take a long and winding route to the place of treatment.

The operation was scheduled to start mid-morning and would take a couple of hours to complete. Afterwards, the patient would stay in the medical house for around one week. Then, all being well, the patient would be discharged into the care of the cardiologist. Consultant cardiothoracic surgeon Mr Alasdair Guthrie was performing the procedure, a highly respected, now retired consultant born in Aberdeenshire, Scotland.

Alasdair had joined POLO a year after its inception, coming out of retirement to help save lives.

This particular house was in the East End of London: a large corner house with a double garage, allowing patients to be delivered into the medical home undetected, entering through a door leading from the garage to the house. The house had been operational for almost as long as POLO had been active and had two operating rooms and three preparation/recovery rooms.

Joining Alasdair today were two surgical nurses, an anaesthetist and another cardiothoracic surgeon. Intensive care nurses would attend later to take care of the patient when the operation was completed, looking after him until he was ready to go home.

While Alasdair was working on the patient, he became aware of cars screeching to a halt outside, doors slamming, and loud voices. One of the assisting nurses went over to the shuttered window and peered out, immediately becoming aware that several police officers were entering the front garden. After alerting Alasdair, he immediately instructed the anaesthetist, the assisting cardiothoracic surgeon and one of the surgical nurses to exit before the police broke in. The nurse still at the table was quick to volunteer to stay, knowing it would mean prison – a courageous young lady.

In the operating room was a cupboard storing various surgical equipment. Inside, at the back of the far-left shelf, was a tiny release lever that you had to expose by pulling back a false panel. The lever allowed a false wall to be pushed back and slid to the side when uncovered. Once behind the wall, it would be closed, and no one would be any the wiser.

Behind the wall was a staircase leading down to a tunnel that terminated under a home three houses up from the safe location, bringing you up a narrow set of stairs behind another cupboard that operated in the same way. As POLO had grown, George Clemons's Tradespeople had built many such escape routes. All the medical staff present could have used this one. But to have done so would have meant certain death for the young man on the table. It still could, as the police might well insist the operation be stopped. But Alasdair was going to give his patient every possible chance to survive.

As the three medical staff slipped behind the false wall, police smashed their way into the front door, quickly entering the operating room. As the lead police officer entered, Alasdair shouted at him.

"Stop, sir. You are placing this young man's life at risk. Whatever you need with us, it can wait."

"You are illegally assisting preservation of life, and I need you to stop," responded the officer.

"I've no intention of stopping until this operation is complete. If you wish to intervene, do so knowing you will be responsible for killing this man," Alasdair fired back.

The officer looked at two of his colleagues, who had entered the room with him. Their look said it all. They did not wish to be the cause of this young man's death. Finally, one of them spoke.

"I see no value in us intervening and causing his death. Let's allow the doctor to finish his work." The other two agreed.

"Thank you," Alasdair responded, relieved that he could continue.

"How long do you need, Doctor?" said the more senior officer.

"Around 30 minutes, but he will need an ambulance to take him to the hospital when we finish."

"I'll call one, sir," said another officer, showing great respect for Alasdair.

There was still a high risk that his patient would die. Alasdair knew that at the hospital, he would be made comfortable but would be unlikely to receive the medication usually administered to ensure recovery, such as antibiotics and blood-thinning medication, warfarin, heparin and other such anticoagulants. The use of a tissue heart valve meant the young man would not require anticoagulants to survive. Ideally, though, he would receive them for the first few weeks or months while the valve settled. Before the operation, a nurse had administered antibiotics. If needed afterwards against infection, approval was unlikely. Alasdair, however, could do nothing about this.

He finished up and prepared the patient for transport to the hospital as paramedics exited the building with the patient. He then turned to his young assistant, hugged her, and thanked her. They were both arrested and led away.

The medics that escaped via a secret tunnel had stayed in the house three houses down. When leaving the medical house, they activated a lock from behind the wall to stop the release lever inside the cupboard from working, securing the secret panel.

Upon arriving at the house further down the street, they transmitted a message over POLO's secure system advising what had happened and giving the names of those who'd stayed in the house: Alasdair Guthrie and Szarlota Wozniak, known as Charlotte.

Although Ed was no longer running POLO operations day to day, he remained fully entrenched and hence received all communications. He didn't know Charlotte but was aware from the message that she had joined POLO six months earlier and was 29 years old. He'd recruited Alasdair before his recruitment group was fully operational.

They had been friends for many years, and Ed had recruited 'Guthy', as he was known, during a dinner at Alasdair's house in Aberdeen on a rare stay over for Ed. Guthy spent so much time vituperating against the LPAS laws that Ed had felt secure in his approach, and Guthy had agreed to join instantly.

A few of Ed's group had previously been arrested and subsequently charged. Such events always made Ed feel down. These latest arrests, however, included the youngest team member to be arrested so far, and also someone very close to Ed. And this made his pain more intense.

Ed put in a call to Jail Sleeks. "Hi, Jail, I assume you've read the inner-circle alert?"

"I have, Ed. We've stood down those who have worked with the two who were arrested. I've asked Covey to stand down Charlotte's recruiter, who by now will be moving to their designated safe house, using their real identity. As you recruited Alasdair directly, there's no recruiter to stand down."

"I'm not concerned about Alasdair giving anything up. I know he won't.

Charlotte, however, is young, and new to POLO. We should prepare ourselves for the possible arrests of those Charlotte has worked alongside. Standing them down isn't enough."

"I agree, Ed. And we haven't just stood them down. We are in the process of moving them to safe houses far away from their usual place of residence. We will monitor their homes and workplaces for police activity. However, they are unlikely ever to be able to return to their previous lives."

"Okay, Jail, I'm guessing we've no clue yet as to how the house became compromised?"

"No clue, Ed. I'll see what our contacts in law enforcement know and get back to you. If those who escaped are correct, this was an LPAS police raid. It could well be that our contacts will have no information."

"Could we have been infiltrated?" Ed inquired.

"I can't rule that out, Ed. I'll have Covey and the team go over recruitment for the past year and plot the movements and work patterns of those recently hired to see if that gives us anything. Do you want to shut down the medical houses, Ed?"

"Yes, we must follow normal protocol. Shut the houses down. We can agree about how long later."

"As good as done, Ed." Even though Jail now ran POLO day to day, there was no question of not seeking Ed's council when he was involved.

Ed hung up and started to give some thought to events. It was the first time a medical house had been compromised without a known source giving the location away – as had happened on two previous occasions, when Collectors were arrested and gave up the house, on one occasion giving up those they worked with too, which was an incredibly challenging time in POLO's past.

Ed's main concern now was that someone had infiltrated the organisation. He knew that, if so, the mole would trickle-feed information, damaging the organisation while hoping not to arouse suspicion.

Later that day, Jail called. "Hi, Ed. I've pulled together the list of all those who knew of the medical house raided earlier today. Brindle has assigned Guardians to watch them and see if that turns anything up.

Meanwhile, Covey has been going over the recruitment data for the past year. I want to interview all those that know this particular house.

However, I'll have to hold off on this, as we will likely spook any fifth columnist, if one exists."

"Okay, Jail. Please keep me up to date. Someone on the inside could cause enormous damage if not identified quickly."

"Clear, Ed."

"Oh, and Jail, what are the chances we could spring the two who were just arrested?"

"That's an off-the-wall question, Ed. You know we can't do that. We'd just land more people in prison."

"Sorry I asked, Jail. It's just that, well, it's playing on my mind more than usual. I think it's having our youngest operative arrested, and Alasdair, a dear friend."

"Ed, I can't help you with your inner demons; I truly wish I could. You have to work them out yourself, and I know you will. Alasdair and Charlotte knew the risks."

"I know. I'm sorry I asked. I was thinking out loud, I guess."

Jail rang off, and Ed went back to pondering on who could have given up the medical house, interleaved with thoughts of Charlotte and Guthy.

The meeting to discuss the raid further was to be held at the old Richmond Bridge boathouse, on the Thames at Richmond Bridge, as the name would suggest. The boathouse, derelict and boarded up, was acquired by Gig's transport company, and awaited a licence to build a copter port.

At today's meeting would be Jail Sleeks, Brindle Llanos, Jesse Omaha, Creak Nooks, Kimberly Marleah, Covey Twinks and, of course, Ed. Ashlin Steeple would not be attending, as no new hires had taken place in the Collectors unit for over two years. For now, at least, this area wasn't seen as a priority.

The team would arrive at different times, coming disguised, as was protocol, with Ed arriving first. Covey was last to arrive, and Ed took the floor.

"This feels strange after so long," Ed commented to the team. "And you won't believe the hassle I had, giving my Special Branch officer the slip!"

"That's why you shouldn't be here, Ed," Jail made clear. "He'll be pissed, and you'll need a good excuse for having done so."

"I know, Jail, I know. I'll tell him I'm having a relationship with a married woman!"

"Anyone who's watched you around Leonora isn't going to buy that, Ed."

"Maybe not, but he'll have to take me at my word. But let's move on. My security arrangements aren't what we are here to discuss."

Jail shut up but was very unhappy with Ed for having ducked his security detail to attend a meeting that could run just as well without him. Although Jail accepted that wasn't Ed's belief.

"Two good people will go to prison because of the raid on the medical house. One of which, as you all know, I am good friends with and recruited personally. Alasdair is a fantastic surgeon and person, and Charlotte, so young and brave, volunteered to stay behind and assist him. It is devastating for them both and for the organisation.

"I know you will all be aware that I haven't attended today due to any lack of confidence in Jail's ability to run operations. However, the events of early last week are serious, being the first time a medical house has been compromised without us knowing how. So who wants to go first?" Ed prompted.

Jail took the floor. "So far, Ed, we've had nothing back from our collective contacts at any of the agencies or the force. Our police contacts advised that this was 100 per cent LPAS police, with no involvement from other enforcement agencies. Our contacts at military intelligence know nothing either but haven't ruled out the possibility that MI5's medical unit is involved."

"Jail," said Ed, looking concerned, "that is by far my biggest concern."

Ed looked over at Covey, asking if she had uncovered anything of value.

"We've not hired anyone new into POLO over the past seven months, except for Charlotte. No one in any department. I'm checking the last four hires into the medical unit, who were taken on between 13 and

15 months ago; and Brindle has assigned Guardians to monitor them for a while. Otherwise, nothing. Sorry."

"Why only the last four, Covey?" Ed wanted to know.

"An initial cut-off, Ed. Before the last four, the previous hire was eight months earlier. We are now well established, and we've slowed down recruitment to ensure added security. We will go back further if we need to, but figured it best to start with these four," Covey explained.

"Good call, Covey," was Ed's view. "Anything to add, Kimmy?"

"Sorry, Ed, no. I've been given no reason to suspect any of the medical team, although I have been soliciting those I trust totally, to see if anyone has been asking probing questions. Nothing so far."

"Jesse?" prompted Ed.

"Brindle is checking the movements of the last four in by tailing them. I'm reviewing their GPS footprints from now on and from six months back, hoping their footprints will give them away if anyone is involved with the security services."

"Good call, Jesse, thanks," replied Ed.

"Anything to add, Creak?"

"Nothing, Ed. None of the folks in question has a Guardian or bodyguard, so no path to follow from my side or Brindle's; historically, that is."

"Okay, folks, I appreciate you all attending. All very troubling, and I'll not sleep easy until we know. Would you please stay focused; leave no stone unturned. We need answers." Ed, highly anxious, felt he had to say something that he viewed was likely on the minds of others, but felt guilty saying it.

"Before we wrap up, I know this sounds unfeeling, but Jail, can you check Charlotte's background and see if your contacts have anything on her. I'm sorry to ask this, but however unlikely, it is possible Charlotte's the mole and is working for MI5's medical unit."

"Don't feel guilty, Ed," said Jail. "I've already kick-started enquiries in that regard."

"Okay, Jail. I say it too often, I know. But I should have known you would have."

"We are likely, Ed, to know if it is Charlotte well before our investigation points in that direction," Jail continued.

"Why, Jail?" Ed wanted to know.

"Because they will go after her recruiter in the hope of taking down many more POLO operatives. Not that they will find her recruiter. But we will know if they make a move."

"I guess that makes sense, Jail." The anguish on Ed's face was plain to everyone.

Ed closed the meeting, and, as usual, left last, arriving back at his apartment late evening. He'd no plans to visit Leonora tonight and was pleased not to have made plans, as his stress levels were very high, and he knew he was irritable. Not a great combination for being with the one you love. And besides, he had spent nearly an hour in an, at times, heated debate with his Special Branch officer, who, as Jail had pointed out, was just a little ticked off with him.

UNnatural Selection –
Not before time

Up at 5 a.m., Ed showered and dressed, quickly gulped down a bowl of bran and mug of instant coffee. Butterflies had been fluttering in his stomach since he awoke, and trepidation permeated his body. For today, Ed was visiting Patricia and Henry, Jennifer Skull's parents, and he was unsure how what he planned to tell them would be received. It had been a little more than two years since Jennifer committed suicide, an event that was still raw, with Ed often experiencing flashbacks, sometimes happy ones, other times not so happy, and even frightening.

Ed missed Jennifer terribly and felt deep, unshakeable pain, blaming himself in part for her taking her own life. It was by far the most significant loss to him, personally, due to LPAS and his founding of POLO. Ed called events that troubled him deeply 'mind scars', and wondered how many he could rake up before they got the better of him. Cirrhosis of the mind, if you will.

He had planned to visit Jelly's parents since her funeral, provide them with a little more information on his friendship with their daughter, and disclose, in part, the letters Jennifer had sent to him and the team before her death. Unfortunately, Ed could not show Jennifer's parents the notes, as carrying them on him was not a risk worth taking. However, he had read them so often he could recite them verbatim, so he could ensure that he made them aware of the most meaningful content.

Ed's journey was somewhat easier than it might have been. He now had an understanding with Special Branch. He would be protected by officers most of the time but would be allowed to duck his protection for personal reasons. Ed didn't elaborate on what these 'personal reasons' were, but the officers protecting him believed he was having a relationship with a married woman, and it suited Ed not to disabuse them of this theory.

When he was going somewhere without his guards, they would ensure no one could follow him, and he agreed to wear a disguise. His agents weren't happy with the arrangement but knew he would kick off if they disagreed and would likely give them the slip anyway. And besides, with a bit of planning, a disguise, and some work to ensure he could not be observed leaving a location, they saw the risk as low.

Jail, however, was furious with Ed, believing he was putting his life at unnecessary risk to do things that Jail thought were not essential. And that he ran the risk of the government formally and, likely, publicly, pulling his guards. Ed disagreed, telling Jail that these things had to be done but could not be done with a Special Branch officer in tow.

This topic, Ed knew, Jail would broach again. For now, his focus was on his visit to Jennifer's parents.

When Jennifer had passed the letters destined for her fellow law-breakers to a correctional officer, asking her to send them, she knew her actions were a risk. The officer had said she wanted to help, but this may well have been a lie, a ploy to obtain information that days of police interrogations had failed to achieve. However, Jennifer knew that the process used by Ed to receive letters, which would continue their journey after being received at a post office box, was slow and secure.

A heavily disguised member of POLO would undertake collection from the PO box and start a long journey around the city, tracked by Guardians, to ensure no one was tailing the messenger. Before leaving the PO box location, the operative would scan the letters to ensure tracking devices weren't present. The member collecting the letters would visit a nearby shop and, under the pretence of buying something, take some items into a changing cubical to check the clothes they were wearing were free of devices, possibly attached while in the post office. A further precaution was that those collecting letters did not carry a cell phone that could be zeroed in on. Precautions complete, the notes would then move from one pick-up point to another, each time ensuring the operative was not under surveillance and using scanners to check their clothing. Only when it was deemed safe were the letters delivered to Ed.

The risk (if it were in fact a ploy) was that it could link Jennifer to an anti-LPAS organisation. Given her intention to take her own life, Jennifer wasn't concerned for herself and had weighed up the risk to POLO. All said, she deemed it a gamble worth taking to deliver an essential valediction to her fellow heads of POLO.

Ed had wanted to visit Jennifer's parents much sooner but was all too aware of the risks in doing so. However, he now believed it was safe-ish. He left his apartment via the underground car park in disguise and got into a car, pre-hired, to drive himself to one of Gig's transport hubs and a copter flight to Lincoln, East Midlands, where he would take a taxi to Nettleton Village.

Arriving in the village, Ed asked the driver to drop him outside the church. Then, entering the graveyard, he sauntered through the grounds of St John the Baptist, making his way to a plot of land at the rear, Jennifer's final place of rest. The words on her gravestone were simple but meaningful, especially to those engaged in the same fight:

Jennifer Skull, Jelly 13.07.2004 – 14.08.2043

Lived and died for the lives of others. She fought bravely to turn the pages on one of the world's darkest chapters.

Ed remained graveside for almost half an hour, his mind flicking through the great memories he had of Jennifer and recalling the many times she made him laugh uncontrollably. Then, as he left, he paused momentarily, turned his head back towards her grave and beyond, to the view over the valley behind the church, and smiled.

Ed wasn't religious, but as he had thought at her funeral, to be laid to rest in such a beautiful setting, a setting that in one's mind you could conjure up when thinking of her last journey, was a wonderful thing. It helped that his memory of her final journey wasn't simply of a grave, but of a beautiful place, one of so many in our amazing home: Earth.

Leaving the church, Ed made his way slowly through the village to a cottage on the edge of a small farm. Jennifer's parents had lived in the house all their married lives.

Knocking on the door, Ed waited patiently. He could hear footsteps slowly moving along the hallway, then the door opened wide, and Patricia greeted him, ushering him inside.

Ed entered the lounge, where Henry shook his hand. "I'm sure you know, but I'm Henry, Jennifer's father. Please, sit down."

Ed and Henry engaged in small talk for around 10 minutes before Patricia walked in with sandwiches, cake and coffee. Sitting down, Patricia turned to Ed.

"When you called, Edward, I'm sorry to say that I couldn't remember you from the funeral. But now I do. And I recall you had a charming lady with you."

"Yes, Patricia. She would have liked to have come today, but for reasons I will go into in a moment, it would have been unwise."

"It's very nice of you to visit us. We've had little contact with any of Jennifer's friends from the city since she died. I'm not complaining. We didn't know many of them, and those we did, we did not know well." Patricia paused for a few seconds before continuing.

"At the funeral, I recall you saying you knew Jennifer from her work at the hospital?"

"Yes, but there's more than Ashlin or I could say that day. You see, Jennifer and I were good friends. Close friends. I loved your daughter as I would a sister. I'm sad to say that I started her on her journey to breaking the law to save others. Jennifer was a member of an organisation into which I recruited her. A secret, 'criminal', if you will, organisation, set up to save the lives of those that the government will not." Ed paused, needing to regain his composure as Henry stepped in.

"The papers never said Jennifer worked for an illegal group, Edward."

"No, the police were not aware. When they arrested Jennifer, it was for illegal life-saving linked to her job as a child oncologist. They never linked her to any organised group working against LPAS," Ed clarified, still trying hard to control his emotions.

"Don't be sad, Edward. Jennifer would never have stood by and watched people suffer and die who she could help," Patricia jumped in, noticing the look of guilt and sorrow that had crept across his face.

Patricia wanted to reassure him that neither she nor Henry blamed him.

"It means a lot to hear you say that," Ed said. "It doesn't take away the pain and guilt I feel, which I know cannot come close to the suffering you've had to endure. Ashlin and I wanted to tell you on the day of the funeral. To do so would have been far too risky, but I had always planned to visit you. I'm sorry it has taken so long."

"We appreciate you taking the trouble, Edward. And as Patricia has said, Jennifer decided to do what she did.

We blame no one except the law for what happened to her," said Henry.

"I want to recite a letter to you that Jennifer wrote to me and others in the life-saving group. I haven't brought it, as it would not be a risk worth taking. But I've read it so often I no longer need it in front of me.

"Before I do, I want you to know that I still find it upsetting, but strangely comforting too. If you'd prefer, I will not recite it." Ed wanted to ensure they were prepared and had the chance to say no.

"Ed," said Patricia. "We want you to tell us."

Ed leant in towards them both, took a deep breath and started to recite Jennifer's letter. As he'd expected, doing so brought it all flooding back, and although he kept going, unlike when he read it to the team in the old mine, he was welling up and struggling a tad. Towards the end, Henry and Patricia were crying too. The three of them ended up hugging in the middle of the room.

After a brief pause, Ed recited the second letter, which outlined her upbringing, hoping this would help too. As he finished, Henry spoke.

"Edward, you'll never know, given the tears, how much happiness your visiting us and sharing Jennifer's letters has brought. When you said you loved Jennifer like a sister, I took it as nice words, but not now. It is clear to me just how much you loved our daughter. Not just from the emotions brought on by reciting the letters; it is also evident the risk you have taken in telling us what you have. Information shared puts you at enormous risk.

Not that it will come to anything. I can assure you of that." Henry paused, and Patricia spoke.

"Henry is right. Your secret is safe with us, and I am so pleased you came to us. Jennifer's words, even though extremely upsetting, have brought us comfort. And Edward, I want to be clear. We do not blame you, and you should not blame yourself. Jennifer was strong. She knew what she wanted to do, and no one could have stopped her once she made up her mind."

Ed again thanked them both, hugging them.

"This won't do, will it now," Patricia said. "Let us tell you some stories about Jennifer."

The three of them spent the rest of their time together talking about Jennifer, laughing and crying in equal measure, and at just after 11 p.m., Ed left. He'd arranged for a taxi to collect him at 11:30 outside the church instead of from Jennifer's parents' house. As he left, he assured them that he would visit again soon. And they told Ed that if they could ever help him, he must ask.

Ed arrived at the church with 10 minutes to spare, sat on the wall, and looked up at the stars. It was a clear night, and with few lights on in the village, the Milky Way was on show in all its glory.

The first time Ed truly experienced the Milky Way was on a trip to South Africa. He was staying with a friend in Hangklip, near Pringle Bay, around 100 kilometres from Cape Town. The house was on the beach, and after a late dinner, they sat outside after midnight looking up at the sky. Ed found the view fascinating.

Now, whenever Ed found the time to look up at the sky for more than a few seconds and could see the

Milky Way – rare, these days, given the amount of light pollution – he always transported himself back to that trip to South Africa. He momentarily smiled, before flipping back to thoughts of Jennifer, which made him smile too, but also feel a tinge of sadness.

Ed's taxi drew up, and within 30 or so minutes, it had dropped him off at the copter port in Lincoln.

As Ed stepped into the copter for his return flight to London, an uncontrollable smile washed over his face. The day had lifted his spirits, relieving some of the pressure that had been with him since her death. He was pleased too that Patricia and Henry had said it had helped them tremendously and that they had not laughed so much since her passing. Ed was looking forward to getting home, but also to his next visit to Jennifer's parents.

UNnatural Selection –
In search of the source

Creak Nooks called an inner-circle meeting to update the team on the medical house raid that had taken place several weeks earlier. The session would take place at Brindle's farm, in the large guest cottage at its centre. Creak had pushed out the invite to the entire inner circle, and at short notice, but made clear that full attendance was the aim.

The eVTOLs started to arrive early morning, with the last touching down just after 11 a.m., with Ed on board. As he walked into the cottage, Covey handed him a large mug of coffee.

"Thanks, Covey. You must be a mind-reader." Ed said, smiling at Covey and again saying thank you. "Okay, Creak, you never call meetings at this short notice. So you've got my hopes up that this will be well worth the trip."

"Maybe, Ed, maybe," responded a serious-looking Creak, who immediately stood up to address the inner circle. "Anyone here heard the name Alvis Riddle?"

Blank looks from everyone, except Marcelle, who said it sounded made up.

"Oh, more made up than Hood!" said George, to which Marcelle responded, "Hood's my nickname, stupid," flipping her finger at George.

"Okay, you two, pack it in," Creak yelled before continuing. "Neither had I, until yesterday. Ashlin has the most amazing patience and focus." Ashlin nodded to thank him for the compliment.

"I pulled a ton of data on the four last in-the-door hires, everything we knew about them, and asked Ashlin to work with other 'equally detailed' POLO operatives to see if they could come up with anything odd. Nothing." Creak scanned the room. "No takers yet?"

"Yes," said Ed. "Doesn't sound like I'll have a good day."

"Patience, Ed, patience," said Creak, with a look of confidence.

"Ashlin, being Ashlin, having done a thorough job, said she would review the information we had on all medical staff in POLO. I know what you are thinking, that's a task to send you mad!

"Ashlin and the team cut and diced the names and information on their history, family, friends and everything we knew about our medics. Then the team ranked them in order based on an algorithm put together by Jesse. A risk algorithm, if you will. Then the detail was fed into the computer, using another of Jesse's programs, to see if it highlighted anything worth following up. For which I must say a big thank you to Jesse. Without her program and algorithm, we'd have been crunching this data for months, if not years.

"The computer kicked out several follow-up points, one of which led us to Alvis Riddle, a career criminal – muggings, burglaries, fraud, drugs. You name it, this guy's into it. Two years ago, sentenced to 15 years, he started to self-harm within a few months, and attempted suicide twice. A career criminal, yes, but as often happens, he could no longer handle prison life."

Ed was by now tilting his head from side to side, staring intently at Creak, his insides knotting up; he wanted to jump in and tell Creak to get to the point but let him run with it, as he seemed to be enjoying saying thank you to everyone...

"In itself, Alvis showing up as a line wouldn't have mattered too much. That is, of course, had he not been released from prison recently."

Ed sat up, knowing something big was coming. "Creak, any chance you can get to the point before I explode?"

"Sorry, Ed, I'm getting there."

"You said he was sent down for 15 years?" Jail asked, making sure he had heard correctly.

"Yes, Jail, and just made it over the two-year mark before being released on parole."

Now Jail had joined Ed in sitting bolt upright and waiting with bated breath.

"This isn't going to be a bloody drawn-out murder mystery, is it,

Creak? Rev Green in the billiard room with the candlestick?" George asked with a grin and a wink. "I want to go home sometime today!"

"I'm all but there, George," was Creak's response, now with a broad grin of his own. "Can I ask if anyone knows Ricki Kranun?"

Now the whole room sat bolt upright, except Ashlin and Brindle, as they knew what was coming, having worked with Creak. Kimberly turned bright red, and her facial expression became one of horror.

"She's on my team and was the theatre nurse who got away from the house the police raided," Kimmy responded in an almost inaudible voice.

"Exactly, Kimmy. And Ricki Kranun is Alvis Riddle's sister!" came the confirmation that Kimmy was dreading.

"Bitch, I'll fu–"

Ed stepped in, stopping Kimberly in full flight. "I understand your anger. Mine is welling up inside me too. I'm not defending her, but for her, her brother's life was more important than the lives of others. That assumes, Creak, that you are saying Ricki is our mole?"

"*Prima facie*, Ed. That's a yes, unless proven otherwise."

"Okay, we need a plan to deal with this, and we need it before we leave this evening." Ed was now up on his feet and pacing the lounge, visibly alarmed at this development. At first sight, it seemed he had the enemy on the inside, which had always been his greatest fear. So many other groups operating against LPAS had fallen for this very reason.

"First, we urgently need confirmation that this assumption is a fact. Then we need to know everything Ricki might have known about POLO, and we have to assume she has given all of that knowledge up." Ed was taking long deep breaths to calm himself.

"We've already taken the necessary steps, Ed," Creak assured him. "We've moved at-risk operatives to safe houses, her recruiter is already on a plane, and the new medical home in which Ricki was due to operate out of has been closed down." Creak paused, and Jail piped up.

"We can't simply assume she has given it all up. And we can't assume we know for sure what she knows. So we have to find out what she knew and what she has given the LPAS police, Ed."

Fear of a different kind was now coursing through Ed's body, as he knew what Jail was suggesting.

"I know, Jail, I know. Get it done." Ed was resigned to the action required: Ricki would have to be taken away and held until she gave up the information they needed. However, this wasn't Ed's biggest concern. It was what to do with Ricki afterwards.

"Creak, did you check to see if any of those at risk were under surveillance before you acted?" he wanted to know.

"Best endeavours, yes. But we couldn't be too thorough; we needed to get them out. I can tell you that no one was following any of them, right up to the final step to safety. We had a lot of Guardians ensuring that didn't happen," a confident Creak replied. "Brindle pulled out all the stops."

"Where's Ricki now?" Ed inquired.

"I've not got the latest, but Guardians have been on her all day, and in Ricki's case, we are sure no one is tailing her."

"Okay, pick her up and find out what she has said and to whom," Ed instructed, even though it made him feel sick to the pit of his stomach.

Guardians were waiting for Ricki to return home. She lived in an apartment block in London with an un-gated underground car park. A Guardian would take down the cameras as she arrived at the car park, then others would follow in behind her and grab her once she'd parked. Guardians already following Ricki had advised that there was still no sign of her being under surveillance from other parties.

Ricki arrived at the car park, locked her car and made her way to the lift. The Guardians made their move: pulled up in a van, grabbed her and, after throwing her in, exited the car park at speed.

Holding her hand tightly over Ricki's mouth, the lead Guardian told Ricki not to scream and she would uncover her mouth, to which Ricki nodded in agreement.

Uncovering her mouth, the Guardian produced a bag. "I'm sorry, Ricki, everything you have, including all your clothing, in the bag – do it now."

Ricki was shaking as she started to undress. Now naked, a Guardian told her to lie prostrate while they scanned her body for tracking devices under the skin.

"Quickly, turn over onto your back," said the Guardian scanning her body.

"Tracker, just below the left shoulder blade," warned the Guardian.

Ricki started to cry, screaming out, hitting the lead Guardian in the face and pulling the side door, managing to open it slightly before being restrained. One of Kimmy's people, who was on the team in case of need, promptly injected her. From flailing around and screaming, within 40 seconds, Ricki was still.

"Give me a scalpel from my bag," said the medic who had just put Ricki to sleep. She made a small incision, and the bug was squeezed out, photographed and destroyed; they then re-scanned Ricki. "All clear."

"And her jewellery and clothing?"

"All clear too."

The van pulled over and a trailing car took the bag of clothes and jewellery, which they would incinerate, just in case. Ed insisted that the abduction team was all female when authorising the snatch, knowing they would need to strip Ricki and knowing she would be scared.

They were now driving to a safe house where a member of Creak's team would interrogate her. Guardians dressed her in white overalls before arriving.

Ricki awoke on a bed in a small room. She noticed the camera instantly, in the top right-hand corner above the door. Still a little groggy and unsteady on her feet, she got up and tried the door: locked, not unexpectedly. As she moved back towards the bed, the door opened.

"Glad to see you are awake, Ricki. Here's a bottle of cold water. Can I get you something to eat?" said a man whose face was covered.

"What do you want with me? I don't have anything of value. You're frightening me. Please let me go." Ricki's face was full of fear, and her voice quivering.

"In good time, Ricki. But for now, can I get you some food?"

"A sandwich, any sandwich... Thank you," Ricki responded. Within 10 minutes, the guard returned with a plate of sandwiches, put them on the bed and made to leave.

"What's happening to me? Please, I'm scared. I need to know what's happening to me." After finishing her sentence, she started to sob.

"I'm sorry, I can't say anything now. Soon, though, very soon," said the guard.

That made her feel even worse, wondering what 'soon' might mean.

UNnatural Selection –
Horrible but necessary

A few hours had passed when the door next opened and a guard escorted Ricki along a corridor to a larger room with a table, chairs and a large mirror on the wall. Ricki was squinting, as the room lights were so bright.

"Ricki, sit down."

As she did, a large man walked in and sat on the other side of the table.

The man who followed Ricki in was Creak, who had decided to interrogate her himself. Six foot two, and although in his early fifties, Creak was well muscled. As one would expect, he was wearing a disguise; and so good was the mask, it sent Ricki into a panic.

"No, please, I don't want to see you," she cried out, leaping from the table towards the door. A guard grabbed her, and Ricki tore at his face with her long nails. Although he was wearing a full latex disguise, she caused a considerable gash to his face, evident from the blood running down his cheek. As Ricki continued to lash out, the guard got control of her, dragging her back to the table, forcing her back onto the chair and holding her in place, while shouting at her to calm down.

As Ricki controlled herself, she tightly closed her eyes for fear that seeing this man would mean almost certain death.

"Please, don't be alarmed. All is not as it appears. I don't look the way you see me. It is just a good disguise. You can open your eyes; I don't want to hurt you."

Ricki opened her eyes and was instantly transfixed by the man before her. She had locked onto his sepia-brown eyes – his natural colour, as he was not wearing contact lenses.

"What's happening to me?" Ricki spluttered as floods of tears streamed down her face, slipping into her mouth.

"That's not how it works, Ricki. I ask the questions, and you will answer them truthfully. Is that clear?"

Uncontrollably crying, Ricki screeched out: "But I don't know what you want with me!"

In a noticeably louder and more sinister voice, Creak said, "I asked you if that was *clear?*"

"It is clear, sir," Ricki replied, still crying and trying hard to control her body, which was starting to shake, and, at that moment, wetting herself.

The mirror was two-way, and on the other side stood Ed, Brindle and Jail.

"We've got to stop this, Jail." Ed was distraught to witness just how frightened Ricki was, having wet herself. "This isn't right. You can see the fear in Ricki's eyes. She's a human being, for God's sake. What are we doing?"

"She is, Ed. Ricki's not a bad person. But she is a major threat, and we need information. So if you can't handle it, you must leave. Don't put POLO at greater risk than we already find ourselves in." Jail pushed back on Ed hard, clarifying that he agreed it wasn't pleasant but was necessary.

Ed knew that without Jail, Creak and Brindle on the team, he would likely already be in prison and his organisation closed down, with thousands of lives lost as a result. However, this was the side of POLO he hated. Fortunately, this kind of thing happened infrequently. Not that that made him feel any better. Back in the room, Creak started to question Ricki.

"Why did you have a GPS tracker injected under your skin?"

"It's a family thing – you know, check up on each other, make sure we are all safe."

"If you lie to me again, it won't end well. Do you understand?"

Tears again rolled down Ricki's face as she nodded, still shaking, holding the table in a vain attempt to keep control of herself.

"I'll ask just one more time, Ricki. Why did you have a GPS tracker injected under your skin?"

"...It was put there by police officers who said they needed to keep track of all my movements."

"And why were they interested in your movements?" Creak probed.

"I provided them with some information to help my bro..." Unable to finish her sentence, she again broke down, begging to be let go, making it clear that she still didn't know what was going on. Her face was covered in red blotches that stood out more due to her bleached white face. An indescribable look of fear made Ed go cold; he was almost unable to look through the double-sided mirror but unwilling to look away, wanting to step in but holding his nerve.

Ed was fidgeting more and more in the adjoining room, placing his head in his hands, then moving them to his stomach, which was beginning to knot. He didn't want to be here but didn't want to leave either.

"Calm down, Ricki, and tell me what the police asked of you." So said Creak in a calm, soft voice, before asking one of the men on the door to give her some water. As Ricki gulped down the large glass, she choked and threw up over the table. Creak jumped up and shoved the table with force into the wall, pulling his chair closer to Ricki and sitting back down.

"Such tactics won't work with me, Ricki."

Ed turned to Jail. "What, does he think she was deliberately sick?"

"No, Ed. He doesn't. But he's letting her know he won't give ground and she will need to do as he asks. It is no good him being nice."

Ed turned to the wall and went to bang his fists when Jail stopped him. "Ed, she'll hear you. You need to calm down too or leave. We know what we are doing."

Ed sat down. The knots in his stomach were now paining him. But he wasn't going to leave. Creak was holding Ricki by the shoulders.

"Answer my question, Ricki."

"I gave them information to help my brother. They said that would be all, but they lied to me. They told me I'd done well, but that without more, my brother would go back to prison and that I would too."

Ricki's problem was that she genuinely didn't know who was holding her, or why. She thought it could perhaps be the LPAS police testing her. Less likely was that it was someone her brother had crossed. She hadn't thought it could be members of POLO. No, that thought hadn't entered her head. "What information did you provide to the police, Ricki?"

Terrified of saying the wrong thing but equally of not answering, Ricki broke down again and started retching.

"It won't get any easier, Ricki, until you answer the questions," Creak said in a soft voice.

Composing herself, Ricki starting to talk, knowing that, whoever was holding her, not talking was every bit as bad as telling all.

"My brother was serving a long sentence and had started to self-harm. The prison let me visit him more often than usual to help calm him down, make him see sense, but he continued to self-harm and tried to kill himself. I had to help him."

"How exactly did you plan to do that, Ricki?" Creak pushed her to elaborate.

"I went to the police and told them I knew of an illegal medical house and that I would provide them with the address, with conditions."

"And they were?" Creak continued to push.

"I said I would only provide the address when the house was in use and that they had to raid it then. I told them that if they did not, I would tip off those who used it, and the police would then get nothing. They pushed me hard for more, but eventually they agreed.

"I told the officer that when parole was official, I would provide the details the next time the house was in use. They agreed, and Alvis, that's my brother, received early parole."

"How did you know the house was in use? Do you live close by?"

"No, I was in the house. I work for the criminal organisation... but the police didn't know how I knew."

"So the police let you go once they discovered you at the house?"

"Not exactly. It's complicated, but I was out of the house before they broke in. When the raid occurred, they arrested two medical professionals. I knew once that happened, the organisation would close the house down, which is why I didn't give them the address earlier and told them they had to act when I did. I didn't want them monitoring the house for a long time and likely arresting more organisation members by following those who attended the house. I think they knew that was my plan, and that is why they told me they required more information."

"So they went back on the deal?" Creak inquired.

"I argued with them that they had broken their promise, but they said Alvis had already mixed with known criminals in the short time he had been out, so they had a right to revoke his parole, but would overlook this if I gave them more."

"So, what did you plan to do next, Ricki?"

"I was planning to run with my brother. He was making arrangements, and once he'd arranged everything, we were going to cut out the GPS device and leave together."

"Okay, Ricki. Enough for now. Return to your room, and I'll visit you tomorrow." Creak made it clear that she wasn't going anywhere yet.

Crying again, Ricki asked if she could leave, and again asked who they were, and begged them not to hurt her brother.

"We've no plans to hurt your brother, and we don't want to hurt you. Get some rest. We will talk again tomorrow."

Guards took Ricki to her room, and Creak joined the others in the monitoring room.

"That was horrible to watch," Ed, visibly shaken, told Creak the moment he entered the room.

"Yes, I know, Ed. I wouldn't say I liked it either. I know she is a decent person. But knowing what she has given away is paramount. I don't need to tell you that, Ed."

"Okay, Creak. What's our next move?"

"I'm sorry, Ed, but I need to go further. What she has told me is good news. She has, or so she says, limited the damage to the original arrests. But I have to be sure that's true. Once I am sure, we then need to decide the important next step," said Creak, fixing his eyes on Ed's.

"That sentence makes me nervous, Creak."

"Everyone in this room with you now, Ed, are your security experts – would you agree?"

"Yes, Creak, I would."

"Okay, so between us, we need to decide how we let her go."

"I'm pleased we are saying how and not if, Creak."

"Ed, we aren't going to kill her, even accepting that there is a risk in letting her go. However, it means those who have moved out of POLO will have to stay out and assume new lives. Painful for them, but they cannot return. However, we want to give Ricki the best chance of not being arrested once we let her leave. I'll work with Jail and Brindle, and we will get back to you, if you are okay with that?"

"I am, Creak, and I'm sorry for my outburst. But this is all still too much for me."

"It isn't a problem, Ed. We understand."

Ed left the building and made his way back to his apartment, feeling better than he had. Ricki had limited the damage to POLO. She was giving up just enough to get her brother out of prison. And Ed, although extremely angry, could understand why she had set up her colleagues. It wasn't something he would have done, and he hoped not too many in the organisation would. But this type of action was always a possibility once the security services had a hold over you. Ed was now hoping that Creak could close it out quickly, as he was travelling to New York in a few days and did not want it hanging over him. Further, he was very concerned about its effect on Ricki, although he accepted it was necessary.

While driving back to his apartment, a concern flashed into Ed's mind, and he immediately put in a call to Creak.

"Hi, Creak, I'm sorry, I've just had an unnerving thought."

"Go on, Ed."

"Ricki was injected with a GPS device, which you destroyed."

"Yes, and?"

"Whoever was monitoring her would have been alerted that something was wrong, and it occurred to me that they would have immediately sent agents out to apprehend Ricki, and, in all likelihood, her brother too."

"Very likely, Ed. Which is why we took him off the street before we snatched Ricki. He's at one of our safe houses, with members of the bodyguard unit, as he's a little more troublesome than his sister."

"Sorry, Creak, I should have known better."

"No issue, Ed. I should have told you, but with all that was going on, it slipped my mind. He is safe and going nowhere. Although he's a little bruised, having resisted the guys we sent to collect him. The boys said he's a real handful. And that's something we have to factor into our release plan. He's a career criminal, which also makes him an opportunist. So I need to leave him in no uncertain terms that any sign of trouble will mean certain death for him."

"Sorry, Creak. I'm not sure I follow. What kind of trouble?"

"Ed, when we help them to safety, they are going to wonder why. It won't take them long to figure out that we are POLO operatives. We are working on a plan to deal with that situation but may not find an adequate one. And if not, her brother knows his sister has information she could give up if she chooses to.

"Okay, we've moved out those at greatest risk. But for some that Ricki worked with, she knows their real names and their day jobs. I don't want that information getting into the wrong hands, even though we have moved them to safety. But tell them they will forever need a fake ID, which will damage their lives permanently, and we will have several miserable people on our hands – and that could become our next issue.

"Of course, that assumes she hasn't given other names to the police already. But I don't want her brother thinking he can sell information and return to his old stomping grounds unhindered by the police."

"Okay, Creak, I get it. And I agree, that's a big concern. What a bloody mess."

"Don't worry for now, Ed. We'll brief you on our plans well before we execute them... The plans, I mean, not the brother and sister!"

"I got that, Creak!"

UNnatural Selection – Before New York

Ed would be back in New York at the United Nations in a few days and was still hoping Jail Sleeks would resolve the internal issue before he had to head off.

Ed was at Leonora's apartment, but Leonora wasn't. She was at a charity event, one of the last she would attend before stopping her work and starting work full time with Ed.

Leonora worked tirelessly for many charities, so extricating herself was a rather lengthy process. Still, she was making headway and hoped it would not be too much longer before she could join Ed on his quest to have LPAS laws consigned to the dustbin of history.

Ed was busying himself around the apartment when the intercom warbled.

"Hi. Ed Thorncroft."

"Hi, Mr Thorncroft, it's Harold at reception. I know Leonora is out, but there's a lady in reception who has a gift for her. What would you like me to do, sir?"

"If the lady is okay about it, I will come down and collect it. If she wishes to give it to Leonora personally, she will be home in about three hours."

Reception spoke to the lady, who said her preference was to leave the gift with the concierge. "That's fine," Ed responded. "I'll be down to collect it soon."

Ten or so minutes later, Ed took the lift down to the concierge and collected a box. He headed back up to the apartment, and as he exited the lift, his phone rang. It was Jail, who wanted to give him an update on Ricki Kranun and Alvis Riddle.

"Okay, Jail, give me a few seconds." Ed put the gift on the side in the kitchen and went into the living room to sit down before asking Jail to go ahead. Jail outlined that he was as sure as he could be that Ricki was telling the truth, after further questioning. He then went on to outline his plan to release both Ricki and Alvis.

"So here's the plan, Ed."

Jail had convinced Ricki that he ran an organisation inside POLO that was involved in what was in effect re-stealing drugs to sell on the black market, and that they took a dim view of anyone who put the organisation at risk.

He'd advised Ricki that he'd give her money and new identity papers for herself and her brother, but that if they ever turned up on his patch again, or he got wind through his contacts in the police that any deals were in the offing with Ricki or her brother, he would come after them.

Ricki responded as one would expect, agreeing to these terms, but she also said she had never intended to damage POLO and that she just wanted her brother free before he killed himself. Jail made it clear that he believed her, but that anything that led him to change his mind would mean death for both her and her brother.

"I put on my most sinister persona, Ed. I think Ricki believed what I told her."

"Jail, I'm convinced that whenever you tell me something, it will happen. I'm sure you scared the crap out of Ricki."

Sleeks was confident this would have the required effect on Ricki. Ed liked the approach and felt it was the best way to protect POLO. "I believe you've come up with the best way of dealing with this, Jail.

However, more broadly, I've become increasingly concerned for the organisation, which now has several issues needing containment, each of which has led to a greater risk of significant exposure. We've had multiple holes to plug over the past year. Furthermore, we have to use many resources to follow ex POLO members, in the hope of effecting further containment if required."

"I hear you, Ed," responded Jail, who was every bit as concerned. "We run a tight ship, but these issues are going to keep popping up. Protocols will limit the damage should anyone decide to give anything up. But I fear we can do no more."

"I agree, Jail. I was thinking out loud. I did not mean to be critical." As Ed finished his sentence, he could hear the apartment door opening. Ed whispered: "Gotta go, Jail. Leonora's back." The call ended.

Ed got up and greeted Leonora in the hallway. As they entered the kitchen, Leonora could see the small gift box and card on the side.

"Ed, what have you been up to?"

"Oh, sorry, Leonora, no – it's not from me. A lady dropped it off with the concierge a few hours ago. I'm also sorry I didn't get her name, but I'm sure the card will say."

Inside the box was the official lapel badge of LPAS. The high-end version, a gold badge. "I already have one somewhere, Ed. So why would someone send me another?"

"Open the card, Leonora," Ed responded.

Leonora opened the card, which was not signed. Just a note: "For when you realise your mistake and rejoin us."

Reading the card sent a shiver down Leonora's spine. "Why would someone send me this, Ed?"

Ed looked at the message.

"It's someone at LPAS who isn't happy with your having resigned your position with LPAS and having announced you are joining me, I'm guessing. Don't think any more of it, Leonora. I think someone is just playing a silly mind game."

Ed cuddled her and said he'd make them a coffee while Leonora changed into more comfortable clothes. Ed, while making the coffee, gave some thought to the gift. He was sure it was no more than a silly stunt, but these types of things worried him. He would have Guardians watch over her from now on, although they'd have to be very careful, as Leonora must not know. He would also raise the subject of the gift with Jail, Creak and Brindle, to get their take on it.

Leonora walked back into the living room, and Ed handed her a large mug of coffee. "Well, Ed. Hopefully not much longer now, and I'll be free from my charity commitments and working alongside you. Hopefully, you'll not regret your decision."

"I'm sure I will not, Leonora. You will be a major asset to the team."

"Thank you, Ed. And Ed... should I worry about the badge?"

"It sounds like you already are. Please don't; I'm sure it is nothing. Just someone who's a little bitter. Don't give it any more thought."

"Okay, Ed. I trust your judgement."

UNnatural Selection – Back at the UN

A great deal of time and effort had gone into garnering support for removing vaccines from LPAS legislation. However, there would be multiple steps to get to an actual ban, which might not happen, and even should it occur, it would take some time to achieve.

With many hurdles now overcome, Ed, with much help, had managed to get the United Nations to agree to a non-binding vote on the question. Non-binding, that was, due to how the LPAS act was structured, which had no provision for such a significant change. Modification of less important articles, yes. A change to a substantial pillar of the act, no.

The act, as passed, stated that a review of its effectiveness would not take place until the year 2070. Bringing this forward would require the Security Council to unanimously put a vote to the Assembly, which would then vote on bringing forward the 'effectiveness review date'. If passed, changes to individual parts of the act, including governance, would be put to the Assembly for a simple majority vote.

Ed hoped that this could be accomplished. He found the rules frustrating – he believed LPAS had found ways to sneak changes in to tighten the laws' grip on the world but would not entertain amendments in the other direction.

An example of this was the withdrawal of treatment for health workers operating in an area experiencing a viral outbreak. Ed believed this to be *ultra vires*, meaning it required legal authority beyond the LPAS framework but was enacted without authority. Still, Ed was happy that a non-binding vote would now take place and recognised that this achievement should not be underestimated.

In his dark role, Benjamin Brown called a meeting to discuss Thorncroft. Attending would be James Brown and Logan Miller, still sidelined from dark LPAS operational activity due to his inability, for now, to make contact with Orpheus, whose unexplained disappearance had become of great concern.

"Non-binding, non-binding – he's pushing his luck!" Benjamin screeched at Logan and James.

"Benjamin, don't concern yourself with this. He has zero chance of getting anything like the votes he would need to move to a binding resolution," Logan Miller put in.

"I'm not so sure," replied Benjamin. "I've been mingling of late with many representatives. A fair few of them seem to have shifted their position. I won't tolerate this too much longer. Even if I have to walk down the hallway and kill the bastard myself!" he shouted, thumping the table, his face filled with rage.

"Ben, get a grip. That wouldn't solve our problem," Miller said forcefully, somewhat surprised at Benjamin's comment. Benjamin was typically a measured character, although often a menacing one too.

"It would get this meddling fool out of our business. Thorncroft thinks he's smarter than everyone else and that the world will miraculously heal itself with a few technological tweaks, extra cash and better education!

He's dangerous. Humanity will end if the LPAS laws are in any way watered down, as that will inevitably lead to their eventual repeal. And that I will not allow. And don't call me Ben, Logan. Had your man done his damn job, we wouldn't be having this conversation! I knew I should have taken charge of getting rid of him myself."

"Fuck you, Ben! I've done more for our cause than you or anyone, so get off my back," Logan yelled while leaning across the table with fury in his eyes.

"Jesus, you two, cut it out," James jumped in. "It isn't helping, you two going at it. Cool down."

Logan and Benjamin took a deep breath and went silent for a few seconds before Benjamin piped up.

"Okay, sorry. I know it isn't your fault. I'm just so mad at this man's interference. We have to get rid of him. LPAS is the only way to keep the world safe, even as more and more people are failing to realise there is no other way."

James and Logan agreed with Benjamin's last point and said they would take a fresh look at options and get back to him.

"Okay, guys, you do that," Benjamin, now a little calmer, replied. "But if I don't like the plan, I am going to take charge myself, clear?"

Logan and James were under no illusion and needed a sure-fire plan.

They could not afford another screw-up.

With an agreement to look again at how to deal with Thorncroft, the meeting broke up. James and Logan were fully aware they had one last shot at getting the job done to avoid Benjamin taking over. Neither of them wanted that to happen.

Ed had been at the UN for a few days and now found himself with some free time to relax with a good book in his hotel room. Engrossed in his reading, he was disturbed when the room's doorbell rang. He went to get up, but his Special Branch minder said he'd answer it. A secret service agent was outside, so there was no risk. His protection officer ushered a man in. And as Ed looked up, he recognised him.

"I'm guessing you're not a police officer, then?" said Ed, standing up from the sofa.

"No, I'm not, Mr Thorncroft, and my opinion that you know more about the person who saved your life in London than you let on hasn't changed."

The man who had just entered the room was the 'police officer' who led the interview with Ed at the hospital after the terrorist attack.

"So who do you work for, and why pretend you were a police officer? Isn't that an offence in law?"

Ignoring Ed's question, the man said: "I'm not here to talk about the terrorist attack or to probe you on your relationship with the person who saved you. We've moved on from that. I'm here as my boss decided to assign me to ensure that no one succeeds in rubbing you out." The man held Ed with a serious gaze.

"Colourful turn of phrase," was Ed's quick reply. "I'm intrigued. Why now? Why not talk to me in London?"

"You seem to have made some friends in high places, Mr Thorncroft. Friends who believe your life is in danger and who do not want to have to explain to the public why the British government failed to protect you should anything happen," the official responded.

"Okay, you have my attention, so what's the deal?" Ed probed.

The man sat down, as did Ed, opposite each other on the two sofas. "You can call me Alan," said the man.

"Okay, Alan, please call me Ed."

"I'm British Intelligence; the specific unit isn't important." Ed knew that was a polite way of saying *don't ask*.

Alan went on to update Ed on information that the security services had received regarding a plot by persons unknown to kill him. He advised Ed that the intelligence service believed the Pink Capitalism terror attack's primary purpose was to assassinate him. Furthermore, he said the man who died at the restaurant where Ed and Leonora had been dining was murdered. Murdered in the hope Ed would compromise himself by administering medical help beyond what was legal.

Ed knew that the security services' interest had peaked due to information his people had provided to their contacts within the service. However, Alan would not have known this to be the case, or that Ed was already aware of the theories he had just outlined.

"I didn't think the bodyguards were for show, and I do appreciate the British government providing me with protection, especially given what you have just said. But why brief me now, in New York? Why alert me at all? Why not just sit back and hope the protection afforded me works?" Ed continued to probe.

"We have the name of a 'person of interest'. And that person just made a big mistake. I can't give you any detail other than to say we believe a further attempt on your life is likely. We don't merely want to prevent your death; we want to snag all those who are in on the planning. These people are involved in, shall we say, other undesirable activities, and we need to stop them." Alan paused, awaiting a response from Ed.

"Am I being used as bait?" Ed wanted to know.

"No, Ed, but cocooning you won't help. Please go about your business as usual while we work on the proof we need to arrest those involved. Hopefully, before they try again!"

"Thanks, very reassuring of you!" replied Ed, scrunching up his face.

"We are working closely with the Americans, and we are confident in our ability to protect you and bring these people to book. And why now, as you asked, is simple: we have recent and reliable information, and we will likely need to change your schedule at short notice on occasion until we put this to bed. You needed to know some of the facts so we can count on your cooperation."

"Okay, you have it. Just let me know what you need from me, and I'll comply, whatever it takes," Ed assured him.

"And," Alan replied, "when I say cooperation, I mean it, Ed."

"Okay, Alan, I get that."

"To be clear, Ed, it might affect your dalliance back in the UK. If the guys say no to an unprotected trip, you listen. Clear?"

Ed was surprised that his fake affair had reached this guy's ears.

Whoever he was, and whatever he did.

"Okay, I hear you loud and clear, Alan."

"Good, Ed. We understand each other."

With that, Alan got up, shook Ed's hand and reassured him again that all would work out okay. Then, as he was leaving the room, he turned to Ed once more.

"Oh, by the way. Let her know that I'm still in awe of her shooting skills."

With that last comment, Alan winked at Ed and left the room.

Around 10 p.m., Ed's Special Branch protection officer left his room, leaving the secret service agent outside the door. Ed put in a call to Jail and Creak, but not before sweeping the room again to ensure no bugs were present.

"Hi, Creak, Jail – at a time I should be feeling far safer, I'm on tenterhooks! I'm checking for bugs much more frequently, I'm forever looking over my shoulder, and I'm calling you from the bathroom with the shower running – pathetic!"

"Well, Ed, that's not such a bad thing," mused Jail. "But what's causing your heightened concern?"

"I received a surprise visitor today. Called himself Alan and said he worked for British Intelligence, although he declined to say which department," Ed replied.

"Ed, given that they are concerned for your life, that isn't unusual," Creak put in.

"I get that, Creak, but I haven't finished. Alan is the 'police officer' who arrived at the hospital with three others in tow to question me about Kai. He said they now had reliable and recent information on what they believe is likely to be another attempt on my life," Ed responded with a noticeable quiver in his voice.

"Okay, Ed, that's more interesting," said Jail. "I can understand you being concerned, but here's my view: whatever name he gave you today is no more accurate than the one he used when he met you at the hospital. It isn't unusual for intelligence officers to be vague about the unit in which they work, so give that no more thought."

"His orders are to ensure you come to no harm. And the fact he attended the hospital pretending to be a police officer doesn't cause me concern either. An armed person taking out a terrorist that the establishment knows isn't someone working for them was bound to garner the attention of the security services. But they've found nothing out, so it isn't anything to worry about," Jail concluded.

"Maybe not, but 'Alan' had a dig about me knowing Kai when he walked in, and as he left, he asked me to pass on to Kai how 'in awe' he was about her shooting skills!" said Ed, rather nervously.

"He's fishing, Ed. He's looking for a tell-tale facial expression or body response. He had a hunch and would like nothing better than to prove it to be true. But that angle is closed, trust me," Creak believed.

"Okay, his gut tells him you know more, but that's it. And they've long stopped looking for Kai. And even believing you knew her would not lead them to think you are running an anti-LPAS organisation. They are much more likely to believe you paid someone to watch your back as you were nervous; no more than that, Ed." Reassuring words from Creak, supported by Jail, both of them knowledgeable in this regard.

"Okay, guys, thanks. I would, however, like to know what it is they think they have uncovered. Is it likely that any of your contacts would know?"

"Something so current? Likely not. Internal chatter probably isn't happening yet, if at all, but I'll ask around," was Jail's takeaway.

With that, Ed thanked them for their input, and they closed the call, allowing Ed to switch off the shower!

Back at the UN building, Ed continued a series of meetings, debates and talks on why LPAS legislation needed to change and why country representatives (UN General Assembly members) should get behind the non-binding vote scheduled in just 11 days. Ed had now been working at the UN, building support, for several days.

Given that the vote was considered an 'important question', being linked to peace and security, a two-thirds majority was required. Ed had hoped to get this changed so that a simple majority would carry. However, he had failed to secure this, which was not, admittedly, unexpected.

The Treaty for Global Laws, approved at the UN in 2028, was what had allowed LPAS to become binding on all members in the first instance. Until this treaty, there was no provision for the United Nations to impose laws on sovereign states, and LPAS was among only a handful that had ever passed under the treaty. However, it was by far the most impactful.

A country could cease to be a member of the treaty if its government chose. However, in doing so, if that country then took steps to unravel LPAS, the remaining member states would apply punitive economic sanctions.

Ed had held talks with political seniors of many countries on their willingness to do this. Unfortunately, none, even those who felt the law to be immoral and unfairly impacted them, were willing to take such a step. The threat of punitive sanctions was too significant, the impact of which would be devastating. Ed therefore knew that unilateral action was not an option, and his only hope of change was via majority support at the UN. And he was acutely aware that getting a two-thirds majority would be challenging, if not impossible. For now, however, he was content to have reached a position where a vote was taking place. In itself, this was a significant step forward.

Now late evening, a little after 9 p.m., Ed left the UN to return to his hotel, exhausted from holding non-stop sessions with senior officials.

Meanwhile, back in London, Jail was busy catching up with a few of his contacts within the security services in an attempt to get information on what they knew of a possible plot to kill Edward Thorncroft. He could not construct the ask in this way; he did not want to give away the link between himself and Ed. So his questions had to be more subtle, which meant he could only inquire about information on dark LPAS, hoping someone would give up the information he was looking for because it was linked. So far, however, he'd drawn a blank.

Arriving home late evening, Jail received a call from a close contact at MI6 – Asia Kellender, someone he'd had a three-year relationship with when working for MI5. Asia was requesting a meeting that evening. He was given the address of a safe house in London and told to arrive after midnight.

Arriving at the house, he was quickly ushered in by Asia. "Coffee, Jail?" said Asia with a beaming smile. Her smile always lifted Jail's spirits when he'd visit Asia at her apartment in London while they were dating.

"No, Asia, not at 20 past midnight!"

Asia made herself a coffee and sat down in the living room with him.

"You asked about illegal activity by LPAS members – the 'dark side' of LPAS is how you referred to it. Well, we've recently had a breakthrough. The name you gave us, Logan Miller – and I'm still intrigued about how you came by it, but I know you aren't going to give up your source – well, it turns out he is working with others within the global body illegally."

Jail started to laugh. "Asia, please tell me something I don't know," replied Jail, hoping she had a little more than that.

"Still the same old Jail. Please let me get to the point," Asia pushed back.

"Early days yet, I'm afraid, so precisely what they are involved in is primarily unknown. But we do know they are planning to assassinate Edward Thorncroft, which was your original brief when you came to us with your suspicions surrounding the London terror attack." Asia paused. "Do you know Thorncroft personally?"

"No, Asia, I don't, but I respect his work and wouldn't want anything to happen to him. Can you give me more?"

"Don't have much. We know at least three members of this inner group, but we suspect that's likely just the tip of the iceberg. We now have confirmation that Logan is involved, and someone named Benjamin – Ben. The other speaker we have on tape wasn't named, but we have the voice prints on all three, so it is only a matter of time before we match these to real people.

"These individuals were involved in an argument about a failed attempt on Thorncroft, which we assume to be the London terror attack. Again, this wasn't clear, so it could just as easily have been referencing an aborted attempt. A heated exchange took place between Logan and Ben, in which Ben said to Logan, 'Your man not doing his job.' So it's sketchy, I'm afraid. We need more pieces."

"Okay, Asia, but it sounds promising. When and where did you come by this information?"

"You know I'm not going to give you that, Jail. But I will say we obtained it 'off the record', so we can't use it directly. It has only served to give us more information, but nothing useable."

"Illegal wiretap?" said a grinning Jail.

"No comment," Asia said, again smiling at him.

"I appreciate you are sticking your neck out for me on this one, Asia," said Jail as he leant forward and kissed Asia on the head.

"Please, Jail, don't, unless you mean it." For her, splitting with Jail was still raw. She had never truly understood why he left her. She had thought they had something that would go the distance. "What went wrong between us, Jail? We had a good thing going, and then it all blew up."

"We both know it was my problem, Asia. I could no longer take the stress of the work you were doing in China. I'd be in England following nutjobs around, waiting for the call to say you were either dead, missing or arrested for spying. It just became too much for me, so I took the easy way out. I know I was never that clear with you, and I'm truly sorry for that."

"We could have dinner one evening, Jail, and catch up for old times' sake?"

"I'd like that, Asia. I'd like that very much. I'll call you. I promise."

With that, Jail got up and went to kiss Asia on the head one more time but stopped himself, given her previous warning.

He had been madly in love with her, and still had strong feelings for her – which was why he had so much understanding for Ed's romantic situation. He too was dealing with demons, albeit of a different kind: his fear of losing her.

Given this, it was strange that he had given her up. But the stress had been too much .

The two had met in their thirties, thrown together on a joint intelligence operation. They never shared a place, but whenever Asia was in the UK, which wasn't too often towards the end of their relationship, Jail would stay at her apartment.

During one of Asia's returns to London, Jail ended the relationship, saying simply that 'it wasn't working for him'. He'd never told her before that it was due to the stress he felt when she was operating in China, so this was news to her.

He arrived back at his place a little after 2 a.m., poured himself a drink and sat down thinking about the fantastic times he'd had with Asia. He would make sure to call her for a dinner date.

Ed was back in London when the non-binding vote took place at the United Nations. The vote failed to reach the two-thirds majority required but surprised many, having failed by far fewer votes than expected. Ed was disappointed but heartened by the numbers who had supported it.

He saw this as real progress that showed that members were thinking differently now about the laws of LPAS. Ed knew that by keeping up the pressure, he could force another vote in the not-too-distant future – and with a much greater chance of success.

Meanwhile, Jail had met up with Asia, not once but a few times. Ed was aware that Jail was dating and took pleasure in ribbing him. Jail had needed to inform the inner circle, as he was dating a member of the security services while running POLO.

At an inner-circle meeting, Jail outlined their relationship. He briefed the team that it was a 'rekindled relationship' and that he recognised the increased risk but was confident it would not be a problem; and he described how quickly his strong feelings for her had returned.

"What is it with you men!" Ashlin teased. "Not happy with a normal relationship, you have to add a little spice, some danger, complexity." Although Ashlin was teasing, neither Ed nor Jail could push back on her. What she'd said was, in essence, true.

"I'd like to say it stems from our past jobs, a need for that added rush. But for Ed, that isn't the case," responded Jail.

"No, quite right, Jail. I could do without the rush. I want to go back to just being a consultant," Ed responded, pulling his sad face.

"It'll happen, Ed. I'm sure it will. You've awakened the world to the folly of LPAS, and it is clear from the UN vote that you are awakening the decision-makers too. So keep going; you and those working with you will win through. I'm sure of it." Such was George Clemons's view.

"Thanks, Gig. I think I agree, for the first time since this evil law was passed. But I know we are still a long way off."

UNnatural Selection –
Cabmen's shelter network

A significant drug theft went south, and police were pursuing two of the Stealers through London's streets. They had lost their haul but managed to evade capture by entering the sewer system and exiting a little under a quarter of a mile from their entry point. However, police numbers were swelling and it was not looking promising for the Stealers. Now out of the sewer, they initiated a call using POLO's network, to a centre set up by Creak Nooks to assist in extracting operatives who were in trouble.

The Stealers advised that two members were in need of 'bringing home'. Then, they initiated special software on their phones that allowed POLO's operations centre to track them in real time and speak to them via the POLO network.

This evening, Brindle Llanos (Overwatch) was the inner-circle member in charge of the extraction centre and took personal control of getting the Stealers to safety. On a large screen in the operating room, Brindle could see the Stealers were five or so minutes away from Bayswater Road, not too far from Lancaster Gate tube station. Speaking to them directly, Brindle advised that he had sent them GPS details to take them to the cabmen's shelter at the Queensgate entrance to Hyde Park, around 20 or 30 minutes away on foot. They started to follow the GPS as closely as possible while avoiding an increasing number of patrol cars and police on foot. One of the Stealers advised the centre that neither knew what the shelter looked like.

"It's small, but you can't miss it. It's green! Let me know when you have it in sight." Brindle then asked a couple of the team to ensure close monitoring of police channels. "I want to know what the police are doing in the immediate area of our Stealers."

"Okay, Overwatch," shouted a control-room technician.

"I think they are likely to get approval to switch on camera tracking software, so we need to ensure that cameras in the immediate area of the park aren't operating," Brindle called out.

"We can have one of the Tradesfolk take out power in the immediate area. Looking at the power map, I can see a final distribution substation that supplies the area close to the shelter. I think taking that down will drop most of the cameras in the area," one of the technicians responded.

"You think? Don't bloody think; I need to *know*," said an angry Brindle.

"Sorry, Overwatch. Checking now," came the response from the sheepish technician.

After a few minutes had passed, the technician advised Brindle that taking out the substation he'd earlier referenced would take out lighting and camera power in the immediate area of the cabmen's shelter.

"Okay, that's good," said Brindle. "Now pick two other areas not too far away from the extraction point and take them down too."

Brindle knew he had to take out a more extensive area so as not to give away the general location that was to be used to extract the Stealers – knowing that if he only took out a relatively small area, the police would flood into the vicinity, linking the failure to their search for the medical supply thieves.

"Let me know when Trades are in place and ready to act," said Brindle.

As the Stealers weaved their way through London's streets, the police were closing down their options. Then, one of the Stealers asked an operations technician if he could speak directly to Overwatch.

"I can hear you. We all can. Go ahead."

"I'm not sure we are going to make the extraction point. The police are closing down the roads, and hence our options, fast," said the very concerned-sounding Stealer.

Brindle was deep in thought. "You aren't too far from the park. Get there and you have a fighting chance. We will see if we can assist."

Huddled in a corner, Brindle and some of the senior technicians started to look at options. The Stealers had altered their route so much that they were now in the Hyde Park Estate. One of the technicians spoke up.

"Overwatch, let's get them to hole up in the estate. We can take out power around Paddington, hopefully causing officers to move in that direction. The Stealers can then head towards Marble Arch and enter the park near Cumberland Gate."

"Okay, that seems like a plan," responded Brindle. "How quickly can we take out power around Paddington?"

"We have a flood of Tradesfolk in the surrounding areas now. I think about 15 or so minutes."

"Okay, but no heroics from our people. It's no good saving Stealers at the expense of losing other members."

"We've told them no unnecessary risks, Overwatch."

The operations centre passed the plan on to the Stealers, and Tradesfolk around Paddington went to work. It took a little longer than planned, but soon a message was received advising that power was out around the area. While eavesdropping on police activity, a technician shouted out across the room.

"We are seeing officers moving into the Paddington area, but we can't as yet tell how many are in the path of the Stealers."

"Okay, no time to wait on that," said Brindle as he got back onto the channel reserved for conversation with the Stealers.

"Okay, go – go now. Head towards Marble Arch and on into the park. Let me know when you are inside."

Entering the park, the Stealers alerted Overwatch that they were heading towards the cabmen's shelter. However, before Overwatch could respond, he heard a commotion. He called the Stealers several times and neither responded. It was clear that something had gone wrong.

The Stealers had stumbled across three park rangers who had challenged them, asking why they were there so late. The Stealers were dishevelled, smelly and looked very nervous, which was the main reason for challenging them, as the park didn't close until midnight.

One of the rangers suspected that the increased police activity in the area could be linked to them, so he pulled out his communications device, and a fight broke out as the Stealers attempted to stop him from using it.

By now, one Stealer was wrestling with two park rangers, and presently had the upper hand. The other was rolling around, trying to get the better of the third ranger, who was much larger, fitter and better trained. As the two fought, the fight became increasingly violent. The Stealer had managed to smash the ranger's comms device, and the two of them, now both back on their feet, were toe to toe, slugging it out.

About 20 feet away, the other Stealer was weakening, but the two rangers, who by now were getting the better of him, suddenly stopped fighting and slumped over. One collapsed on top of him, the other to the side on his knees, slumping forward. Pushing the ranger off him, he jumped to his feet, noticing his colleague getting up off the ground, the third park ranger lying prostrate nearby.

It was only now that the pair noticed a smartly dressed man, alongside a woman dressed up to the nines, holding what looked like guns.

"What the hell?" said the Stealer closest to the pair. "Who the fuck are you?" The second Stealer nervously moved forward towards the pair. The Stealers weren't just banged-up; they were unsure what had just happened.

"Calm down, and don't look so worried," said the lady. "Overwatch sent us. He thought you might need a little help in the park, being the most exposed area. So on your way, before we are all caught."

The Stealers looked at each other momentarily, then started running towards the shelter, and the two POLO operatives walked off hand in hand, like lovers out for a stroll. They'd used tranquilliser guns to subdue the park rangers. Not a perfect solution, as using enough of the drug to take someone out quickly also puts them at significant risk. But Overwatch had authorised their use if required.

As the Stealers ran towards the green hut, one said, "I can't believe they killed those rangers."

"I don't think they did. I've been around guns my whole life, and I didn't recognise what they were holding. So I don't think the rangers are dead."

"If they are, it won't be five years we get."

"Call on channel five, Overwatch," one of the technicians called out.

Having switched channels, the loving couple informed Brindle they'd used darts and that the Stealers were now only around five minutes from the shelter.

"Okay, good, thanks. Get yourself out as quickly as you can. You've ditched the guns?"

"Yes, of course."

Switching back to the Stealers' channel, Brindle asked for an update.

"We can see a green hut, Overwatch."

"Good, hold fire; don't move any closer until I give you the all-clear."

Brindle had sent two miniature-drone operators into the area of the shelter and now asked them to launch their drones and check the site was clear. By now, power was out in several locations, including around the hut. The concealed hatch in the shelter floor was powered by the underground network, as were the pods, so they would not be affected by the outage.

"Update, please," Brindle called out to the drone operators.

"Still checking the area in infra-red, Overwatch."

"Check faster; we don't want to lose them now."

A few minutes later, the drone operators relayed the all-clear message to Brindle.

"Okay, make your move to the shelter. There's a side door with a digital panel. The 10-digit code is being transmitted to your phones now. Let me know once you're inside."

Once inside, the Stealers alerted the control centre.

"Okay, stand on the side of the hut that has the orange bar across the top of the roof. You will see a small screen in the left corner. Touch the screen to activate it, and when it prompts for input, hold your phone up to the screen with the one-time random picture code I've just sent you."

As one Stealer pointed his phone at the screen, the floor at the other end of the small hut started to open. "Wow, that's bloody cool," said the other.

"Forget cool. You've seen nothing yet," remarked Brindle. "Climb down the ladder to the small platform area. I'm afraid it's a long climb down, so make sure you clip into a safety belt. When you reach the platform, push the red button on the right of the platform to close the upper hatch. A small pod will arrive within a minute, and the doors to the tunnel will automatically open. With the hatch closed, communications will go down. Once in the pod, we will be able to speak to you again, understood?"

"Yep, understood, Overwatch."

With the hatch now closed, low-level lights illuminated, and they could now see the tunnel. As advised, a glowing blue pod arrived.

"Oh man, this is fucking awesome!" said one of the Stealers.

"Just get in," said the other. "I don't figure we are safe yet."

As they stepped into the pod, the outer and inner doors closed and the pod started to move off, gathering speed quickly. Then Brindle began to talk to them over the pod's speaker system.

"Okay, we had many options, but the pod is taking you to a cabmen's shelter across the river, at Temple Place. There's no abnormal police activity in the area. Get your disguises off when you are inside the shelter. One of the team will be there to provide you with clean clothes. Check in again when you arrive home, or if you encounter any problems. Clear?"

"Understood, Overwatch. We can't thank you enough for getting us out."

Brindle had transmitted the codes required for them to exit the pod and get up into the shelter. As he had advised, a POLO operative was there to bag up their disguises and provide them with clean clothes.

"Clean up best you can in the sink before getting dressed. I don't need to tell you that you smell a little!" said the POLO operative.

"No, you don't. We're aware."

Thanking the operative, the Stealers exited the hut, making their way to their respective apartments.

Thankfully, they'd got away. Arriving home, Stealer One sent in a safe home message, and within 50 minutes, the second Stealer did the same.

"Okay, team, great job. Can we get confirmation that all those involved in bringing the Stealers home are also safe?" said Brindle.

"Doing that now, Overwatch."

"Okay, I'll be in the end office. Update me as you get news."

During their time running the centre, Brindle and other inner-circle members had used the huts to get POLO members out of harm's way.

Ed had purchased the remaining cabmen's shelters for £100 each when the charity supporting them went bust. He had done it for one reason only. Some years earlier, he came to know that an extensive tunnel network had been put in place linking the shelters. So he had his people build a vacuum tube network that would enable small two-person pods to zip around under the ground, powered by tapping into the tube network's power.

Brindle made himself a coffee and sat in the office, awaiting updates. The extraction had been too close a call, with many resources needed to bring them home, thus putting many other members at significant risk. A couple more hours passed before Brindle was alerted that all involved had checked in and were safe. A close thing at times, but Brindle was pleased it had ended well.

Unusually, Brindle called Ed and briefed him on the day's events.

"I know the team are having to deal with issues all the time, Brindle. But it's unusual for any of you to call and brief me. Should I be concerned?"

"I don't think so, Ed. But we are experiencing more close calls these days, as you know, and I'm wondering are the intelligence and police services getting closer? Are we taking greater risks? Maybe a bit of both. I guess I called really to replay it in my mind. I'm sure it's nothing to worry about."

"Okay, I hear you, Brindle. I'll speak with Jail. I'll not say you called me, and I'm not suggesting I'm concerned with Jail's leadership – and I know you aren't saying that either. But me stepping back in for a few days can't do any harm."

With that, they ended the call. But Ed was concerned. During the life of POLO, they hadn't lost many operatives. The number in prison stood at 23, and two were dead. It wasn't a number that Ed would forget, as each was a source of pain. So it is, Ed thought. Time to call a special inner-circle meeting. Aside from what was driving Ed's decision, he would look forward to spending time with the inner circle. It was so rare, now, for him to spend time with them all. One of the things he missed most.

UNnatural Selection – Ed's in control

True to his word, Ed spoke with Jail, informing him that he wanted to hold an extraordinary inner-circle meeting as soon as Jail could arrange one. The session would run more or less for the entire day, which meant a Sunday meet.

As POLO's finances had grown, they had purchased many safe locations. As a result, meetings once held in derelict or empty buildings, usually uncomfortable, damp, smelly and generally unpleasant, were now primarily held at POLO facilities. Still not all meetings, but the lion's share.

The day had arrived, and the meeting was on a narrow boat near Shillingford Bridge, Oxfordshire. Observers had been in the area for a few days to ensure it was safe. In addition, inner-circle members' bodyguards would travel to Shillingford and spread out across the surrounding area.

As was nearly always the case when he attended meetings, Ed would arrive first, and today would travel in a fully autonomous eVTOL (drone copter) operated by Gig Transport. His landing site was a farmer's field not far from the mooring, a plot of land that was part of an old farmhouse owned by KAIGuard. Other members would also arrive by drone, with some opting to drive.

Ed arrived at the copter port just after 6:30 a.m., boarded by 6:50 and landed in Shillingford by 7:20, equidistant from the farmhouse and the boat mooring. No longer an active farm, Kai mainly used it as a recreational house for members of the bodyguard team to take their families on long weekends.

Most, but not all, of the guards officially worked for KAIGuard. Working for an established close protection organisation made it far easier for POLO bodyguards to move around the UK. The company gave them cover, and Kai's company performed extensive bodyguard duties for senior figures within the UK, Europe, North America and parts of Africa and South America. Kai's company was successful before she started working for POLO, and the company had received very little financial support from the POLO organisation.

Having arrived, Ed made his way down to the Thames and walking along the river until he spotted the name of the narrow boat.

The boat's listed owner was Rage Millstream, an inner-circle member responsible for a highly skilled group of Forgers. Rage herself was an accomplished painter and sculptor before turning her hand to forgery while living in Australia. The boat Ed was looking for was named *Brown Fleur*, which was interesting, as Ed knew that Rage's birthname was Fleur Brown.

Having found the boat, Ed stepped on board and went inside, picking up an old magazine and starting to read to pass the time before the rest of the group turned up.

Next to show was Ashlin Steeple, whom Ed hadn't seen for over six weeks, as hospital shifts had kept them apart. Hugging Ashlin as she arrived, he kissed her on the forehead.

"Missed me, Ed?"

"Yes, Ashlin, I have. It's been too long."

"You are looking well, Ed. And I can sense the excitement," Ashlin commented, a little excited herself.

"I feel good, and yes, I am excited. It's a while since I've met with the inner circle, and I've not even managed a one-on-one with some members. So I've been looking forward to today."

As Ed finished his sentence, Jesse came down the steps. Again, Ed reached out and gave Jesse a hug and kiss, and the three of them started to catch up, with Ed's opening comment being that the gap between Ashlin and Jesse's arrival was too close in his view.

Thirty minutes later, Gig arrived, followed within 20 minutes by Jail. The conversation, small talk really, was in flow when Kimmy arrived. Ed greeted Kimmy with a hug and a kiss, and Kimmy commented that Ed always looked a little sad when she entered a room.

"I do, Kimmy. But that is not a reflection on you. I love catching up and spending time with you. But when I first see you, I can't help thinking of Jelly, who I miss so, so much."

Kimmy leant forward and kissed Ed, saying she missed her a great deal too and that she didn't take it personally. Over the next 90 minutes, Covey, Marcelle, Rage, Brindle and Creak all arrived.

All members now present, Ed took the floor.

"Well, I must say, this is the smallest venue in which we've held an inner-circle meeting."

"Rage thought you'd like your first meeting in a while to be snug," Jail quipped.

"Well, it's snug all right, Jail. But let me get to the nub of today's meeting. I'm keen to hear from you all what you've been up to of late, and I welcome an open conversation.

"I'd like a brief on recent operations, and focus on those that didn't go as well as they might have. And most importantly, I've missed spending time with you all. It is the one thing I can say I've lost out on now the day-to-day operations are in the capable hands of Mr Sleeks."

"That's a relief," said Covey. "I thought something had happened, or you were planning some big changes."

"No, Covey, no big changes. You all do an amazing job, and I've zero plans to change anything."

"That may be so, Ed. But I know you, and I can't help thinking that your concerns prompted the timing," said Jail, pushing Ed to be clear on his reason for calling the meeting.

"Jail, you've always been the super-brain among us, and if I wasn't entirely honest with you, I know you'd see through it. So let me–"

Brindle interrupted. "I prompted it, Jail. I called Ed after the London steal went bad on us. I wasn't calling to worry him. I just wanted to talk, really, so I picked up the phone almost without thinking. So please don't take it as me having a go at you. It wasn't like that."

"I take Ed at his word, Brindle, and you too. I'm not concerned. I just wanted the trigger out in the open."

With everything that Ed wanted to get from today detailed, and Jail happy that he had the trigger event, they got down to discussing the increase in close calls over the past few months.

Jail discussed recent operations, outlining those that had failed and those that had almost resulted in losing one or more operatives.

"The trend is worrying, Ed. No question. I pored over the data and there isn't a single cause. I think the security services are anticipating our moves better after they realise an operation is in flight. I think it is also likely that we've grown a little too confident. I've started to address the trend with Marcelle and Ashlin mainly, but I've also been talking with Jesse and George."

"Okay, so give me your read on the incident that Brindle and I discussed," Ed prompted.

Jail advised Ed that very experienced Stealers were involved, and that one of them knew Marcelle and had worked with her on a couple of steals.

Jail then outlined the mistakes made, advising Ed that they stayed on the job too long, which had aroused the suspicion of one of the site managers, although they had got out of the facility before the police arrived. Officers quickly tracked them down, and a car chase ensued, which led to them crashing the van and high-tailing it on foot.

"Why did they stay on site longer than was planned?" Ed asked Marcelle.

"Over-confidence, Ed. They had a list of drugs to collect, which would have taken no longer than 20 minutes. However, they decided to take more, which meant they were on site for almost an hour, and the site manager became suspicious, knowing that the list presented to him should not have taken that long to load. Fortunately for them, the main barrier was easy to drive through. Otherwise, it would have been game over."

"And they recognise their error?" Ed asked Marcelle.

"Oh yes. They know just how close they came to a great many years in prison. And I made them acutely aware of just how many people risked their freedom to keep them out of the hands of the authorities. I've stood them down from further operations and told them it'll be at least three months before I approve them for active ops."

"Okay, I understand most of that. But I don't know how our Stealers were able to take more. Surely the warehouse staff are sourcing the drugs listed on the paperwork?"

Ed had hit on something that neither Jail nor Marcelle had been keen to air.

"Well?" Ed prompted again.

Marcelle went to answer, but Jail stopped her. "I'll take this, Marcelle."

"We've moved on in the way we steal drugs, Ed. The days of one- off steals with fake paperwork or outright hits on warehouses are mainly in the past. We've set up several dummy companies that are part of the system, to acquire far more significant hauls than we once could and do so using a repeatable process. No one investigates, as it's all above board. Or so they think.

"These two Stealers have been regular collectors of drugs from the warehouse in question. They had a good relationship with the warehouse staff, and while they sipped coffee, our folks would take the drugs off the shelves and load up."

"Disguise is still normal practice, Jail, right?"

"Yes, Ed. No one operates without one, and full-on prosthetic disguises and gait adaptors are in use for the likes of Stealers. We've not changed those rules, nor would we."

"Sorry, Jail, but I had to ask."

Ed, his eyes transfixed on a corner of the boat, had drifted off into Thorncroft World. And that was terrible news for Marcelle and Jail, who were both acutely aware of why he'd gone there.

However well meant, it was clear to Ed that the mistake these Stealers had made had far more significant consequences for POLO, and it made the reason for Brindle's call much more apparent. Brindle knew that once Ed became involved in reviewing operations, he would dig deep and get all the facts on the table. Brindle, more or less subconsciously, had been concerned for some time, and the London steal going wrong was the one that tipped him over.

Brindle had the utmost respect for all the team members, and especially Jail. But he was concerned, and felt Ed needed to be involved, although he hadn't wanted to directly out Jail. Nevertheless, POLO was Ed, and Ed would not accept unnecessary risks, especially ones that bordered on stupidity.

"Okay, that should have been the first piece of information you gave me. No need to answer, as I know you know that too. It's one thing to screw up. It's entirely different to do so because you are so cocksure of yourself that you take unnecessary risks. There's no room for arrogance in POLO."

As Ed spoke, Jail and Marcelle started to feel uncomfortable. They knew Ed well, and his body language bespoke the slow build-up of his anger.

"Jail, keeping mum isn't you, and I'm disappointed that you did. I'm guessing you wanted to give the Stealers the benefit of the doubt and knew I'd likely throw them out. For me, if that's your thinking, it's the bigger issue causing what I'm feeling in my stomach right now. It doesn't matter if you and I do things differently. But don't keep things from me.

"As for the two Stealers, I want to meet them. If I feel it was an aberration and they've learned from it, they can stay. Otherwise, they are out."

"They're good Stealers, Ed, among the best."

"I don't care, Marcelle. Don't defend fools. It'll bring the house crashing down."

Marcelle said no more, and neither did Jail, both of them aware that Ed was at that point just before the cork popped. "So, who's briefing me on the damage they've caused?"

Jail stood up and sat opposite Ed, handing him a report that he'd worked on that related to the Stealers in question.

The existence of a report made Ed feel just a tad better, as it was clear Jail had planned to brief him fully.

Although evidently after the dust had settled, hoping that Ed wouldn't overrule Jail's decisions by then.

"Okay, so give me an abridged version," said Ed.

"We've had to abandon the dummy company they worked for, and we've given other members of the company a couple of months off. The entire team wore disguises, had fake paperwork, identities, et cetera, so I'm not expecting any arrests. But the cost of pulling out has been considerable, financially and otherwise. So much of what we'd accumulated we had to ditch. We did get some of the drugs out on the night but couldn't risk going back, as we knew the security services would be all over the company and its premises. And they were."

"They were? Can you expand?"

"Security services raided all the premises linked to the company in the early hours of the morning. Actually, within four hours of us getting the Stealers to safety. I'd anticipated it, and every one of our people was out of their home address, whisked off to safe houses."

"How many, Jail?"

"Twenty-seven, Ed."

Ed was acutely aware of what that meant. Their possessions in their rented houses gone; and their bank accounts would be frozen. Cars and anything else they had acquired: forfeited. In Ed's mind, this was the most negligible impact. You can replace material things. Yes, some items have sentimental value, but essentially material possessions are just about money.

What wasn't about money, however, was that the lives 27 people had built had suddenly ended. Okay, they knew the risks when they agreed to become a different person and live under an assumed identity. But that didn't lessen the impact of a life built and lost. Friends made that they could never see again. And months changing their appearance, possibly their accent too, to move to a new assignment or revert to their true identity, which most would likely do unless POLO had other roles for them requiring a false identity.

Many would voluntarily leave POLO. And everyone who left became a risk.

Ed's feeling of excitement had long since left him. Instead, he was now feeling a little discouraged, although his anger was ebbing away.

"This is one hell of a mess, Jail."

"I know, Ed, I'm sorry, and I should have raised it with you at the time."

"You should have, but it isn't your mess or Marcelle's. And I'm sorry, but I've changed my mind. I don't want to meet them. I want them out."

Marcelle let out a loud gasp. "Ed, these–"

Ed shut her down. "Enough, Marcelle, enough. I don't care if they are the cream of the team. Their misjudgement is way too big a deal for them to continue in POLO. And yes, I recognise the risk we take in letting them go. So, Brindle, I want around-the-clock surveillance on them both, once we've cut them loose. Jail, as they're already in a safe house, get them processed out as quickly as possible. Set them up a new identity if that's their preference, or a return to who they are. Give them enough cash to sort themselves out and exit them."

"Ed, can we–"

Ed stopped Marcelle once again. "No, we can't. It isn't up for discussion, period."

"But Ed–"

He jumped in again. "Drop it, Marcelle." His tone was now angry. Marcelle dropped it.

"I'm going to step through the things on my mind. Just jump in, Jail, if it's already taken care of. Clear?"

"Clear, Ed."

"Everyone we know and the Stealers know, outside of the 27, that are working under a fake identity must also be moved to safe houses and given new identities or revert to their old selves." Ed looked up at Jail.

"Already done, Ed."

"Everyone they know that work using their true identity must stop all POLO work for 12 months, maybe more if we find they are the subject of surveillance."

"Already being done, Ed."

Ed was hoping this wasn't going to amount to too many of his people.

As he thundered through a list of things to do, it was clear to Ed that, not unexpectedly, Jail had everything in motion. And as the debate continued, it dawned on Marcelle just how big a screw-up this was and how many lives would be affected by it. It didn't take too long before she recognised that Ed's call was the right one and that it was one she and Jail should already have made, holding herself responsible for almost begging Jail not to kick them out.

The team remained focused on the clean-up underway, plus work still to be carried out now and way into the future. They finally closed out on the subject around 6 p.m., with Ed assigning a sub-team to run everything that would be needed now and further down the line to ensure that POLO stayed safe. Gig, Creak and Brindle were all assigned.

"Let's do no more today," he concluded. "Let's grab some food and a drink and sit out on the deck while there is still a little heat in the air."

Some wanted to admire the view as they sat on the boat, while others struck up conversation. Finally, Covey and Kimberly sat down beside Ed, and the three of them used the time to catch up generally.

"I visited Jennifer's parents not so long ago. I'd always planned to, but knew I had to leave a respectable amount of time to reduce the risk that they themselves might still be under surveillance."

"I bet that was emotional, Ed," said Kimmy.

"It was, in part. Certainly when I stopped by Jennifer's grave before heading to the house. And then at the house when I let her parents know just how close we were, and the risks Jennifer took to save lives that they weren't aware of."

Ashlin, one of Jennifer's closest friends, joined in the conversation. "Ed, I overheard you saying you'd visited Jennifer's parents. I wish I'd known; I would have joined you."

"I know you would have. That's why I didn't tell you. I figured the first visit would have been risky. So I felt I should do it alone. But I've promised them I'll go back. And when I do, I'll be sure to let you know, and we can go together."

"I've heard so much about her and I feel I know her," Covey commented.

"Covey, you and Jennifer would have got on so well. You both have that zest for life and an almost permanent smile on your face. In many ways, you remind me of her," Ed replied.

George joined the conversation, along with Rage, both recounting stories of time spent with her. The conversation continued while Ed withdrew to the back of the boat with a glass of wine and sat staring out over the Thames towards the bridge. Marcelle walked over and sat down beside him, speaking in a low voice.

"I'm sorry, Ed. I'm so sorry. I'll understand if you have a mind to replace me."

Ed smiled and put his arm around her. "Replace you? Are you nuts! Your skills and the skilled people under you have saved thousands of lives. I've been in awe of some of the fantastic steals you've pulled off and been scared to death at the risks you've taken to acquire medicines. Too often, you've been putting your liberty on the line.

"Don't blame yourself for the errors of those who work for you when you could not have foreseen their mistakes."

"But I defended them, and I pushed Jail not to dismiss them."

"Okay, that's yours to own. All I ask is you learn from it. So please don't dwell on it any longer. Finding a better person to head the Stealers won't happen, Marcelle. I've already got the best."

"Marcelle hugged him tightly, thanked him and moved back towards the other members, sparking a conversation with Creak Nooks, while Jail walked over to Ed.

"I wanted to apologise, Ed, for holding back. I should never have done that. I knew it at the time, and, well, I've no excuse. It was foolish."

"You knew I'd likely force them out of POLO, Jail, correct?"

"Yes, Ed, and that makes it worse, as I withheld telling you to keep these Stealers on board."

"I'm not happy with your decision, Jail, but I know you recognise it was wrong. So we need not discuss it further."

"Thanks, Ed."

Jail's decision had been abysmal. He wasn't just super-intelligent but had a lengthy background in MI5, so he should have known that the two Stealers, however good they were, could not stay in POLO. Instead, he wavered, in deference to Hood, for whom he had great respect. A rare mistake, and one he would not make again.

As the group departed, Brindle asked if he could catch a lift with Ed on his drone back to London, which breached protocol. However, this was a rare ask, so Ed agreed. With everyone now departed except Brindle and Ed, they made their way back to the farm, where the drone was waiting. Lifting off, Ed turned to Brindle.

"You didn't ask to hitch a lift because you like my company, Brindle."

"No, Ed, I didn't. I wanted to apologise if I've caused a rift between you and Jail. I started to feel bad as the day unfolded and I realised just how angry you were. It was not my intention to cause a problem; I was just concerned that more issues were arising, and I thought – no, I knew – you'd dig deep and add the kind of value only you add. I'm not sucking up; I just thought it was time you got back in the hot seat for a while."

"Brindle, you haven't caused a rift. Jail and I are cool. But more importantly, you were 100 per cent right doing what you did. We are a tight group; we all get on well. But that doesn't mean we do not challenge each other when necessary. That's a must, given what we do. It's in part why we've stayed safe for so long. We must not stop challenging each other."

"I hear you, Ed. But I should have challenged Jail directly. He must be fuming that I went behind his back to you."

"He isn't. He's way too smart to allow emotion to get in the way of his thinking. He knows you did so because going to him would likely not have changed the outcome. You did the right thing. Jail will now focus more attention on the failures of the past, and that's a good thing."

"I appreciate that, Ed. I'm glad I raised it with you. But it has been worrying me all day."

"It's forgotten, Brindle. It was the right call. So, let's discuss the Guardians you'll assign to watch these two over the next year. I'd like a bit of insight into those you've selected."

Ed's last comment was to get Brindle off the subject and think about something else. It was evident that Brindle was deeply concerned with his decision. But, hopefully, Ed had reassured him it was the right one. And one to be repeated in similar circumstances.

UNnatural Selection – High to Low

Early Sunday evening, Ed and Leonora were drinking champagne in celebration of Ed's progress. Seniors at the United Nations and several heads of state had come round to his view on vaccines, and a vote on the issue was supported, although not won. However, the vote was closer than expected.

Then, out of the blue and out of character, Ed cut away from their conversation on watering down LPAS.

"I only drink champagne when I'm happy and when I'm sad.

Sometimes–"

Leonora interrupted him.

"Ed, You've gone off-piste and are, oddly, quoting Lily Bollinger."

"Likely correct on both counts. Although I'm unsure if I've gone off-piste or if I am piste!"

"Which are you now, Ed?" enquired Leonora. "And no, I don't mean off- piste or pissed!"

"I am sober enough to have worked that out – just, I think!"

"So?" Leonora said.

"I'm happier than I've ever been, almost exclusively down to you, with a hint of happiness from a growing light I can see in chipping away at LPAS."

"That's a lovely thing to say, Ed. Thank you."

The couple were close to emptying a second bottle as the conversation bounced between serious and frivolous. Both a little tipsy, Leonora placed her glass on the table and straddled Ed, wildly kissing him. Ed, surprised but pleased by the move, tried putting his glass down on the side table, but dropped it on her rather expensive Turkish rug!

"Damn it, let me clean that up," said a flustered Ed, attempting to get up.

Turning him to face her, Leonora said sternly, "Leave it," as she cast off her nightie and got right back down to kissing him.

As things hotted up, she removed Ed's T-shirt, and Ed responded by sitting up while holding her, carrying her into the bedroom and dropping her on the bed, before joining her there. Thirty or so minutes later, Ed, lying down, arms above his head, Leonora on top of him, continued the conversation they'd started before Leonora became amorous. Then, out of the blue, she asked:

"Ed, why have you a tattoo of a red syringe under your arm?"

Ed started to chuckle, and a broad smile washed across his face.

"We've been together how long? And now you wonder?"

"No, Ed, I've always wondered. I just never got round to asking. I only think about it when I see it when we are, you know, naked. And when we are, we are not usually talking too much!"

Ed chuckled again and kissed her on the forehead. "A few of us at medical school made a pact that when we graduated, we'd each get a tattoo that represented our profession in some way. So I chose a syringe."

Leonora smiled, saying, "Couldn't you have chosen something a little more important or exciting?"

Ed smiled. "I chose it carefully, Leonora. It is so simple but yet so indispensable in my profession. I would go as far as to say it is the most necessary device we use; it has helped save millions of lives."

"I never thought about it like that, Ed. I have, though, often thought how out of character it was for you to have had a tattoo."

Kissing his chest, Leonora continued: "Now, where were we…"

Rather unromantically, her question had got Ed thinking about the tattoo that had inspired his codename. The word 'syringe' is from the Greek word *syrinx*, and the reason Ed chose it as his handle. Then, still, deep in thought, his thoughts were broken by a raised voice, a half shout from Leonora.

"Ed, Ed, I said where were we! You've gone back into your own little world. Snap out of it!"

"Sorry, Leonora. So… where *were* we," Ed dittoed as passion again took hold.

With Ed's busy schedule, they had been apart for some weeks, and Ed sensed it was going to be a long, sleepless, but enjoyable night!

Monday morning, and Ed was up at 6:45 a.m., making coffee and breakfast for the two of them before waking Leonora. Between sex and talking, they had finally fallen asleep around 3 a.m. Ed had taken five days' holiday and had not scheduled any meetings connected to his fight against LPAS. So the five days were solely to relax and spend time with Leonora, who had ensured that she had no charity obligations either, which hadn't been an easy juggling act, given that she was winding everything down to join Ed full time.

Ed had prepared Eggs Royale, with a mug of strong black coffee, just in case Leonora felt as he did. He was regretting overdoing it!

He took the breakfast tray into the bedroom, placed it beside the bed and gently stroked the top of her back to wake her up.

"Yes, Ed, thank you; I'm awake, but it feels early?"

"I've made breakfast, Eggs Royale, and a mug of coffee." So was Ed's response, ignoring her indirect ask.

"Great, but you didn't answer my question."

"Twenty-five past seven, Leonora, a great time to start the day!"

Leonora wasn't amused. She'd planned to be asleep way past nine after such a late night. Now awake, however, breakfast smelled good, so, propping up her pillows, she sat up in bed.

Breakfast over, as they sat sipping coffee, Leonora turned to Ed, peering deep into his laurel-green eyes. "When you left weeks ago, with a busy schedule planned, my spirits fell knowing I'd not see you for quite a while. When you walked into the apartment yesterday, you stole my breath, and I felt a little giddy. Feelings I haven't had since I was a lovesick teenager, and rather silly now... but it made me realise just how much I love you."

Ed stood up, removing the tray to avoid another accident, cuddled up to Leonora and said, "I don't like being away from you either, and I'm glad we both feel that way."

"There's a point to me telling you this, Ed." Knowing just how much Ed protected his independence, Leonora was about to take a risk. "Ed, why don't you move in with me?"

Since he'd returned from Kenya, he had planned to discuss their relationship but hadn't figured out how to approach it. But even with such thoughts bouncing around in his head, Leonora's ask caught him off guard.

"I'll take your slow response as a no, Ed. I'm okay with that; I just felt I needed to broach the subject."

She had followed up before he had responded, and although saying she was okay with it, he sensed a tinge of sadness, and his joyful mood dimmed.

"Leonora, I've not felt the way I feel about you with anyone else. I don't know what I would do if you were not with me. But I worry that sharing a place, being in each other's shadow, will give you a window into the real me, and when you see me looking back, you'll leave; and I can't risk losing you."

As Ed finished, he welled up, kissing Leonora on the forehead.

Looking at him, it was abundantly clear to Leonora that this wasn't an excuse to let her down gently. Staring into his eyes, she knew he genuinely believed what he had just said.

She hugged him tightly. "Ed, I know the real you. You are allowing the fear from the introverted side of you to dominate your thoughts, seeding doubt in your mind. I know you oh so well, Ed. I won't be going anywhere, and you are stuck with me."

Ed wasn't allowing his introverted self to dominate. He had so many skeletons in the closet he couldn't open it for fear they'd all come tumbling out!

"I feel bad, Leonora. Give me a few weeks, and I promise we will talk about this again. I'm sorry that isn't the answer you wanted to hear."

Leonora sat upright. "Well, I've managed to dampen both our moods, haven't I? So let's say no more on the subject."

Ed made a show, jumped up and collected the breakfast bits, saying, "We should get ready and go out," all the while feeling crumpled inside. Leonora had bounced back, but as with Ed, it was a façade. She was annoyed with herself for having asked, and was worried, not so much about Ed's rejection of the idea but about his reason, which she could not fathom.

She got into the shower while Ed took out the dishes. He returned, took off his dressing gown and got in the shower with her, holding her tight and apologising once more.

Kissing him, Leonora said, "We need say no more, Ed. Let's get back to how we felt when you woke me up!"

Ed, exiting the shower and kissing Leonora, backed her into the bedroom, falling on the bed, soaking wet, their downbeat conversation oddly driving up their desire.

Now just after 10:30, they'd showered again and dressed. They left the apartment for a walk through Holland Park and lunch in Chinatown. They had exorcised their low feelings for now. But Ed knew he needed to have a serious conversation in the not-too-distant future, which meant dealing with his concerns, or face losing her.

The week's break passed all too quickly, and Ed was returning to work on the Sunday. They had packed a lot in and had a fantastic time, with both pretending to put Leonora's request behind them. But neither had.

Ed felt guilty and sad. Leonora could not know he wanted to be with her more and more and would love to move in with her.

His fear of her inadvertently stumbling across something terrified him. If she learned about his secret life, it would expose the bed of deceit on which their relationship was formed, bringing his world crashing down. Just thinking about it filled Ed with dread, sending shivers around his body, his heart racing, and a tightening of his chest. He loved her so much and now felt that it could well be his refusal to commit that could end their relationship. It was a terrible plight, with no option without risk.

Leonora was sad too at Ed's unwillingness to commit to moving in together. It left her questioning Ed's love for her, although these were thoughts she did not want to be having, and when she focused, she was sure he loved her as much as she did him.

Try as she might over the past few days, she could not understand him when he'd said that she would leave him if she saw the 'real' Ed.

Leonora could not comprehend why he would think that. Was there a dark and sinister side that he had somehow managed to conceal? The instant this thought landed, she banished it. She knew Ed better than that...

She knew that it would likely be a few weeks before they could sit down and discuss his concerns. From Sunday, he would be teaching at Chelsea and Westminster Hospital for a minimum of three to four weeks, and she did not expect to see too much of him during this time. The thought of not seeing him for a month, possibly longer, left her empty. His response was front and centre of her thoughts, and she knew that would be the case until she got a proper answer.

UNnatural Selection – Good news?
Leonora and Brindle

Alan, or whatever his name really was, visited Ed at the hospital. Ed invited him into an empty office and closed the door. It had been some months since meeting Alan during his UN trip, and he'd had no further conversations with the security services relating to his safety.

"You'll be pleased to know, Ed, that from the end of the week, Special Branch protection will cease."

Ed was pleased in many ways but surprised by the news. "What's changed, Alan?" he inquired.

"Circumstances have altered the threat level against you. The powers that be no longer believe you are in imminent danger," replied Alan.

"Okay, that's good. And you agree with this assessment?"

"I'll be as straight as I can with you, Ed. I don't know all the details, but what I do know leads me to believe you are no longer under any immediate threat. At least not from the quarter we were investigating. I can't give you the information I have on why. You'll have to trust me.

Another US security agency took control of operations, so my folks and those we worked with within the US were shut out. All I can say is the immediate problem no longer exists."

"Cryptic, Alan, cryptic. But I know you aren't going to elaborate, so I'll not probe further. Thank you. I appreciate the update."

"I doubt we will see each other again, Ed, but for what it's worth, I support what you are doing. I also believe the LPAS laws are morally wrong and deeply damaging to society. So I wish you all the best in your quest to get them overturned."

With that, Alan left, and Ed sat, puzzled by how the threat had been neutralised, given that nothing had hit the news concerning arrests or the like. Still, he trusted the British security services and was relieved that he would no longer have Special Branch in tow, allowing his Guardians and bodyguards to resume their work. He would put in a call to Jail and get the three spooks to see if their contacts had picked up any information on the security service grapevine.

Ed had called Leonora and said he had some spare time because of the cancellation of a class he was due to teach and would like to pop in for lunch.

Leonora was still busy closing down her charity commitments but was at home and was pleased Ed had called.

Ed walked in, greeted her and hung up his jacket. "Smells lovely, Leonora."

"Just a stir fry, Ed. I hope you like it," Leonora commented as she put the bowls on the table.

"I was in two minds whether to call you, as I know you are busy. But it was good to get a few hours off, and I could think of no better way to spend them."

"I know it hasn't been too long since we spent a few days together, Ed, but to be honest, I've been feeling a little anxious."

"Anxious, Leonora? Anxious about what?"

"Oh, I don't know. Rather silly. I've become a little worried our relationship might be drifting."

Ed got up from his chair, pulled her up from hers, held her tightly and said, "Leonora, don't be crazy. I said to you before, I could no more give you up than the hands I have to save lives."

Ed's words caused Leonora's eyes to well up, and a tear ran down her cheek. She knew he meant it, but his inability to commit to furthering their relationship, and the fact he'd never mentioned marriage, had her thinking he was gamophobic.

"Hey, don't get upset. I hate seeing you upset. When this teaching stint is out of the way, I'll book some time away for a romantic entanglement!"

Leonora raised a brow and laughed out loud.

"You mean a dirty weekend, Ed?"

"I guess you could put it that way, but there's no need to make it sleazy!" They both laughed. Then, wiping tears from his face, Ed kissed her, saying how much he loved her, and they ate lunch, which was now barely warm.

Lunch almost over, Ed zoned out. He was himself becoming more and more worried now. He was terrified of losing her due to his lack of commitment. And equally, he feared moving in together and Leonora stumbling across his life in the shadows.

"Ed, Ed, Edward!" Leonora screeched.

"Oh, I'm sorry, I dropped–"

Leonora stopped him. "You dropped into Thorncroft World. Maybe you should see someone about that, Ed. You do it so regularly. Where did it take you this time?"

More lies, Ed thought to himself. He couldn't even tell her the truth when his mind wandered.

"I was just thinking about where we should go," he managed.

"Oh, is that all? There'll be plenty of time to work that out," Leonora replied, feeling a little down.

Her dismissive words worried him, born as they were from what she saw as his uninterest in furthering their relationship. She was hoping he was thinking of something more meaningful, and he was, but she didn't know what, and that just made him feel worse. Fearful as he was, Ed was going to have to make up his mind or risk irreparable damage to their relationship.

"I caught up with some of my ex-colleagues yesterday, Ed. We had afternoon tea and spent a few hours catching up. It made me realise I'd missed them and should make more of an effort to see them."

Leonora had flipped the conversation, and that was also not a good thing.

"Are they still enjoying catching the good guys, who they think are the bad guys, Leonora?"

"Now, Ed, tut, tut, there's no need for that. Most of them are doing admin, but a few work in operations. Unfortunately, there are still a great many people who support LPAS," Leonora continued.

"Lydia, one of the admin seniors I worked with, shared some sad news with me that had upset her quite a bit. A senior operations manager based in New York whom she knew very well – I believe she had a secret crush on him, as she spent a lot of time with him while he was on assignment in London… But I digress. Anyway, her friend was killed in a car accident in Vermont. And what's more, it happened the same week that another New-York-based operations manager committed suicide by jumping off the Verrazzano-Narrows Bridge."

"That's truly sad, Leonora. I'm sorry for your friend. I don't like what they do, but I don't wish them any harm."

"Thank you, Ed. She was so upset, but I think it helped her being among friends and talking about it."

"It's always hard losing someone close or someone for whom you have feelings. Vermont is so lovely, and I guess he was enjoying a well- earned break?"

"She didn't say, Ed. She just said Benjamin was such a lovely man, and whenever in London, he would make a point of taking her to dinner. She didn't know the gentleman who committed suicide that well.

Although she had met Logan a few times."

Ed's interest level shot up, and his body language showed it. "Ed, you seemed startled by that name? Do you know a Logan? Someone you've met on your numerous visits to the UN?"

"Yes, actually, I think I might have met him. Very sorry to hear all this bad news. Can we talk about something more upbeat?"

With that, they moved on to discussing what Ed had called a weekend of romantic entanglement. However, his mind was now in overdrive. The name Logan was familiar. Could it be the same Logan he knew to be involved in at least one attempt to murder him?

The inner circle were meeting at Ed's request. Ed had already briefed the three spooks, Brindle, Creak and Jail, on his conversation with Leonora. Now, Ed opened the conversation.

"So Jail, Brindle, Creak, have you learned anything new?" He was both curious and strangely nervous.

Jail took up the story. "The LPAS operations manager who died in the car crash in Vermont was Benjamin Brown. It just so happens it was the same Benjamin who was caught on an illegal wiretap having a conversation with the known dark operator Logan Miller.

"Logan Miller is the Logan that Leonora spoke of, who committed suicide by jumping off the Verrazzano-Narrows Bridge." Jail paused, then continued. "What Leonora didn't know was that another gentleman by the name of James Brown – no relation to Benjamin – was arrested within a few days of these events for possession of cocaine, in sufficient quantity to see him charged with dealing. He's still awaiting a hearing and has been fired from the department of LPAS at the UN, but is protesting his innocence, saying he's the victim of a fit-up."

Everyone turned and looked towards Ed, who had become transfixed on an uninteresting part of the warehouse wall. Then, snapping out of it, Ed said:

"This is way too big a coincidence, especially given my conversation with 'Alan'."

The three spooks were all nodding in vehement agreement.

"Is it likely that the US government have…" Ed paused. "…God, it takes my breath away to say it… had these guys murdered?"

"Government maybe too strong. Security services, perhaps. Especially given that another US Intelligence service took charge of the operation, most likely the NSA. We know Logan was corrupt, and we know he was in cahoots with Benjamin. James Brown, who knows. But my initial intel said three persons had been in the room that the intelligence services had eavesdropped on.

"Arresting them once they had evidence they could use legally would have caused significant embarrassment to LPAS and the UN. In all likelihood, it could have significantly damaged LPAS. So I think it is highly probable that these guys didn't die in an accident or commit suicide. And if I'm right on that, a fit-up is more likely on the guy arrested for dealing drugs," was the way Jail figured it could have played out.

"There's a problem with that, Jail. If it's true, the security service has severed the only lead to others working for the dark side of LPAS. That is, assuming the reports on how they met their ends were a lie. Given that US Intelligence would be acutely aware of this, it could be that they had evidence of an imminent plot to have another crack at you, Ed. Maybe US Intelligence felt they had little alternative but to remove a significant embarrassment," was Creak's view.

"I've mixed emotions about this. I'm happy that people hell-bent on doing me harm no longer can. But I'm not at all comfortable to learn that governments are still knocking people off!" Ed commented.

"Ed, this isn't something you should have in focus. It's not our issue, wasn't – if that's the way it happened

– our action and wasn't something we desired. And you know, it may just be that it happened as reported. Who are we to assume otherwise?"

Ed was shaking his head. "Okay, folks. Let's wrap this up. I feel like I'm living in an alternate reality!"

Most of the inner circle had exited the meeting location. Only Ed, Brindle and Creak were left, awaiting their time slots. Brindle turned to them both. "Who are the good guys?" The conversation had stirred up deep emotions within him.

"Come again, Brindle," Creak responded.

"Who are the good guys? Is it us, LPAS, Dark LPAS, the governments of the world, the secret security services, who?"

"Brindle, you're mixing up many different things," Ed responded. "My point earlier about living in an alternate reality, for me at least, is true. My life has changed in ways I could never have imagined, and I am seeing things happen and causing them to happen that I'd prefer not to.

"However, to answer your question, *we* are. We might not like how the world has changed and forced us to change. But that does not make us wrong. I believe you once told me that yourself, Brindle?"

"I did, Ed, and I get what you've said. But here's the thing.

"The UN, supported by the majority of countries, passed LPAS into law, believing it to be the only solution to the almost inevitable extinction of the human race. In their view, they had no choice but to impose these appalling restrictions on life-saving intervention.

"Having passed those laws, our world leaders created a behemoth to administer and police the law. This behemoth spends millions a year tracking down and imprisoning people for the crime of saving lives. People like us. In their view, people like us undermine what the LPAS laws were created to achieve.

"We now know for sure that a darker side of LPAS exists, spawned from the concern of some within the organisation that, if they do not stifle all resistance, it will lead to a watering down of the laws, and their eventual revocation, bringing humankind back into the danger zone."

"And then there's us, and hundreds of other groups like us, saving lives where we can, knowing it is wrong to allow thousands to die needlessly. To do this, we break the law. And we think we are right." Brindle paused, then continued. "We can't all be right. So who are the good guys?"

"I can see you are troubled, Brindle," said a worried-looking Ed. "If you feel what you are doing is outweighed by what others have done or are doing, I won't criticise you for that. If, and I hope I am wrong, you are starting to feel that what we are doing is wrong, say it out loud."

Ed paused. "Are you thinking of leaving POLO, Brindle?"

"No, Ed, I'm not thinking of leaving, and I believe wholeheartedly in what we are doing to save lives. LPAS is wrong. I'm just trying to make sense of where we are as a race, how we got here, when will we exit, and will it be a better place when we do?"

"There is no simple answer, Brindle," Creak put in. "Conflicting priorities, late to the party, wrong choices, greed, power, differing beliefs, differences in desired outcomes, political ineptitude – all this and more got us here. What's important to me is human decency. And that's why we save lives. It's that simple." With that, Creak looked down at his watch. "Sorry, guys, I'd like to continue this conversation, but I have to be somewhere else."

As Creak exited, Ed walked over to Brindle and took him by the shoulders. "Brindle, if ever you are troubled, please talk to me. You've helped me on many occasions to deal with my doubts and fears. You say you've no doubts and I'll take you at your word. But if something is troubling you, I am always a call away if you want to talk, get drunk, or both."

Brindle's face lit up with a big smile.

"Thanks, Ed, and please don't be alarmed. I'm not about to walk, and I haven't lost faith in our cause. I'm just troubled more than usual about how and when this nightmare ends. I'm just a little down today, Ed, no more than that."

A few minutes later, Brindle left, leaving Ed to think about what was the first conversation with a member of the circle that had truly worried him, and, for a few minutes, causing him to ask himself the question, "Are we right?" But he didn't take too long to tell himself, "Yes, we damn well are."

UNnatural Selection –
A bridge too far

Another full-on day teaching at the Chelsea and Westminster Hospital. Ed gathered his belongings ready to leave for the day and stopped off to grab a coffee. He'd agreed to collect tickets for a friend at the Chelsea Football Club megastore, given that Stamford Bridge was less than a 15-minute walk from the hospital. Within a few minutes of leaving, his phone rang, and he picked it up by tapping his earpiece.

"Edward Thorncroft. Can I help you?"

"Hi, Ed, it's Hans. I need to meet you urgently," Hans said, his nervousness denoted by a quiver in his voice.

"Are you okay, Hans? You sound, well, nervous."

"Maybe just a little, Ed. I've got some news, something important, something of concern that I must discuss with you now."

"Okay, Hans, what is it?"

"Not on the phone, Ed. I really need to see you."

Ed was intrigued but also concerned. Hans's odd behaviour was out of character and not typical of a neurosurgeon. "Alright, Hans, come over to my apartment in about an hour."

"No, Ed, I'm in a taxi on my way over to you; you're at the Chelsea and Westminster, right?"

"No, Hans, I've left; I'm walking to Stamford Bridge to collect some tickets."

"Okay, Ed, that's good. You will pass the old Brompton Cemetery. There are gaps in the boards that you can step through; walk up to the domed chapel, and I'll meet you there."

"Hans, this is all a bit cloak-and-dagger. Can't we meet in a wine bar or somewhere less ghoulish? Are you in trouble, Hans?"

"Ed, please, we are good friends; I need you to understand. So please do as I ask. I'll be there in 20 minutes."

Ed agreed to Hans's bizarre request but was perplexed. Hans sounded nervous and stressed. And what did he mean by "need you to understand". What had he done?

Ed was now in the domed chapel. Given that the entire site had been boarded up since 2035, he was surprised about its condition. Plans to redevelop the area had been significantly delayed due to legal arguments over a memorial park and stone to honour Emmeline Pankhurst, buried here in the summer of 1928. There was also a solid objection to the redevelopment of the graveyard. Ed remembered the year, as it happened to be the same year Fleming discovered penicillin.

It was a full moon this evening. A cupola crowned the chapel's dome, and multiple windows were set into the walls, providing ample but subaqueous light. Ed was admiring the stonework when Hans arrived.

"Thank you, Ed. I appreciate you meeting me," said Hans, his breath shaking.

"How could I not, Hans. I find this all rather intriguing. So, what's going on?"

Hans got right to the point: "I've evidence that Ashlin is involved in anti-LPAS activity."

Ed's mood instantly plummeted, and he stumbled back against one of the Corinthian columns supporting the dome. An alarm sounded loudly in his mind as he stood, stunned into silence.

He reached down to his wristwatch, twisting the dial one half turn before engaging with Hans. All inner-circle members had well-known watch brands, modified to act as a transmitter in times of need. Once activated, the transmission was picked up by the member's bodyguard. In Ed's case, there were usually two guards, and Kai was ever present as his primary protector.

On the periphery of the cemetery grounds, Kai heard the high-pitched beep in her earpiece as Ed activated his device.

"Wow, Hans, I must say you've stunned me with that laughable accusation. What makes you believe such a tall story? Idle gossip?"

"No, Ed, straight from the horse's mouth!"

"That's absurd, Hans. You want me to believe that Ashlin, knowing your stance on LPAS, would have told you this? What is this about, Hans? What game are you playing? Ashlin is your friend, our friend; we go back a long way. That's not the truth, Hans, is it?"

"Yes, Ed, it is… But no, Ashlin didn't tell me directly; I overheard her on the phone to some guy named George," Hans responded, still nervous, but adamant.

"Ashlin was where? In the canteen? Not a care in the world, talking about breaking the law. Is that it, Hans?" quipped Ed, trying to make light of it even while his chest started to tighten with fear.

Hans had said George, and that name meant Hans had to know something. Ed needed to know what he knew and what objective evidence he had.

"No, Ed, she wasn't in the canteen. I was up in my usual thinking place, on the roof of the hospital. I go up there sometimes to clear my head. Anyway, Ashlin appeared and was speaking on the phone. She hadn't noticed me, as I'd been peering over the edge at the comings and goings in A&E, and an air-conditioning unit largely obscured me. I was about to call out to her when she mentioned a consignment of vaccines that needed moving quickly. Intrigued, I flipped my medical recorder on."

A bombshell. Whatever Hans had picked up, he'd tapped it too.

"Hans, what are you like. She's a doctor who's having some vaccines collected; big deal," Ed pushed back, anxiety journeying through his body.

"No, no, Ed," Hans responded, trembling with fury at Ed's dismissal. "She was deep in conversation with this man. She was talking about an operation arranged by someone named 'Hood'. These might not be real names, Ed; they could be made up." Hans paused, then continued:

"Ashlin said this Hood fellow had asked her if she could arrange to have a consignment of vaccine vials collected and moved to a safe location, as Hood was on another job and couldn't get to them and had failed to reach George, the guy Ashlin was now speaking to." Hans paused again.

"Ashlin told George that a Stealer who was moving them had to dump them in a bin while running from the police after legging it, having been caught up in a random stop and search. Ashlin wanted this George guy to get the vials picked up before anyone discovered them. She told George that a tracker was attached to them and gave him a code."

Ed's mouth was dry; anxiety was now free-flowing through his body.

"Okay, Hans," he responded. "So we need to have words with her, right?"

"No, Ed," Hans hit back aggressively. "I needed you to hear it from me first hand. I have to report this to the police – but I wanted you to have the full story, hoping you would understand. I'm going to Shepherd's Bush police station directly from here."

Ed's eyes lit up, anger now overtaking all other emotions. "No, Hans, I don't fucking understand. Ashlin is one of our closest and dearest friends. *Your* dearest friend. Stop this crazy talk of going to the police. You aren't going to throw her to the wolves."

"Ed, we've different views on LPAS, I know. But you must understand that I can't keep this secret. Ashlin has broken the law, and I must report this."

The pair argued back and forth for almost an hour. With every minute, Ed was fighting back the anger coursing through him, unable to comprehend Hans's intention to give Ashlin up, knowing the outcome would almost certainly mean a lengthy prison sentence. The back-and-forth became even more heated; then Ed escalated it by shoving Hans backwards, causing him to crash into a support pillar and fall on one knee. He jumped up and lunged at Ed, pushing him hard.

"What do you think you are doing, Ed? Back off!"

Ed toned it down, having one last forlorn attempt at changing Hans's mind. "Don't do this, Hans. Ashlin is your friend; she will spend years in prison for saving people's lives. Is that what you want?"

"It isn't about what I want, Ed. You've never resolved yourself to the law's absolute necessity, have you? It is about Ashlin breaking a law that is required to save the human race."

"Is it, Hans? Is it saving us? Can't you see that this law is turning us against each other, aside from allowing millions to die? Is what Ashlin has done so bad that she should spend the best part of the rest of her life in prison? Can't you see that Ashlin is saving lives?

"That's what all of us trained for and why we entered med school. It's what we have done our entire working lives. The law is wrong, Hans. I'm begging you, please, don't do this."

Ed's anger briefly took second place to his sadness as tears bubbled up in his eyes before streaming down his face.

"Man up, Ed," Hans shouted, showing a total lack of empathy or concern. "I should have gone straight to the police instead of wasting my time with you." He turned to leave the chapel.

Ed leapt at him from behind, spinning him around and hitting him with full force in the face. Hans staggered back but gained control and lunged forward at Ed, hitting him several times in the body. Hans had been an excellent amateur boxer and knew how to take someone down. Especially someone not trained or toned to fighting level. With two last savage blows to Ed's stomach, Ed went down hard, winded and in severe pain. Hans looked down at him and shouted:

"You're pathetic, Ed. We aren't kids in the playground. What were you thinking? We must all obey the law. The consequences of not doing so are too dire."

Hans started towards the chapel's entrance, exiting and walking along the cemetery path, heading to West Brompton station, less than 10 minutes' walk away. He would catch a train to Shepherd's Bush, being the closest police station to the cemetery.

Less than 30 seconds later, Ed's phone rang. "Syrinx," said Kai, "I heard it all. I almost came down when you started fighting but thought that would have been a mistake."

Ed, still winded, blurted out, "Stop him, Kai," forgetting to use her codename.

"Syrinx, what do you mean stop him?"

"He must not reach the police station."

"Syrinx, you need to be clear with me. What do you mean *stop* him?"

Ed, his heart pounding, chest tightening, fear twisting his gut, quietly said: "Kill him."

Kai hung up the phone, immediately called her back-up, whose codename was Tan, and started after Hans. Tan answered his phone.

"Tan, it's Honu. Move in close to my position. I need you to be my eyes. I have to stop Hans."

"Stop him, Honu?"

"Yes, you heard me right: stop him."

"Honu, you need to use a knife. You cannot shoot him; it will raise too many questions."

"Do you think I'm the Italian Mafia! I'm not carrying a knife," Kai angrily responded.

"*I* am, Honu," came Tan's reply. "You be my eyes. I'll do it," he said reluctantly.

Neither of them wanted to do this, but they both knew it had to be done and were damn sure that whatever emotional turmoil they were in right now, it was nothing compared to what Ed would be going through.

Kai and Tim Lawton (Tan's real name) started to close in on Hans about halfway to the train station. As Hans entered a side street off the main drag, using it as a cut-through to save time, Tan moved in. As he got to within striking distance, a beep in his earpiece from Kai let him know he was clear. Tan spun Hans around, momentarily locking eyes with him. He thrust the knife into Hans's chest at an angle. Tan knew precisely where the blade would be most effective.

Hans let out an ear-piercing howl of pain as he fell into the side of a building, staggered on for about 10 feet, then fell to the floor clutching his chest.

Tan, himself distraught at what he'd had to do, quickly took Hans's wallet and wristwatch before making off for all he was worth. Kai, standing in the shadow of a building at one end of the street, quickly headed off down an alleyway, disappearing into the night. Tan had done the deed.

Kai was now heading back to Brompton Cemetery, concerned for Ed and knowing she had to get him out of the area. Meanwhile, Hans was discovered, still alive, and an ambulance was called. The paramedics instantly recognised Hans, and while one of them desperately started work to save his life, which, ironically, was against the law, the other, using an emergency clearance system, put in a request for permission to work on him. Cato Thon (the hospital administrator) and Gordon Jefferies (the LPAS administrator) were among several seniors linked to this unique clearance system.

Gordon Jefferies responded in less than a minute, clearing the paramedics to intervene to save Hans's life. While working on Hans, a senior doctor arrived and took charge, battling frantically to save him.

The attending doctor pronounced Hans dead 18 minutes after arriving on the scene.

Kai arrived back at the cemetery to find Ed sitting on the floor, his head on his knees, his hands on his head.

"Ed, we need to go. We can't hang around here."

Ed looked up and, in a barely audible voice, said: "Is it done?"

Sorrow shredding her insides, Kai responded: "Yes, Ed, it's done."

Grief already turning his body into an empty shell, Ed asked: "Was it painless? Was it quick?"

"Ed, don't do this to yourself," Kai begged him.

Crying and spitting his words, Ed rounded on Kai. "Answer me, Kai. Did he suffer?"

"I think he did, Ed," Kai responded, feeling numb all over. She continued: "Ed, we need to go. I can't imagine what you are feeling right now, but we must leave."

Ed heeded Kai's concern, got up and left the cemetery, with Kai making sure he got safely back to his apartment before putting in a call to Creak to brief him on the evening's events. It was the hardest debrief Kai had ever given, and she felt hollow with sadness.

Ed was drinking in the dark, running through what he had done, over and over. Then, at a little after 23:30, his phone rang. Looking down at the phone, he could see it was Kine, Hans's wife. Ed froze. The colour drained from his face, and the guilt, fear and sadness that had been with him since he gave the order coursed violently through him, causing him to start to shake.

His mouth was dry, his eyes deep red, and tears pooled in his lashes. He took a couple of deep breaths and answered the phone.

"Hi, Kine, late call. How are you?" What a bloody dreadful and unfeeling way to have answered the phone to Kine right now.

"Ed," said Kine, followed by a long pause that left Ed desperately trying to hold back his tears and steady his voice. "Hans is... dead." As Kine finished this briefest of statements, she broke down, and Ed heard another voice.

"Hi, Ed, I'm Stacey, one of Kine's friends. Hans was attacked earlier this evening. The police believe it was a mugging that went bad. He died from a single stab wound to the heart. Kine wanted to call you; she insisted, saying you had to find out from her. She's a mess, Ed, as you can imagine. She's in no fit state to talk. But don't worry about her.

There are a number of us at the house, and we'll stay with her."

Ed, in floods of tears, responded as best he could. "Sorry, I'm having trouble processing this. Would you please look after Kine and tell her I'm terribly sad and will get over to see her? And thank you for looking after her."

Kine's friend acknowledged Ed's words and said she would pass them on once Kine was in a better state. Ed thanked her again and put down the phone.

The first person Kine had called was Ashlin, for she was not just a long-time friend of Hans but also Kine's friend. Ashlin knew that Kine would also call Ed and, although deeply upset herself, was now making her way over to Ed's apartment. While in the car, Jail phoned her.

After Kai had briefed Creak Nooks, her boss, Creak told Jail Sleeks in his capacity as head of operations. Jail instructed Creak that no other member of the inner circle must know, and that what had happened must be kept to as small a number within POLO as possible.

Ashlin picked up, but before Jail could speak, Ashlin said, "I'm sorry, Jail, I can't talk now. I'm a little messed up and on my way over to Ed's place. You've heard us talk about Hans in the past? He was murdered earlier this evening, and I know Hans's wife will have by now told Ed, who will be taking this even harder than me. So I want to check in to ensure he is okay. Maybe I also need comforting; I don't know, really. I'll call you tomorrow."

Jail didn't want Ashlin going to Ed's, but how could he stop her? Too late – Ashlin hung up.

He was now in a quandary. Should he intercept Ashlin? Should he go over to Ed's? He had a key card for the front door and Ed's apartment. Should he call and warn Ed that Ashlin was on her way?

Although he wanted to do something, he knew he would have to stay clear and let Ed deal with it. Not a great choice, but it was, in Jail's mind, the only one.

Ashlin arrived at Ed's apartment block and buzzed his door. After a minute, she buzzed again. Still no answer. She rang his phone, and after a long delay, he picked up.

"Ed, I'm outside your apartment. Where are you?"

Ed, his speech slightly slurred, advised Ashlin he was home.

"Ed, I know you know about Hans; I can't believe it. I'm devastated by the news. Please buzz me in."

Ashlin arrived at the apartment, entered the living room, and as Ed stood up, wobbling on his feet, Ashlin hugged him and started to cry. Ed held her tightly as a flood of tears rolled down his face.

Within a few seconds, Ed's legs buckled, sending him down to the floor on both knees. The cause wasn't so much the drink he'd poured down his throat in a short space of time as the ground swell of emotions. Ashlin went down with him, saying:

"Ed, I can't believe it either. It's so sad, and for what? No doubt a few pounds in his wallet. The killer must have known their reward would not have been a mountain of cash. I suspect Hans resisted, but why kill him? Why not run away and find an easier victim? I don't understand the minds of these people. They've taken the life of a man whose talent has saved hundreds of lives and who would have gone on to save a great many more. This wicked deed, I suspect, was to feed their filthy little addiction."

Ed pulled back slightly from Ashlin, looked into her eyes and kissed her on the forehead. Then he stood up, took a few unsteady steps back and sat down in the chair. Ashlin got up and sat beside him.

"Ed, I know you've had your fair share of run-ins with Hans of late, but I know how much he meant to you. It is obvious how upset you are, but we must be strong for Kine. She is going to need us." She flung her arms around him again and held him.

"Ashlin, I appreciate you coming over. I know you are a mess too. Thinking of me at such a time is typical of the person you are. You are a great friend."

They chatted for an hour or so, which allowed Ed to sober up a little. Most of the conversation was about the great times they'd had with Hans. Then, a little after 2 a.m., Ashlin left, saying she would call him in the morning and that she intended to ring Kine.

The conversation about Hans had only served to deepen Ed's revulsion at what he'd done. He had found the conversation extremely difficult, breaking down every so often, driven by his grief over the death of his friend and the fact he had ended his friend's life.

He reverted to trying to make sense of what he'd done. He wasn't looking to justify it. No amount of thinking about it would achieve that.

He had often thought LPAS, which had led to his founding POLO, had changed him in ways he found repulsive. But this act was undoubtedly the ultimate betrayal of his beliefs; his moral values had sunk to a painful new low in his fight against an immoral law.

What has become of me, that I could have ordered the murder of another human being? he asked himself. Perversely, the pillar of strength keeping him from an almost inevitable meltdown was his belief that even after analysing his decision, he would still have ordered Hans's murder. A diabolical strength, and cruelly comforting, although it did not help him deal with how cold he had become.

Ed awoke. Not that he'd slept much, having spent almost the entire night staring up at the ceiling. He had a text from Creak, saying that he and Jail wanted to meet him today, if possible, and suggesting they do so at Brindle's farm.

Ed called in sick and prepared to head to the farm. Upon arrival, he found the two of them deep in conversation, and as he walked in, they both got up and said how sorry they were.

"Thank you both; I appreciate your concern. I haven't fully taken it in. I feel a great loss. Severe anxiety set in immediately after I gave the order. I'm hurting in a way I never have before. And yet I feel

I have no right to be, and that's creating a painful conflict that is tearing me up inside."

Ed paused, then continued.

"I'm scared to close my eyes, for doing so transports me to a frightening place." He paused again, then went on. "Closing my eyes brings a rush of negative thoughts, fear, and a terrifying picture of Hans lying on the floor, screaming in pain. And when I fall asleep, it gets worse. The same picture, but Hans reaches up to me and asks me why."

Creak responded. "Those high moral standards you have that forced you to constantly listen to your internal voice telling you what's right and what is not, those values are the driving force behind the way you feel. They are the same lofty values that drove you to set up POLO."

Creak continued.

"Those same high values brought you to give an order that every fibre of your body was resisting. I cannot begin to imagine what that was like, or how broken you must feel."

Ed looked at Creak and gave a half nod to say he respected his view. "I no longer see myself when I look in the mirror. I see someone I don't recognise and don't want to be. But I know the man looking back at me is saving lives and that I have to live in him to do so." Ed paused to compose himself. "How can I face Kine? How can I sit in front of her, comfort her, knowing it was I who caused her the greatest of losses and unimaginable pain? How can I allow others to comfort me over Hans's death, knowing I sanctioned it?"

Ed broke down and Creak placed a comforting arm around him.

Jail, who until now had kept quiet, piped up.

"Ed, I'm not going to pretend that I can begin to understand the grief, the pain and the guilt you feel right now. I can't help you quell the loathing for what you believe you have become. And I can't help you deal with having to face Kine, knowing you are the cause of her grief and pain. I cannot offer help in these areas any more than I have been able to help you deal with the guilt of being in a loving relationship built on a foundation of deceit. And I'm sorry I can't. But here's what I know: I know Edward Thorncroft."

Jail paused before continuing. "I've never known a more decent, thoughtful, caring or compassionate human being. Had you not started POLO, well over 100,000 people would now be dead. So many young adults and small children are among that number. No doubt many of them will go on to have careers saving lives; and none, not one of them, would have had such an opportunity had it not been for you.

"You made a decision so hard, so painful, so much against your instinct, that I cannot begin to comprehend the conflict and turmoil this is causing you. You were in an impossible position. Do nothing, and Ashlin would have gone to prison for the rest of her life. With the names on the tape, the authorities would almost certainly have found Hood. George is a common enough name. But Hood – nickname or not, I think they would have found her. And you, being so close to

Ashlin, would have become a major person of interest, which would, in all likelihood, have damaged your reputation and your political efforts, and possibly have led to your arrest."

Creak and Jail left Ed up at the farm, first telling him, through what would doubtless be a long and torturous journey of the mind, to understand and come to terms with what he had done. He must view it through multiple lenses, taking everything into account. Then they left, reminding him that they were both just a phone call away should he need to talk.

Standing in the doorway of the cottage, looking out over the beautiful Kent countryside, Ed reflected on Jail's views. However, Ed would not justify his actions by twisting them into a warped idea of a good deed. Whatever the events that had transpired, it was his call to make such a heinous decision.

He knew, however, that he could not have stood by and allowed Ashlin to rot in prison. He had promised himself that he would never allow harm to come to any of his team if he was in a position to stop it. And he had – heartbreakingly, undeviating – held to that promise.

Leonora picked up on the news that Hans was the doctor murdered in London and was now concerned about why Ed hadn't called. They hadn't spoken since a few days before Hans's death, but Ed had texted her the day after the murder, saying he was busy and would call her in a couple of days, making no mention of Hans. So Leonora decided to go over to Ed's apartment.

Arriving at Ed's place, she let herself in the main door, taking the lift to the third floor. A few seconds after ringing the doorbell, Ed opened the door. Immediately, upon seeing her, he started to fight back the tears. Leonora hugged him and they stood in the doorway, Ed still trying desperately to control his emotions. Stepping inside, Leonora shut the door and they went into the lounge.

"I'm so sorry, Ed. I know how much Hans meant to you. I came over as soon as they announced on the news that Hans was the doctor who was murdered."

At this moment, more than at any other time in their relationship, Ed felt sick to his stomach at the way he had deceived Leonora and continued to do so. Wracked with guilt and loathing, anguish permeated his body, causing a sensation of pins and needles all over. These deep feelings that were contorting his face were impossible for Leonora to miss.

Ed's chest tightened as if the cam of a vice were slowly being twisted. He wanted to yell out who he was and what he had done, exposing the double life he led.

Leonora leant in to hold him again. "Ed, I know this is hard for you. Talk to me; you need to let go of the pain. You know better than most that bottling it up is damaging."

Ed was on the verge of doing something that would have incalculable consequences. Pushing Leonora back and staring deep into her beautiful storm-blue eyes, he held his breath, trying to compose himself.

"I can't bear it," he yelled out loudly. "The grief, the pain, the guilt. I can't close my eyes without seeing him lying there alone, dying in hideous pain."

As Ed stopped, Leonora could see and feel his heart beating rapidly, as if ready to burst. Now crying for him, she held his face tightly, sweat oozing from his head and face as it would if one were suffering from craniofacial hyperhidrosis.

"Ed, I hate seeing you like this; you're scaring me. You must calm down. Have you sedatives in your bag? We need a doctor; you're going to have a heart attack if you don't calm down. Breathe out, Ed, breathe. This isn't your fault. You cannot take on the guilt for the wrongdoing of others."

Ed, turning blue from not breathing, let out a huge gasp and yelled, "Leonora, I…"

Ed was at his apartment, readying himself for work. He'd stayed in ever since Hans's death. Ed had come within a whisker of telling Leonora that he was responsible for the murder of his friend. As one would expect, he continued to struggle with grief and guilt (the two 'g's, as Ed called it). It was a growing problem, and Ed was finding everyday functioning more and more difficult.

His intense guilt caused Ed time and again to see Hans lying on a backstreet pavement, blood pumping from a chest wound, holding his chest and writhing in agony, looking up at Ed and asking – Why?

This recurring scene happened day and night. And it had caused him to cancel a few operations that other surgeons had to pick up.

Leonora had ensured that she gave him space. It was evident to her that consolation was not what he needed, nor wanted. She knew he was a strong man and needed to work this out on his own.

Hans's funeral was fast approaching, and Ed knew he must get a grip. He had done what he had to. He had to deal with this to enable him to continue fighting for and saving people's lives. He had to put it behind him but feared he might not be able to.

UNnatural Selection –
Funeral; Ed on the edge

Ed had not woken at 4 a.m., as he hadn't slept. He had spent much of the night sitting in the corner of his living room, looking out at the sky through a gap in the curtains. It was a beautiful clear night, the stars glistening brightly, and there seemed to be more of them than usual. It was the kind of night that made Ed feel alive. Unfortunately, that wasn't the case tonight. Outside was beautiful, but inside, Ed felt ugly.

A large part of the night was tearful, and the guilt of having ordered the execution of his best friend ate away at his sanity. Ed questioned who he was ever more frequently.

Hans's funeral was today, and Ed was delivering the main eulogy. His wife made it clear that her husband would not have wanted anyone else to do it. Under any other circumstances, Ed would have insisted on doing the honours, even though to do so for his best friend would be emotionally challenging; but emotionally challenging did not describe what he was going through right now. He was in danger of transcending the barrier between knowing that life was worth fighting for and seeing death as the better option. Suicidal thoughts had been flashing through his mind over the past few weeks. He had latched on to a few of them, given them credence, and more significantly, expanded them to add detail to the various methods that came into his mind.

Ed felt he had turned into a Jekyll-and-Hyde character. A good person, capable of unspeakable acts. He was tormented not just by having ordered the murder of his best friend but also by the fact that having been let loose once, Mr Hyde could escape again. And what would he do next? As yet, he hadn't realised that he was bordering a breakdown.

Ed arrived at the funeral early, accompanied by Leonora, and a chapel member escorted them to a waiting area reserved for close relatives. Kine was already waiting with two of her closest friends, one being Ashlin. Kine got up, rushed towards Ed and embraced him – no tears, but her gaunt features took his breath away. And what was more, the weight loss was genuinely frightening, especially given that Kine had always been petite.

As she hugged him, the full gamut of emotions tore through him. And right at the top were sadness and disgust. Ed held her tight, trying desperately not to cry and to keep enough composure to enable him to speak to her.

"Kine, I cannot begin to understand your pain. I'm deeply sorry for your loss. I want so much to find a word, a sentence, that will relieve some of your suffering. But I have none."

Kine looked up at him, grabbing his face. "You being here helps me, Ed. And it is *our* loss. I know you loved him too." Her words only amplified Ed's guilt and self-loathing. No longer able to stop the wall he had built in his mind to keep his emotions at bay from crumbling, he broke down.

As they embraced, both in floods of tears, Leonora leant in, hugging them, and all three stayed in the embrace for a while before Ed and Kine composed themselves. A few minutes of diverting small talk took place, helping them calm down and gain control. A few minutes later, they received a five-minute warning that the car carrying Hans was nearby and that they should move into the chapel. Ed would go outside to meet the hearse, for one of his duties today was as one of the pallbearers, along with close family and other doctor friends of Hans.

Ed and the other pallbearers took their seats with the coffin in the chapel as the funeral celebrant opened the service. Five minutes later, Ed received his cue to step up and give his eulogy.

Ed spoke for 20 or so minutes, telling stories of his and Hans's antics at medical school, which brought laughter to the service. Ed recalled how he first met Hans at a party for young doctors. When Ed arrived, Hans was mopping the dance floor in his underpants, having dropped six pints over himself and the floor on his way to the table.

Ed told those at the service that he unintentionally spent the entire evening chatting to Hans, such was his presence.

"Hans was authentic, interesting, a storyteller, but most of all he was edutaining. You learned and laughed with Hans. And let's face it, that night he had to have a strong presence. And so it was that I spent the evening in a three-piece suit, talking to a man in his shreddies! His description, not mine, and army slang for underpants." Laughter filled the chapel briefly.

Bowing his head and falling silent, Ed looked back up. "Hans made me feel alive and gave me confidence. I have no words that can come close to describing how I miss him and the pain and guilt I feel over his death."

Guilt was not a word Ed should have used, but he did so without thinking. He had not scripted his eulogy. He fell silent as tears ran down his face. Leonora got up and guided him back to his chair.

Within 30 minutes of Ed ending his eulogy, the committal began, with Hans's coffin being lowered out of sight. Before leaving the chapel, mourners took a few minutes for individual thoughts and prayers, then left the service to pay their respects to Kine. Hans had no siblings, and his parents died in Africa a few years earlier while on a three-month safari.

Kine opened the wake by telling all in attendance that Hans would want them to have a good time, not be sad, and exchange stories of their time with him.

"I don't want to see any more tears, people," she said while wiping tears from her face.

With that, Kine signalled to the band to play Hans's favourite tune. A slow, romantic song, which Kine told everyone summed up the man she loved. Stepping down from the stage, she walked over to Ed and asked if he would dance with her. As they moved onto the dance floor, Kine whispered in Ed's ear:

"Ed, I don't expect you to stop missing Hans. I know you, too, are in pain. But please do not feel guilt. You weren't there. And if you were, you likely could not have saved him. You might have suffered the same fate."

Ed pulled her tightly to him. It took all his ability to focus, not to break down again, and thoughts of ending his life resurfaced. He felt that no one could sink lower. A vision of Hans still tormented him, one he now experienced both when asleep and when he simply closed his eyes.

He would see Hans dying. Blood pouring from a massive wound to his chest. Alone and in pain on a dimly lit street. As Ed realised he was going to lose control, he moved Kine slightly away, kissed her forcefully on her forehead and said:

"I'm so sorry, Kine. I can't stay, I need to leave, I'm sorry, forgive me, please forgive me."

With that, Ed made a hurried exit, forgetting that Leonora was with him. He hadn't even acknowledged Ashlin the entire time he was there. As Kine started after him, Leonora stopped her.

"Let him go, Kine. He needs time on his own. His grief is not like yours, but I do know he is majorly cut up over Hans's death. He beats himself up all the time. I tell him constantly that it wasn't his fault, but he seems hell-bent on blaming himself. I will check on him tomorrow."

The two hugged, and Kine thanked Leonora and asked her to tell Ed that she wasn't mad at him for leaving the wake.

When Ed had rushed from the wake, his last words to Kine weren't as Kine had interpreted them. He was not asking to be forgiven for leaving the wake but for ordering his friend's – her husband's – murder. Ed was now almost at a point of no return.

Ed didn't make it home. Instead, he went to a London park and sat alone with thoughts that were bringing him ever closer to, at best, a breakdown, and at worse, suicide. Cold, confused, despairing, Ed's instinct, honed by years as a doctor, told him he was in a dark place and in deep trouble. Reaching for his phone, he called Creak. When Creak answered, there was silence at Ed's end. Creak waited a few seconds before saying hello a second time, but again there was no reply. He could hear sobbing and the mumbling of someone clearly in distress, but he could not discern who it was. He knew it had to be one of the inner circle, as the call had come through on POLO's secure system. He suspected it was Ed but wasn't sure.

Calmly speaking, Creak said, "Please calm down, speak to me, tell me where you are, and I'll come to you."

Ed blurted out, "It's Ed; I'm in Richmond Park."

"Stay where you are, Ed, I'm coming to you. Don't go anywhere."

Creak jumped in his car, immediately calling Ashlin and asking her to meet him at the park, outside Peg's Pond Gate, and to bring medication to calm a profoundly distressed person. It was clear Ed was in serious trouble.

Creak arrived at the gate first, with Ashlin arriving not too long after. By now, it was just after 1:30 a.m.

The pair set off to find Ed, calling his phone for directions, but Ed did not answer. Richmond Park is huge and finding Ed without an idea of his location would be challenging.

As they hurried through the park, Creak continued to call Ed's phone, and after several attempts, he answered, telling Creak he was near the Isabella Plantation café. Nearing the café, they could see the outline of a man huddled by a tree. As they approached, they could see he was shaking and could hear he was crying.

The sight of Ed in this condition took Ashlin's breath away; she instantly welled up, looking skyward to focus on something else. Creak dropped to the ground, pulling Ed towards him and hugging him like a brother. As he stared into Ed's eyes, the look of anguish was clear.

"Get his jacket off, Creak, and roll up his sleeve."

Creak pulled Ed's jacket off and, using a penknife, cut off the cuff buttons so that Ashlin could set up an intravenous catheter, through which she would administer midazolam, a strong sedative that would calm his brain and nerves. They sat with him for around 10 minutes, allowing the drug to enter his body before picking him up and making their way back to the gate, Creak telling Ashlin to leave her car.

"Can we take him to your place, Ashlin?" said Creak, deep sadness in his eyes, a look that Ashlin had not seen before.

"Sure, but would he not be better at home?"

"NO!" shouted Creak. "No one must see Ed like this, especially Leonora. Who knows what he'll tell her?"

"What do you mean, Creak? What do you think he will tell her?" Ashlin knew that Creak knew what had caused Ed to get into such a state and was convinced that it had to be more than grief for his friend, knowing how strong Ed's character was.

"I'm going to tell you something, Ashlin. Something that Ed made me swear never to repeat, never to discuss outside of those who already knew through necessity. Only a few within POLO are aware of this, and I shouldn't be telling you, but Ed needs your help, and it is right that you understand why."

"Okay, Creak. Let's get Ed back to mine, make him comfortable, and then we can talk."

Arriving at Ashlin's, they stripped Ed down to his underpants and put him in the spare room. Ashlin ensured that he was comfortable, and he was quickly asleep. Then, entering the living room, she poured Creak and herself two large drinks, sat down and said: "Well, what's going on? I've seen enough people on the brink, and he's most definitely on it. He's a hair's breadth from a breakdown – why?"

"You might want to sit down, Ashlin." With that, Creak downed the large whisky that Ashlin had poured out for him and asked her to refill his glass. Ashlin downed hers and refreshed both glasses. Then, sitting no more than six inches from Creak, she said, "I'm listening."

"Ashlin, I'll give you the shock headline. Then, when you calm down, I'll tell you why, okay?"

Ashlin, more apprehensive than she could ever remember being, said: "Okay, Creak."

Creak breathed in deeply, expelling the air slowly. "Ed ordered Hans's murder!"

Ashlin, instantly enraged, jumped up, dropping her brandy glass on the floor. "NO, no, no, he'd never do that – no, why did you say that? It's a lie, and you know it. So what are you hiding?"

Creak jumped up and held her. "I'm sorry to have blurted it out like that, Ashlin. But it's true." She pulled away from him, screaming at him that he was lying and how disgusting it was that he would say such a thing.

"Ashlin, calm down, please, calm down. It isn't a lie; it's the truth. So calm down and let me explain."

She hit out at him, catching him on the left side of his face, causing a small cut. Creak grabbed her, holding her tight to stop her lashing out. "Ashlin, stop it, stop it; this isn't helping. Let me explain." As he felt her body calming down, he released her.

Ashlin sat down; the colour had drained from her face, and she was crying. She knew Ed well; he wouldn't do that. But she also knew Creak well, and he wouldn't lie. So she was left confused and questioning her judgement. Creak knelt beside her, held her arms and said, "Listen to me."

Ashlin took several deep breaths, wiped the tears from her face and sat silently waiting for Creak to explain.

Creak asked Ashlin to think back to when Ed was teaching at the Chelsea and Westminster Hospital. It was during this time that Hans was attacked. Ashlin acknowledged it, unsure why it mattered. Creak told her that Hans called Ed and wanted to meet him urgently, as he had to tell him something. Ed knew it was serious, as Hans sounded nervous, scared even. Ed then met with Hans at the old Brompton Cemetery, as Hans had insisted it couldn't wait.

Ashlin interjected, "Why the cemetery?"

"Ed was passing nearby on his way to Stamford Bridge to collect some tickets."

Creak continued. "When Hans arrived, he launched into accusations about you. He told Ed that he knew you were a member of an illegal organisation, and that it was important to him that Ed understand why he needed to take this information to the police."

"Creak, I don't discuss POLO, and I hardly mix with Hans. So he couldn't have known. And if he suspected, he couldn't have any evidence." After finishing her statement, she fell silent. She was pushing back, but deep down she wondered if it was possible she had tripped up somehow.

Creak continued. "Hans told Ed he'd heard it, as he put it, 'straight from the horse's mouth'."

"No, that's a lie; that's simply not true, Creak."

"Ashlin, he told Ed he was on the roof of the hospital. A place he often went to gather his thoughts. He was hidden from your view as you entered the roof space. You were on the phone talking to George."

Ashlin turned pale. She remembered the event to which Creak referred.

"Stay focused on me, Ashlin," Creak continued. "Hans told Ed he was about to call out to you when he heard you mention a consignment of vaccines that needed moving quickly. He then dropped a bombshell on Ed, telling him he was intrigued by what he had heard, and immediately flipped his medical recorder on and stayed silent."

Creak explained that Ed pushed back, but that the evidence was building, and it was clear that Hans had enough to put her away for a long time, possibly for life.

"He taped you talking about a Stealer having to dump the vaccines while running from the police and saying that the vials needed to be retrieved. Ed and Hans's conversation became more heated, eventually ending in a fight, which Ed lost. Hans left the cemetery, heading straight to the police station. Ed knew you'd go down and that it would bring them very close to POLO."

Ashlin, ashen-faced and trembling, stared at Creak. Giant blobs of water rolled from her eyes. Wiping them, she responded.

"He killed his best friend for me – is that what you are telling me? It's my fault, then. He killed the man he loved most, the one man he looked up to, loved as a brother, for me. No, this is insane. Why would he do that?

"No, I don't accept it. It can't be true." Ashlin leapt up to run into the bedroom to wake Ed. Creak grabbed her, pulling her to the floor and holding her tightly, which wasn't easy, given her rage.

"No, Ashlin, he did what he had to do to protect you and POLO. No one is blaming you, least of all Ed. He made a decision, and Jail and I believe he made the right one."

"He should have given me up. I'm confused. I can't think straight. This can't be real. It cannot be true. Ed's..." Ashlin fell silent for a few seconds. "I know Ed. It's not in him to do that."

"Ashlin, we all do things we did not think possible when circumstances leave us no good options. Ed had no good options, and God, how difficult it must have been for him to have given that order."

"He loved Hans," Ashlin repeated.

"Yes. He did and still does. But he made the only call he could have, and it's destroying him."

Ashlin couldn't take in what she'd heard. Creak released her from the floor and pulled her to his chest.

"I know this is a lot to take in, Ashlin. I know this is very hard for you. It was hard enough for Jail and me. I knew telling you would be bad. But given Ed's state, you needed to know. Ed needs you now more than ever. You have the medical know-how; you have his trust. He loves you. I feel that only you can get him through this. Stop him from falling into an abyss from which he will be unable to climb out." Creak took a breath.

"Ashlin, if you tell him he made the wrong call, you will finish him. Do you understand that?"

Silence filled the air for what seemed an eternity before Ashlin spoke.

"I get it, Creak. I'm devastated that my lapse caused this. I've broken a man I love because I didn't follow protocol."

"Ashlin, stop. I don't need you and Ed going off a cliff. It isn't your fault. Events happen, and we react as best we can. You were dead unlucky than Hans was on the roof at that time, and that his hatred for anyone breaking LPAS law drove him to keep quiet. He kept quiet, Ashlin. Kept quiet to get what he could on his friend: you. So he could put you away for life. Let that sink in before you allow your guilt to overcome you as it has Ed."

"I'm numb, Creak. I know what we do has had, and will have, undesirable consequences. Jesus, we killed a police officer who was doing his job. We all knew how bad that was, but we told ourselves we had no choice. We were saving thousands of lives. But this is different. It is so hard to take in. What are we becoming that we can do these things? Can we still be right? I'm not sure I know."

"At any time, Ashlin, we can quit. We can go back to our day jobs, and we can stop saving lives. Is that more moral than taking a few to save thousands? Had Ed given you up, do you think it would have stopped there? It would not. The authorities would have dug deep into your friends, colleagues, acquaintances. Okay, maybe it would not have brought POLO down. But be assured it would have seriously impacted operations and our ability to save lives. Ed had no choice. Can you imagine how hard it was for him? I can't. I cannot imagine the strength you would need to have made such a call. And we now need to help bring him back from the brink."

"Creak. Isn't that the LPAS argument? Allow millions to die, to save billions. So are we both right, and could it be they are *more* right?"

"Ashlin, you sound like Brindle."
"Brindle? What's wrong with Brindle?"

"Nothing, Ashlin."

"But you said–"

Creak stopped her. "Forget I said that; it isn't important now. Don't allow your mind to entertain that argument. The LPAS laws are in place so that millions will die. That is their sole purpose . We've made a few mistakes, yes, some terrible ones that have cost a couple of innocent lives. All of us feel the pain of that. But it is not the same."

Creak paused, then continued.

"We need to focus on getting Ed through this. He's been trying to do it alone, and it isn't working. We all need to be strong for him."

Ashlin got up and poured them both another drink.

"I'll have one too." Ed was standing in the doorway to the living room. "You told her, Creak. Why did you tell her? What must you think of me, Ashlin?"

"I'm sorry, Ed. I needed her help. *You* need her help. I couldn't fob her off with a story that she would not have believed."

"Ashlin, whatever you think of me, I think worse. I did what I had to do."

Creak was getting anxious, not knowing what Ashlin's reply would be.

"Ed, when you say you did what you did to protect POLO, I know that's true. But I'm not sure that if one of us wasn't also in danger, you wouldn't have just closed the operation down for an extended period. Lives would be lost, yes, but we've taken this action before and will probably have to again. My failure contributed to placing you in an unfathomable position. The pain must be unbearable. I'm surprised you've managed to hold it together for as long as you have."

Ed looked over to Creak and back at Ashlin.

"Ashlin. POLO would not have been in danger but for the information that Hans uncovered. In that sense, you are right. Had one of you not been in the mix, the problem would not have arisen. However, that does not make you responsible. In those seconds before making my decision, I saw a side of Hans that I never expected to see. He could not have known that it could have brought down the house of POLO. But he did know that he would be condemning one of his best friends to life in prison. And why? Yes, for breaking the law. An unjust, immoral and discriminatory law that governments the world over should never have passed.

"I saw in front of me a man who would put one of his closest friends in prison for the crime of compassion. For doing your job, *our* job. We all, you, me and Hans, trained to save people's lives and make their lives better."

Ed paused, then walked into the room, as he'd started to feel weak while standing in the doorway. He sat down and continued.

"Ashlin, it was not a single concern that led me to make the most traumatic decision of my life. I feared our organisation would need to shut down to protect itself, and that it would likely shut down for a considerable amount of time, causing the loss of many thousands of lives.

"Yes, I feared for you. I lost Jennifer due to my inaction. I could not have that happen again.

"But most of all, Hans – a man I respected, looked up to, and someone who had taught me a great deal, who had on numerous occasions guided me when I needed it most, someone I loved as I would a brother – had forgotten why we entered the medical profession, such was his belief that LPAS was the only way forward."

Choking up, Ed paused, putting up his hand as Ashlin moved to console him. Then, regaining control, he continued.

"I will never get over what I have done. I will never forgive myself. But I now know I can learn to live with it. I must, as we still have much to do, thousands more to save. Yesterday I was at my lowest point, forcing me to reach out. Had I not, and had Creak not responded so quickly, maybe, just maybe, we wouldn't be having this conversation now. But we are, and I will go on fighting these laws until the world's leaders see sense."

Ashlin and Creak got up, and the three of them embraced.

"It will take some time, Ed, for you to fully recover, but you will," said Creak, feeling for the first time since receiving Ed's call that Ed was going to be okay.

"I don't even know how you are awake, Ed," said Ashlin. "I gave you enough sedative to take down a horse."

"The inner me doesn't want to sleep, to rest, to be at peace. My conscious self reluctantly supports what I had to do. My unconscious self refuses to."

Ed asked Ashlin if she'd pour him a drink.

"Ed, you know as well as I that you should not be drinking alcohol with the medication I've given you."

"I know. But just the same, I'd like that brandy."

Ashlin didn't argue; she got up and poured him a small glass, putting her arm around him as she handed it to him.

"I am lucky to have such strong, caring friends around me. I've always known that. But no more so than tonight. Thank you both for being here for me. I don't think I'd have left Richmond Park had you not come."

UNnatural Selection – The PM,
open protection, red-faced

Some time had passed since Ed's low point, and he'd steadily got back into his work and had shaken off the images of Hans's death. With every day, he was learning to live with what he had done.

It was early Monday morning, and he was up, dressed and ready to leave Leonora's apartment. Today, he had a private lunch with the Prime Minister. The PM requested the lunch, which pleased Ed; as yet, he had not managed to get air time with the PM or his closest advisers. As the PM's fiancée would be attending, Leonora would too. Lunch was at Number 10, which Ed saw as recognition of his work.

Hans's funeral had been a turning point for him. He knew that ordering the murder would stay with him until his death, and that he would never get over it; but living with it was now more manageable, and getting on with the job of weakening the LPAS laws and the eventual repeal of the laws was what mattered.

Ed had done a lot of soul-searching over Hans's murder, and it had taken its toll on him. A piece of Ed died too on that evening in the domed chapel.

The Prime Minister had been in office for three years, with a general election due to take place in May 2050, a little over two years from now. Joshua Robinson, Conservative, had a large parliamentary majority and was well respected across the house. No children, and never married, he had become engaged a year into his premiership to Yasmin Corders, a long-time friend and one of his key advisors before he became PM.

Lunch was to be in the garden unless inclement weather dictated otherwise. However, the day was bright, if a little chilly. Nothing that should stop an alfresco lunch.

Ed and Leonora arrived at the back of Number 10, as the Prime Minister did not want this to be a highly publicised meeting. They were ushered in by security and escorted by one of the PM's staff to a lovely corner of the garden with a pergola and outdoor dining furniture.

"The Prime Minister will join you shortly. Can I get you something to drink while you wait?"

"Water" was the joint response from Leonora and Ed.

Five minutes later, the aide reappeared with a large bottle of still water and four glasses. "I'm sure the PM will not keep you waiting too long. So please relax and enjoy the lovely garden," said the aide as he left.

"Relax – he said relax. Do I look like I'm not relaxed?" said Ed, turning to Leonora while pouring them both a glass.

"You are not relaxed, Ed. You're fidgety."

"Oh, sorry, I'll try not to be," said Ed, taking a few deep breaths.

"Ed, calm down; it's unlike you to show signs of nerves. You've met senior figures all over the world, so why you are so nervous I don't know."

"Neither do I, Leonora. Maybe it is just that getting the UK to soften its support for LPAS would be such a big win. On the other hand, perhaps I'm scared I might say the wrong thing."

"Ed, you'll be fine."

Ed continued pacing up and down and poured himself another large glass of water.

"Ed, will you sit down and stop pacing."

"Is my pacing bothering you, Leonora?"

"Yes, actually, it is. You are making me nervous too!"

Ed sat down but was still moving his legs up and down as if he was walking.

Twenty-five minutes had now passed, and no sign of the PM. "What is it with people and tardiness? Maybe some people think they are more important than others?" was Ed's comment to Leonora. As he commented, he got a reply from an unexpected source.

"I'm sorry, Ed. I don't think I'm more important than you. I got caught up on a call with the Home Secretary."

Neither Ed nor Leonora had seen the Prime Minister arrive from the other side of the pergola, and Ed was a tad embarrassed.

"I'm sorry, Prime Minister. That was rude of me. Please accept my apology."

"No need to apologise, Ed. I've had much worse said about me," responded the PM, chuckling and reaching out to shake his hand. "And this must be your better half?"

"Nothing could be truer, Prime Minister," said Ed as Leonora stepped towards the PM.

"Happy to meet you, Prime Minister. I'm Leonora Annabelle-Hawkes."

"It's great to meet you both. And Ed, I have been looking forward to meeting you – you are making quite an impact. Let's sit down. Yasmin will join us shortly; she is holding a phone call with the President of France!"

Ed knew that was a humorous dig at his comment. Smiling, he and Leonora sat down with the PM, and after around 15 minutes, Yasmin joined them.

Lunch had gone well, and the conversation had covered many aspects of LPAS. Ed was polite but forceful when speaking of his deep concerns about the law. He pointed out its clear responsibility for many deaths and also spoke at length concerning the long-term implications on society. He'd pushed the PM, but the PM gave little away.

"Ed, I'm listening, truly I am. I know I've avoided answers that commit me one way or another. I would, however, say that I do not believe I would have voted in support of LPAS had I been PM. However, I understand why it received support, and like it or not, it is significantly reducing the world's population."

Ed, leaning forward, tried to interject but was cut off by the Prime Minister.

"Please, Ed, hear me out. I've heard all your arguments on alternatives, and yes, maybe that is the way we should have gone. But the world didn't, and we left it too late. That brought us very close to a possible global conflict, in the judgement of many government security agencies worldwide. When LPAS was voted for, the world had little choice. And moving away now isn't an easy option, given that it is working. We cannot risk a catastrophic event."

"I don't wish to be insulting, Prime Minister, but when you say 'working', I hear 'mass murder'. Even as late in the day as February 2040, we could have tried alternatives. Costly alternatives financially, yes. But undoubtedly better than allowing people in their millions to die needlessly. That's against everything we have worked to achieve as a race.

"I recognise that, having made the call, changing direction now is hard. But eroding the impact of LPAS on the people of the world is of paramount importance, as is the repeal of these obscene laws. No one will convince me to the contrary."

The conversation continued a while before the Prime Minister said he had only 15 or so minutes before he would have to leave. He told Ed that he wanted to meet with him again and would assign a minister to work with Ed's team on what alternatives would look like and how the UN could help support and introduce them globally. Ed felt this was a good outcome, and more than he expected.

"Before I go, Ed, I want to share some information with you that will shortly hit the press. I do so, as in large part we are introducing this legislation due to changing threat levels to senior politicians, including yourself."

The PM informed Ed that his government would soon introduce legislation to parliament that would allow senior figures of other political parties to employ licensed armed bodyguards. He said they had considered extending government security support but that it was too costly and that deciding who to protect would become far too political. Hence, allowing senior politicians of other parties to choose was deemed the better option.

Right on cue, an aide appeared to remind the PM that he needed to leave for his next engagement. So, goodbyes over, the PM and Yasmin left, and Leonora and Ed were escorted out – again via the back door.

Ed was feeling good. He knew that the legislation to which the PM referred would allow Kai and her team to protect him openly, affording him much closer security.

A government car took the couple back to Leonora's apartment. They sat debriefing the conversation with the PM, making notes to update Ed's political team and, unbeknown to Leonora, POLO seniors too. Notes completed, Leonora got up to shower, and Ed went off to one of the other bathrooms. Sitting on top of the toilet seat, he started to send a message to Jail and Creak to give them a heads-up on the legislation and asking them to prepare the way for Kai to come out from the shadows.

As the Prime Minister had said, the new legislation was announced, debated and approved, becoming law just eight weeks later. Kai was elated at not having to be in disguise and could now have her and her team stay very close to Ed. Her agency was already government listed, and it took little time for those who were to protect Ed to become certified to carry a weapon. Ed then invited Kai to meet Leonora.

Kai arrived for dinner at Leonora's apartment. Ed wasn't yet back from the hospital, so Leonora greeted her and ushered her in, asking her what she wanted to drink.

"Water will be fine," said Kai.

"Okay, I'm going to have a glass of red wine. Are you sure you won't join me?"

"Later. I'll start with water, thank you."

Leonora continued to prepare dinner, and the two of them started to get to know one another. Leonora's phone rang; it was Ed. He was going to be very late. A severe accident had come in and was within quotas, so he was heading down to the operating room. He'd be a while, so they should have dinner without him.

Leonora turned to Kai. "It seems it is just you and me for dinner. Good luck with protecting him. You'll be keeping all sorts of unsociable hours."

"Oh, I don't mind, Leonora. No different to what I am used to."

"So, how did Ed find your company so quickly?" asked a curious Leonora.

"We've done work for people Ed knows when they were travelling overseas. So Ed knew of my company, and we had met." Now Kai was having to lie to Leonora.

"Your company?"

"Yes, KAIGuard. I started the personal protection company when I left the United States Secret Service."

"Oh, I see. Did you protect the President?"

"At times, yes. But I was never one of the key guards, and I mainly focused on undercover work."

"What made you volunteer to watch Ed's back personally?"

"I believe in what he is doing, and I believe that Ed's profile in his fight against LPAS puts him at significant risk. I will act as his primary guard, but I will have a team supporting me."

"Have you ever needed to react to a serious incident?" Leonora was still probing.

"On a few occasions, yes. I've had the person I've been protecting shot at, attacked by a knife-wielding madman, had people try to accost them, things of that nature. But the person I've been protecting has never been injured, if that's your real question?"

"I guess in part it was. But more generally, I'm curious. You've chosen a difficult profession, so I guess I'm wondering what drives people to do what you do?"

"I can't talk for everyone's motives. But for me it is about protecting people that I believe give much to the world. That's worth putting my life on the line for."

Leonora had no clue, of course, that it was Kai who had saved Ed's life at the opening of Ed's friend Aurora Giordano's club. Leonora was probing because she wanted to know that if Ed was to have armed guards, they knew what they were doing; but there was also just a hint of jealousy, given that Kai was so attractive.

"So, what do you do in your spare time, Kai?"

"I work out at the gym, practise martial arts, spend time at the gun range. You know, the usual things!"

Leonora laughed.

"Okay, sorry. Enough of the inquisition. Please, join me in a glass of wine. I've taken the liberty of making up one of the rooms for you. If, however, you'd prefer to go home, I'll arrange a driver for you."

"Very good of you, Leonora. Thank you, I'll have that glass of wine, and I am happy to stay over."

The two of them chatted for hours, losing all track of time. They got along well, and soon it felt as if they'd known each other for years. They led very different lives, and they found learning about what each of them had done interesting. Then, just after 2 a.m., Ed walked in, looking tired and bedraggled in crumpled and oversized scrubs.

"You never wear your scrubs home, Ed."

"I know, I had to change the ones I was wearing in the operating room, as I needed to go up and talk to the family, and the operating scrubs were a mess."

"How did it end up, Ed?"

"Hopefully, a good outcome. A young lady, 27, caught up in a road accident. They had to cut her out... multiple broken bones and internal bleeding. She's in an induced sleep and on a ventilator now. All being well, we will wake her in 48 hours. After talking to the family, I just wanted to get home. I didn't even grab the car keys. One of the nurses gave me a lift."

"It must be so stressful, having someone's life in your hands," said Kai.

"Yes, it often is. There was a time when I didn't want anyone coming through the door mashed up and in need of urgent surgery. But now I do, knowing that many don't make it into surgery. For every patient that enters surgery, 20 or so exit the hospital via the back door in a body bag, having received no help. That's the true cause of my stress."

Leonora got up, hugged and kissed Ed. Then, turning to Kai, she said, "I imagine it is stressful for you too. Guarding someone, hoping no one has a go at them."

"Yes, it can be. But I'm sure it isn't the same as having to put someone back together as Ed does."

"Ladies, you might be expecting me to go to bed. But give me 15 minutes to shower and I'll join you both for a drink." With that, Ed wandered off to the bedroom to shower and change.

"He's a good man, Kai. Please look after him."

Kai sensed the concern in her voice.

"I will, Leonora. As will my team. There are no guarantees in this business. But we put our client's life before our own."

"Having spent time getting to know you, Kai, I'm not sure I like the sound of that. But I know it's your job, and you choose to do it. All the same, I want you, Ed and your people to be safe."

"I am sure we will be, Leonora."

Ed walked back into the room, heading straight for the drinks cabinet. Grabbing a large brandy glass, he poured his favourite bedtime drink, then he sat down next to Leonora and Kai.

"So, I hope you two are getting on?"

"We've been getting on just fine, Ed," Leonora responded.

"Yes, Ed. I am hoping all the work I do for you will be as rewarding as this," Kai added.

"Good – because if the two women who will be closest to me don't get on, I'm in trouble!"

"We are all good, Ed. Although I must admit I wasn't expecting your bodyguard to be so darn good-looking," said Leonora, winking at Kai.

"I chose Kai for her skills, nothing more," said Ed as he too winked at Kai.

The three of them settled into conversation, eventually heading off to bed around 5 a.m. As Ed got into bed, he felt oddly relaxed. Odd, as it had been a long and challenging day. But more and more, he was starting to believe that real progress in curbing LPAS could be made, and sooner than he had initially hoped. A few minutes passed, and Leonora moved up beside him, kissed him passionately and said, "I know it's late, or early! And you've had a terrible day. But I hope you're not looking to go straight to sleep."

Sleep they did. But not until well after 6 a.m.

Ed got up around 11 a.m. His mind was racing; he had many meetings scheduled and needed some quality time to make notes and plan his approach to each session.

Pulling on a pair of sports shorts, he grabbed his phone and headed off to the main bathroom so as not to disturb Leonora. Opening the door, he walked in to find Kai sitting on the loo, naked.

"Oh God, sorry, Kai," said Ed as he made a hurried exit.

Scurrying to another bedroom, he locked himself in. He started to catch up with the news and sent out a few emails to his political team about the upcoming meetings.

Leonora got up an hour later and made breakfast, calling Ed and Kai to the table. A sheepish-looking Ed sat down, grabbed some toast and buried his head in his phone.

"Ed, please, don't be so rude at the table. Put the phone down," said a disappointed Leonora.

"I don't think he means to be rude, Leonora. I think he's embarrassed at having walked in on me while I was naked on the toilet!"

"Ed!" exclaimed Leonora.

"Kai, I'm so sorry. I am embarrassed."

"Ed, I'd have been embarrassed too had it not been for your face. I laughed as you scurried out of the bathroom. Think no more of it."

"Ed, isn't our en-suite good enough?"

"Yes, obviously, but I didn't want to disturb you, and, well, I wasn't thinking about other people being in the apartment."

"No, you weren't thinking. And going back to your comment last night about the two women closest to you getting on – you've now seen both those women naked!"

"Leonora, I couldn't be more sorry. Can we drop it?" said Ed, who was turning bright red.

"I know he is super-embarrassed, Kai. When we first made love, I told him the next morning that I'd learned a few things–"

Ed jumped in. "Leonora, stop it. We don't need to go there."

"Ed, shush, don't be such a prude... As I was saying, Kai. First, Ed thought I was talking about learning about his life. Then, when he realised what I meant, he turned a lovely red. But not as red as he is now!"

Both women burst out laughing, and Leonora stood up and pecked him on the forehead. "Yes, Ed. Enough said. Lucky for you, Kai has accepted your apology and is less embarrassed than you."

"Yes, yes, thank you, I know, I am truly sorry, Kai. And Leonora, we don't need to discuss intimate details with–"

Kai interrupted him. "With the *staff*, Ed?"

"No, I wasn't going to say with the staff. I was going to say with anyone, for God's sake! I think you two are enjoying this way too much." He started to get up, but Leonora pushed him back down.

"Okay, Ed. We've had our fun."

UNnatural Selection –
Twice scared, priority crystal clear

Ed had dinner with Gabriel Meyer in January while visiting the United Nations, and they'd kept in touch ever since. Gabriel was in London meeting with senior parliamentarians and the Prime Minister to discuss the growing problem of 'skirmishes', as no one wanted to use the word 'war'. These 'skirmishes' were breaking out in different parts of the world over water and land. LPAS would stop that happening, according to the legislation. Conflicts of this nature had initially reduced, but over the past year, the incidents were increasing once again.

Gabriel and Ed had planned for dinner during his trip, and Ed said he would host it at his apartment. Gabriel's security detail arrived first, checking out the apartment complex, garage and general area. Gabriel arrived around 7 p.m. with two close-protection officers, who gave Ed's apartment the once-over before withdrawing to stand guard outside the door.

"What can I get you to drink, Gabriel?"

"The wine I see on the side looks rather nice."

"A glass coming right up."

Ed poured them both a glass of wine and then went into the kitchen to check on dinner. He'd kept dinner simple, as he wanted to make the most of his time with Gabriel.

"I hope you like fish?"

"I do, Ed. Very much so."

"Good, as I've prepared a cold lobster salad to start, followed by a fillet of seabass with char-grilled vegetables."

"Sounds great, Ed. If it's good, I'll visit more often," said Gabriel, laughing at his own joke.

As they talked over dinner, Gabriel advised Ed that he felt he had enough commitment from delegates to win a non-binding vote on excluding vaccines from LPAS control.

Ed froze. "Wow," was his response as he leapt from the chair in excitement. "I wasn't expecting you to bring such great news. I'm stunned. I never thought we'd get to vote on vaccines again for some considerable time."

"Don't get too carried away, Ed. I still have to get the vote itself tabled and agreed. But if that happens, I'm reasonably sure we have the numbers to win it."

Ed was finding it difficult to contain himself and rushed off to the toilet to relieve himself, such was the impact of the news. In all his work against LPAS, this was the most significant development by far. The sheer idea that the votes were there was unreal and showed how the tide had started to turn against the LPAS laws. Suppose they could genuinely get enough 'yes' ballot papers to exclude vaccines, albeit in a non-binding vote. It would set the scene for a move to bring forward the date for voting on fundamental change to LPAS.

Ed returned from the bathroom still buzzing from the news, cleared the table and made them both a double espresso.

"I'm lost for words, Gabriel. You've made my decade."

"As I said, Ed, we've work to do to get a vote on the agenda, and the longer that takes, the more at risk the outcome will be. But I am hoping we can get it on the register by year end."

"It feels surreal. We only spoke on the phone a couple of weeks ago; you didn't know then?"

"I did know then, Ed. But having planned to be in London, I wanted to tell you in person and witness your reaction. And I must say it was worth it."

"I can't explain the emotions going through me at this moment. I'm so happy I could kiss you!"

"Had I known that, I've had told you on the phone!" quipped Gabriel.

"Seriously, Gabriel. I can't even remember what I was going to tell you before you dropped that bombshell."

"It couldn't have been that important, Ed. So why don't you pour us a glass of that red, and you can update me on how it's going with Leonora and why you haven't married her yet before she gets fed up with waiting."

This was the second time a friend had warned him regarding his relationship. Ed topped up their wine, and they headed into the living room, Ed sitting on the small sofa with his back to the window and Gabriel opposite, facing out.

"Not the best view, Gabriel. You'd prefer to look out of Leonora's windows. Much nicer view."

"Nice segue, Ed. So how are things with your lovely lady?"

As Ed started answering Gabriel's question, he heard a dull thud, followed by another. Turning, he could see two small white marks on the window, with what seemed like capillary-type squiggly lines emanating from all around the spots – what you'd expect to see on glass if you'd hit it with something. As Ed started to turn away, he noticed another appear, and another. He leapt to his feet, launching himself at Gabriel, who had a look of shock on his face, and he and Ed rolled over the top of the sofa and onto the floor.

"Stay down, Gabriel."

"Ed, what are you doing?"

"Someone's firing at the window!"

"What!"

"Just stay down." Ed belly-walked his way to the door and leapt to his feed in the hallway, opening the front door and screaming at the guards: "Someone's firing at the window!"

As one guard started talking to the security detail on the street, the other pulled his gun and ran into the apartment. Within a minute, he re-emerged, dragging Gabriel along the floor.

"More security are on their way up. We are safer in the hallway. Both of you, stay where you are."

The guard took up a position at the front door while his colleague kicked in the door opposite and slightly to the left of Ed's apartment, assuring the occupant they were safe, then took up position in the doorway. Soon, several guards appeared, telling Gabriel and Ed that they'd secured the underground car park and were taking them down to a waiting car.

The guards closest to them received the all-clear, grabbed Ed and Gabriel, and pulled them towards the lifts, almost throwing them inside.

This is cosy, Ed thought to himself. He and Gabriel in a lift meant for six people in the middle of at least eight! The doors opened, and two Range Rovers with blacked-out windows were immediately in front of them. A guard launched Ed and Gabriel into the back seats, and both cars sped up the ramp. The road was kept clear by other officers as the sound of police sirens grew louder.

"Sorry to be so rough, gentlemen," said a large, fit-looking man in the front passenger seat. They knew he was an officer with Special Branch. All Gabriel's guards were, except the two that accompanied him to the UK, and both were still at the apartment.

"We're going to take you to a government safe house until we understand better what's gone on tonight. We need you well away from anywhere people would expect you to be."

Gabriel turned to Ed. "I'm sorry, Ed. I don't know why anyone would want to kill me, but I'm sorry to have brought this to your door."

"Gabriel, it's not a problem, as long as you pick up the tab for the new window."

Gabriel gave a nervous laugh, followed by an equally nervous laugh from Ed. The Special Branch officer didn't seem to see the funny side.

As they continued their journey through London, Ed couldn't stop thinking that just maybe it wasn't Gabriel who was the target. Perhaps it was another attempt on his life?

At the safe house, one of the protection officers handed them coffee, then left the room, telling them that his boss would visit them soon and not to worry, as the house was very secure. Still in shock, both Ed and Gabriel sat sipping their coffee in silence before the officer from the car reappeared.

"You'll both be staying here tonight, and the PM is coming over to meet with you in the morning to convey a personal apology for what has happened this evening."

"Okay, thank you. And please thank the team for putting themselves in harm's way for us," Gabriel responded, downing the last of his coffee.

The officer grabbed the mugs and refilled them from a large pot on the side. "We still don't know much, but we've sealed off the apartment used by the gunman. Unfortunately, we found two people inside – we believe they were the owners. Both shot through the head."

Gabriel, a practising Catholic, touched his forehead and mentioned "the Father", then completed the cross by touching his right shoulder while saying "spirit". A prayer for the dead. Ed, an atheist, put his face in his hands at the loss of two innocent people, feeling sadness and guilt about their deaths.

"Earlier in the day, our people checked out the apartments opposite yours, Mr Thorncroft. And days before that, our team spoke with many of the occupants, including the couple found dead. We believe the shooter had come in late to minimise the risk of discovery, although we don't yet know how he got past security in the area."

"How do you know he hadn't been holed up a while in the apartment?" Ed asked.

"The lady of the house was dead in the hallway and her husband on the sofa. I don't wish to be graphic, but both bodies were warm."

Ed retched, holding his hand over his mouth in case he vomited up his seabass. "What kind of heartless bastard would do that?" he responded.

"Often the paid kind," the officer replied. "The would-be assassin cut a hole in the window and waited for you to enter the room. Lucky you've such good glass, Mr Thorncroft."

"What's that mean?" Gabriel asked.

"Bulletproof, Gabriel. My windows are bulletproof."

"Why, Ed?"

"It's linked to the terrorist attack I was caught up in. The security services believe I was the target."

"I never knew that, Ed."

"It isn't something anyone wanted in the public domain. But many changes were made as a result. One was the installation of bulletproof glass in the apartment. Although honestly I thought it was a waste of time, given that they could take me out on the street, or at the hospital. Any number of places."

"Could you have been the target, Ed?"

Before Ed answered, the officer interjected. "No,

Mr Thorncroft wasn't the target. The target was you, Mr Meyer."

"How do you know that?" came Gabriel's nervous response.

"Forensics have already measured the angle, and the shooter was aiming for you. On the fourth shot, I figure he recognised he wouldn't penetrate the glass and made his exit. We closed the area down very quickly, but as yet we've turned nothing up."

"That's why you asked us where we were seated on the way here?"

"Yes, Mr Thorncroft. It was important we knew early on who the target was," responded the officer.

Ed felt some relief but also deep concern for his friend. What would killing the UN secretary-general achieve? Ed thought to himself.

Only one UN secretary-general had ever been murdered, a murder not proven until 61 years after his death in a plane crash, and still disputed by many.

Ed woke early, still in his clothes, and wandered into the living room. Gabriel was already up, sipping coffee, and looked worn-out.

"I didn't get much sleep, Ed."

"I'm not surprised, Gabriel."

"No, I don't mean I sat up all night thinking about the events; I've been on calls almost non-stop, and I've had to put the mobile on silent, I'm receiving so many text messages."

Ed experienced one of those dreadful heart-stopping moments.

"Oh, shit, I haven't called Leonora. How did I not do that? My phone is at the apartment, and she must be wondering where I am."

"No, Ed. She won't be. Our names are all over the news, as is your apartment block. I think she knows."

"Can I–"

Gabriel interrupted him mid-flow. "Yes, Ed. Take the phone."

He called Leonora, and her voice gave away her emotional state. "Hello, Leonora speaking..." She hadn't recognised the number.

"Leonora, it's Ed. I'm sorry, I–"

She broke in. "I was out of my mind for hours until it came on the news that you and Gabriel were safe. And you couldn't have called me, Ed?"

"It was thoughtless, I know. I can't explain why I didn't."

"No, Ed, you can't – but I think I can." Leonora hung up.

Ed, panicking, called out to the guard, telling him he needed a car.

"Problem, Ed?" Gabriel said, a look of disapproval on his face. "How the hell did you not manage to call her?"

"I don't know, Gabriel. How bloody thoughtless and stupid."

"I agree. And telling her you left your mobile at the apartment isn't going to cut it."

"Thanks, Gabriel, nice piece of advice – not!"

The senior Special Branch officer entered the room, advising Ed that he could go if he wished, and they'd have a car take him where he wanted to go, but that the Prime Minister was due soon and didn't he want to wait for him?

Gabriel jumped in. "I don't figure he wants to tell his girlfriend he was further delayed because he had to speak with the PM."

"You're not helping, Gabriel," Ed snapped.

"I know, Ed. I do not intend to. Get off. Get off and let Leonora know how much you love her before she gives up on you."

Ed got in the car and gave the police driver Leonora's address. He was scared last night, and even more so during the terror attack. But not as scared as he was now. He couldn't fathom why he hadn't called her.

What's the matter with me? he thought to himself. Momentarily, it crossed his mind to propose when he arrived, so Leonora would understand how much he loved her. But he knew she'd see that as a reaction to his grievous oversight, and that it would likely alienate her.

Arriving at the apartment, Ed went up in the lift and knocked on the door. A minute later, he knocked again. Leonora opened up, and her look of anguish was frightening. Her face was a mess from sobbing, and her top was wet and snotty. She walked away from the door without saying a word. Ed stepped inside and grabbed her shoulders from behind, attempting to turn her around. Leonora shook him off, turned and hit him square in the face with an open hand.

Ed sucked it up and leant in, holding her shoulders again, only to be pushed back and slapped again. Leonora had never behaved like this.

"Leonora, please, I want to say let me explain, but I can't explain how I was so thoughtless."

Leonora, still saying nothing, her face etched with pain, walked over and sat on the sofa. She raised her eyes to Ed, making him go cold, such was the devasting look on her face.

"For hours I called your mobile; it just rang and rang. I left voice messages, I sat clinging to my phone, waiting – no, praying it would ring and I'd hear your voice. I called the police. I called anyone who might be able to let me know you were okay. No one knew – or wouldn't say. I eventually curled up in the fetal position; I couldn't cry anymore. I feel guilty when I say I didn't feel that sick, that much pain, even when my father died. And then a friend called, saying she was so relieved to hear that you were okay."

"Imagine her surprise when she realised I didn't know. I should have jumped for joy, relief, excitement, happy you were alive. And I *was* relieved. The pain ebbed away, and my friend said she'd catch up with me later and that she'd let me get on. I know what she was thinking because I was thinking it too: how humiliating to be told your boyfriend is safe by a friend calling you. Imagine that, Ed. Imagine, along with the grief, convinced as I was that I'd lost you, hearing it from a friend and not you. That says a lot about how you feel about me, doesn't it?"

Leonora fell silent for a few seconds. "Leave, Ed. Please leave. I can't deal with this now. I need space."

Ed was terrified that if he left, it would be over but was also gravely concerned about what would happen if he pushed it.

"Leonora, please, let me stay. I'll say nothing; I'll sit here. I don't want to leave. I'm scared that if I leave now, it will never be the same for us."

"Ed, I love you so, so much. I can't imagine loving anyone the way I love you. But your work at the hospital, your political work... it is what gets you up in the morning... it's what drives you, gives you life... Oh, yes, I'm sure you love me. But I have to recognise that I come a close second. And I'm sorry, but that's not enough for me."

Ed was rudderless. He had no clue which direction to take the conversation but knew instinctively that he had one shot at getting it right. In deep thought about what to say next, he stopped analysing and just said what came naturally. Kneeling beside Leonora, he said:

"Leonora, please hear me out. Please don't shut me down. Let me speak." He paused briefly, hoping she would say nothing. She didn't respond.

"I've no excuse. Yes, I could give reasons, none of which would justify my not calling. Tomorrow I'll resign from the hospital, and I'll leave politics too. I told you that without you, I didn't know where my life would be, and I meant it. Without you, life would just be miserable. I would not find happiness with anyone else in the way I have with you.

"Don't shut me out, don't end what we have. The pain and hurt I've caused you, I could see it when you opened the door. But I'll never allow that to happen again."

Ed fell silent, continuing to look at Leonora, hoping for a sign she'd listened. Leonora looked up at him, her eyes dark red and leathery, like third-degree burns, her face blotchy and puffed up, snot in her hair and round her nose. And then a stream of tears rolled down her face. Ed took a gamble, leaned in and pulled her towards him. What seemed an eternity passed before Leonora gave eye contact.

"I want to hit you, Ed. I want to hurt you, tell you to go. You've hurt me so much and I can't understand it, even more so as you can't, either. But I never thought you would give everything up for me.

"I know how vital a part of your life it is to save other people's lives. And I know that your political work fighting LPAS is for that same reason.

"If you had tried to justify not calling or made excuses, had you said anything other than what you did, it would be over between us. And that would have been the most heart-rending decision I could ever make. I could not imagine life without you. But I could not live with being second place and living with the possibility of going through what I went through last night all over again."

"Leonora, I know it will take time to forgive me, to forget what you've gone through, because of my incomprehensible lack of..." Ed paused. "...lack of just about everything decent. Seeing you when you opened the door floored me. I can't forgive myself and I can't justify it. But tomorrow I'll put it right."

You had to have been close to Ed over the previous years to grasp the extent of what he was giving up for Leonora. And Leonora knew it to be a huge testament to his love.

"Ed, I could see it in your eyes and feel it in your body language. You meant every word of it, and I know that, without me intervening, you would give it all up tomorrow. But that would be selfish. People would die who don't need to. And it would set back the chance of pushing back the LPAS by many years. I can't let you do that. Every fibre of my body wants to. But I could not live with myself if I allowed you to give up what you do.

"It is enough for me to know that you would. I needed to hear that, although I never thought I would."

Ed grabbed Leonora's face, kissing her, but she pushed him back forcefully.

"I'm sorry, Leonora, you need time; I understand."

"You're right, Ed. I need time. I need to clean up my face and shower.

Then you can kiss me."

Leonora went to the bathroom, leaving Ed in the living room. As he sat on the floor, he questioned his thinking. Not calling Leonora was as thoughtless as anything could be, and he genuinely did not know why he hadn't. And not just why he hadn't, but why he hadn't even thought of it. It reinforced just how much was going on inside his head, and he knew he needed a break.

It was clear to Ed that she did not want him to give up his medical career or political work. However, he needed and wanted a break from both – no, all three – of his jobs. The stress and high workload were the only explanation he had for screwing up so badly. He now needed to set out a plan – and he would surprise Leonora by announcing a lengthy sabbatical. A period during which he could focus on their relationship.

And he would start by asking her to marry him.

UNnatural Selection –
Announcing his intent

Ed's inner circle were gathering at the farm in the big cottage, and, unusually, Ed would be last to arrive. At around 8 p.m., Rage Millstream shouted, "Quiet," and added, "Ed's arriving – I can hear the drone." Ed had called the meeting at short notice, telling them it wouldn't take longer than an hour, and asked that, if possible, they make themselves available. This gave rise to significant disquiet. And when Ed entered the cottage, you could hear a pin drop.

"Who's died?" he commented as he sat down.

"We were hoping you are going to tell us, Ed," Covey Twinks replied, never one to hold back.

"I get it. You think I've come bearing bad news. I've not, but it is important news."

"Okay, Ed. Spit it out. The suspense is killing us," replied Ashlin, who was trying to tighten the hands on a clock she'd knocked over just before he had arrived.

"Yes, out with it, please, Ed. Before Ashlin breaks anything else," said Brindle.

Ed explained that he planned to take a long break from POLO, politics and the hospital. But he needed to close everything out cleanly first. Kimmy asked how long he planned to be out.

"I figure three months," Ed responded.

"You said a long break," Gig commented.

"Two weeks would be a very long break for Ed, I know, so three months is like a bloody lifetime," was Jail's view. "I think it's the right thing to do, Ed. You've been at it full time almost every day for the best part of a decade."

"Thanks, Jail. I do far less on the POLO side now anyway, so I'm sure you'll not miss me."

"We'll miss you, Ed. Your drive, energy, encouragement, critiques of plans you read, and general guidance, are ever present. But we'll do just fine." That was Jesse Omaha's opinion, and everyone nodded in agreement.

"Any idea on timing, Ed?" Creak wanted to know.

"Not sure; sometime after the LSU meeting with Charly."

"Ed, I told you I should deal with that, especially while there is still a high risk. It makes sense me doing it until we are sure."

"Thanks, Jail. But we've had this conversation ad nauseam. We've vetted the group all we can, and we've promised Charly a meeting with the head of POLO. If we are going to work with this group, they have to trust us just as we need to trust them. So I'll go ahead with the plan and exit POLO activity shortly after New York."

"Still going ahead with the NY trip, then?" Brindle inquired.

"Yes, Brindle. New York isn't about me. It's about Leonora's first big step into fighting LPAS. It's her show, and I won't cancel that. I'm looking forward to learning from her. She's an amazing speaker."

Jail returned to their first point. "Okay, Ed. It was worth a try, though." He knew Ed wouldn't change his mind about meeting Charly but had wanted to push it one more time.

"Rage, Hood, nothing from either of you?"

"You'll be missed, Ed. That's all I have to say," said Marcelle (Hood).

"Only thing I want to say, Ed, is recharge – but come back." It was clear from the way she said it that another possibility concerned her.

"Rage, I'd miss your blow-ups far too much to leave for good."

"Thanks, good to know that's all you'd miss about me!"

"Now, Rage, I'm joking. And I'll miss you all, for a great many reasons. I do need the time off, though. I didn't realise just how much until recently. I'll come back so refreshed you'll be wishing I hadn't returned after a week!"

"You're unusually quiet, Ashlin."

"I won't lie, Ed, I'm a little worried, and a little sad, too. You've given your all for over eight years; so, yes, you deserve a break. You've endured so much more than any of us. Frankly, I don't know how you've kept going. POLO will be fine; Jail's a great leader. But I think the political arm will slow a little, as it is clear that all the driving is happening because of you.

"However, my main worry is the hospital. There's no other A&E doctor that comes close to what you do or has anything like the respect you command. That's where the more significant impact will be, in my view."

Ashlin and Ed were extremely close – closer than Ed was to Jennifer, so it was always clear that Ashlin would feel it more than the other team members. Ed wasn't going to say it now, but he planned to get some time alone with Ashlin before his break.

"Thank you all, and thank you, Ashlin. I said it wouldn't take long. So unless you've more questions, we can go home."

"What, no long goodbye, Ed?" Brindle quipped.

"I haven't gone yet and I don't like goodbyes."

Ed asked Gig to arrange transport for them all, advising he'd go last. He stepped outside as the first drone arrived, and as each member was leaving, he hugged them and shared a few private words. Ashlin was the last to fly out, as Brindle lived at the farm. He hugged her, and she got a little teary.

"Hey, cut it out. I'm just taking a break. I'll be back before you know it." Ashlin kissed him and climbed into her ride, and as the drone took off, Brindle approached.

"We'll watch out for her, Ed. You've been the constant in her life at the hospital and in POLO. But we will take good care of her."

"I know you will, Brindle."

As Ed's drone touched down, he hugged Brindle, thanked him for all his support and got inside.

Ed had found the meeting hard. They were a close-knit group and only had each other to speak to about their work. He'd miss all of them, and the job too. But his health, and more importantly to him, his relationship with Leonora, was paramount.

Ed was up early, as today he was meeting with the hospital board.

He was going to let them know that he would be taking time out, and there was no guarantee that, when he was ready to return, a role would be available. But that wasn't something that caused him concern. When his political work started, he took the lead in A&E less frequently, giving up a number of responsibilities to other consultants. So taking time out from A&E would be less impactful, but he realised it would still affect the hospital.

Suited and ready to go, he sat on the bed beside Leonora, kissing her shoulder and inadvertently waking her up.

"You off, Ed?"

"Yes, wish me luck."

"You don't need it. They'll be fine. They'll likely try and get you to reduce your time off. But otherwise it'll be fine."

The plan was for three months out, but he'd been vague with Leonora on this point. He hadn't mentioned that he would be doing the same on the political side. And of course she knew nothing of POLO.

Leonora was now more involved in politics and had started to speak at conferences against the LPAS laws, having given up almost all her charity work. And soon she would be on a bigger stage, in New York. Something Ed was looking forward to.

He had held back enough of his plans so that it would still be a big surprise when he told her at the end of their NY trip that they'd have three months together without interruption. He felt like a big kid and couldn't wait to have that particular conversation.

Walking into the hospital boardroom, Ed felt like a naughty schoolboy going up before the headmaster. He sat in front of the board and outlined his plans for a break, advising them that it would be at least three months, and maybe six. When it was time to return, he wanted to focus on politics first, followed by POLO, then ease himself back into his work as a consultant. So advising them that it would be three to six months seemed appropriate.

As Leonora had suggested, the board spent some time trying to persuade him otherwise, including the guilt trip. Finally, realising it wouldn't work, one of the directors stupidly advised him that there might not be a job for him when he was ready to return.

"I fully understand that, and I've no problem with it. I'll take longer off until something comes up somewhere else."

It was clear that a few of the members weren't happy with their colleague's comment and quickly assured Ed that they'd be sure to get him back on board when he was ready to return, which somewhat embarrassed the director who'd said otherwise.

As Ed left the room, Cato came out and told Ed he'd miss him. "Steady, Cato. You're dropping your guard. I'll start to think you like me if you're not careful."

Cato laughed, again telling Ed he'd miss him, and Ed said likewise before heading back down to A&E to finish his day.

A nervous Ed walked into the studios of a holographic video company. They operated the most advanced holographic video service available. Nothing was physically in the room other than a chair and desk. The system would project the image of virtual participants into the space.

The technology was so good it never took too long before you forgot that the other participants weren't in the room. They all sat at the same style of slightly curved desk, and all would be seated at a different part of the desk in their room from where other participants sat. Each room was the same size, and engaging the system made it appear as if everyone were sitting around a large round table together.

The number of people now reporting directly to Ed in the political wing of POLO – not that they knew they were part of POLO – was 15, and all, with three exceptions, were stationed outside the UK. Those stationed in the UK spent a great deal of time in other countries or at the UN, as was the case today: only Ed was in the UK for the session.

Ed opened by explaining his plans for a long break and that at present not even Leonora was aware that he would be taking a sabbatical from his political work. He had to ensure they would not tell her, as many of them now worked with her too. There was some concern, but not to the same extent as he had experienced with his POLO leadership team or the hospital board. They feared a lack of direction but agreed that it was right for Ed to take some time off.

One of the team asked when his break would start. Ed answered that he planned to begin his vacation immediately after his and Leonora's trip to the US, where Leonora was to speak at some universities, open gatherings and at a couple of UN forums.

Ed would accompany her, but he had a light political schedule, with few meetings. The trip was predominantly Leonora's show, and he wasn't planning to break until afterwards, as she was very much looking forward to it, as was he.

The team wished him well, told him to enjoy his down time, and that some of them would see him in the US before the break.

"Mum's the word, folks. Please don't slip up in front of Leonora."

Olivia Olsson, whom Ed had hired after meeting her in Kenya, teased him, saying she would get on the phone with Leonora and spill the beans. Ed jumped up and playfully lunged at her, forgetting she wasn't there. That caused everyone in the virtual room to laugh, realising that Ed had momentarily forgotten.

"That single act proves you do need a break, Ed," Amelie chided him. Amelie was the analyst Ed had met and had offered a job, an offer she took up some weeks later.

"That aside, Amelie, I can assure you I do." With that, Ed closed the session.

That was the last act of informing people about his plans, other than to come clean with Leonora about stopping all activity and that he would do so for three months. Having done the hard work of notifying everyone, he started to feel relatively relaxed and noticed that his stress levels had dropped dramatically over the past few days.

He'd started to read a novel, something he hadn't done for a long time. Feeling more chilled, his mind gave flight to a minor concern: that maybe he wouldn't want to return after three months. But no, he knew he would. He'd return re-energised and, unbeknown to anyone else, he'd also be engaged to the most amazing woman.

A little voice popped into his head as he had that thought: *She might say no!*

"Geez, she might."

Ed quickly pushed the thought away. However, the reason he had had this qualm would become apparent when he proposed...

Ed walked into Leonora's apartment, went up to her and started a passionate session, undressing her and himself while moving her towards the bedroom.

"Ed, what's come over you? It's three in the afternoon."

"The time doesn't matter. I've been thinking of you since I left."

"Ed, you've not been gone that long, and we had sex less than eight hours ago!"

"That's a no, then?" He started to back off.

"Don't be silly," came Leonora's reply.

Ed recommenced undressing them both, moving steadily towards the bedroom. Leonora commented that if the mere thought of reducing his workload had this effect, maybe he should make it permanent.

UNnatural Selection –
Sad last visit, for a while

Above the domed chapel at Brompton Cemetery, not too long after midnight, hung a clear sky and full moon, just as it had been on a night that had haunted Ed ever since. That was the night Ed gave an order for his best friend, Hans Pelletise, to be killed – *stopped*, as he first put it, having been too scared to say out loud what he meant. Stopped to ensure Hans could not expose Ashlin Steeple for her work against LPAS.

Hardly a week passed without Ed recalling that night, and that was the reason that at least once each month, Ed returned to the chapel to think of his friend. Hans wasn't just his best friend. In Ed's view, he was one of the best, if not *the* best, neurosurgeons in the country.

Ed knew the pain and grief would forever stay with him. It would always grieve him to have to use the past tense when thinking of his friend. Past tense because of his orders.

He was squatting on the floor in the chapel beside one of the Corinthian columns. It appeared to Ed as if someone was playing a holographic movie, so vivid were the pictures in his head, seemingly projected in front of him. Pictures of himself and Hans discussing, arguing, then fighting over Hans revealing Ashlin's involvement in an anti-LPAS activity...

At that time, the cemetery grounds had been boarded up for 10 years while a legal battle ensued around a memorial for Emmeline Pankhurst, a political activist best known for organising the suffragette movement. Within a few months of Hans's death, Ed had purchased the site. The owners were glad to see the back of it, and Ed agreed to a large memorial for Emmeline.

Ed's plan, selfishly, would see a beautiful garden built, with large stones scattered around the grounds in tribute to good people who had died worthy of remembering. The stone he wanted to lay most was a stone for his friend, Hans.

As he left the dome, he knew it would be his last visit for a while, as work was due to start on restoring the chapel, colonnades, catacombs, and as many of the original graves as possible, including significant landscaping work. Ed couldn't wait to see it finished and lay a stone in memory of Hans.

A little after 1 a.m., as Ed left the cemetery, a motorcycle officer pulled up to investigate as he saw Ed squeezing himself out of the grounds between the broken and twisted boards.

"Sir," the officer shouted, "you shouldn't be in there."

Ed walked towards the police officer, saying, "I'm sorry, I was just trying to picture it as it will look when restoration and the new park are complete." As Ed got a little closer, the officer recognised him.

"I'm sorry, Mr Thorncroft, I hadn't recognised you at first."

"That's okay, officer."

"It's a nice thing you are doing, sir," responded the policeman.

"Thank you. There isn't enough open space in London anymore, since planning permission and rules protecting historic buildings changed in the early 2030s. As a result, building projects are now consuming all open space."

"Yes, sir, but with over 12 million people living in London, what choice do we have?"

"Quite," Ed responded. "But I'm sure that problem will be solved in short order by the destruction of life caused by the LPAS laws."

"I know you are fighting hard to have the LPAS laws changed, sir. I watch you whenever you are giving speeches on the changes needed. I too believe LPAS is wrong. It surely can't be right letting so many people die when it needn't be that way. But while the law is in place, I must uphold it." With that, the officer said, "Have a good morning," and rode off.

UNnatural Selection –
Meeting Charly – LSU head

Ed and Covey would travel to the Lake District to meet the head of LSU, an organisation involved in illegal life-saving in the same way as they were. Charly Bemelle had set up and ran the group, and both Creak and Covey had been working to ensure it wasn't a dummy group for more than a year. Creak had met Charly and other key LSU folks on three occasions, although it was Covey who took the lead, and hence the most significant risk, meeting Charly on four occasions before Creak. All the intelligence on the group and Charly had checked out, so Ed would now meet Charly himself. This would be Ed's last outing before taking a break. Leonora thought he was away teaching.

The meeting was to take place in a large rented house in Underskiddaw, Cumbria, in the north-west of England, a beautiful location close to Lake Bassenthwaite. It was chosen as it was far away from Ed and Charly's operations and an easy place to guard. Since forming POLO, Ed had always believed that forming alliances with other groups in the fight against LPAS would be beneficial.

The main reason this hadn't happened sooner was the enormous risk attached to hooking up with other groups. There could always be a dummy group set up to catch those fighting the law. Or it could be that their security wasn't as effective as POLO's; or perhaps they were under surveillance. Not that POLO itself was immune to many of these issues.

Ed and Covey would travel separately, albeit on the same train, to the Lake District and then on to the house in separate hire cars.

Guardians had been in the area for several weeks, along with an advance group of bodyguards. They had encountered nothing suspicious in the area, so far. They had also staked out the house for over a month, including bugging the house and using sophisticated listening equipment.

Handles initially used had been swapped for real names as the relationship grew tighter between Charly, Covey, Creak and a couple of Charly's inner circle. Ed would not use his handle when meeting Charly, as, quite obviously, Charly would know him immediately, such was his public profile. Jail had warned Ed against the meeting, saying that he should do it, as head of POLO operations. Ed agreed that it was high risk, but he had well-thought-out ideas about how such alliances could work and wanted to run any integration or cooperation agreement himself.

"Ed, why not let me take this one? Give it a few more months, and if all is well, you can then step in."

"I hear you loud and clear, Jail. I've heard you loud and clear every time you've suggested it! I'm not down-playing the risk, but it is my risk to take, not yours. I wanted this to happen, and should it go south, I want you and as many of our folks as possible protected. Continuing to offer yourself up isn't going to change my mind."

"Ed, you are far more important to POLO than I am. You *are* POLO."

"Nice of you to say, and true at the start, but not now, Jail. I have a strong team, and you, Brindle or Creak could run the group comfortably. Honestly, you run it better than I do. Your operational skills are much better than mine; that's why you now run the day-to-day. It wasn't simply to give me time for the legal side of our operations. I knew you'd do a better job operationally than I could ever do."

"I appreciate your confidence in me, Ed. But it makes me so nervous, you stepping in to meet these folks. Sure, we've vetted them best we can, and all looks to be above board. But my doubts are still playing on my mind."

Ed and Jail talked a while longer, and Jail warned Ed about one of Charly's sidekicks, whom he knew from conversations with Creak, and who Ed would take a dislike to.

"Ed, if he's present at the meetings, try and ignore Hagen Crumbier. Telling him to piss off at your first meeting with Charly won't help cement the relationship!"

"Jail, you don't normally see fit to warn me in this way. Especially about someone you haven't met. So why this guy?"

"Creak has briefed me on all the players he has interacted with thus far. Hagen, according to Creak, has your pet personality hate by the bucketload! He told me, 'Crumbier is likely the most obsequious person I have ever met.' He also said his fawning over Charly made him want to puke."

Jail explained that Hagen was a gofer, for want of a better description. Creak had found him to be insecure and of low ability, which explained his nature. Creak said he saw him as a "person of concern", and within the security circles, someone with such a personality would be unlikely to make the cut.

"So all I'm saying, Ed, is don't blow your top with him. If you're lucky, he didn't get an invite."

"I hear you, Jail, and I wish Creak had seen fit to warn me. Has Creak discussed with Charly the security concerns he has?"

"No, Ed. Not yet. He felt we needed stronger relationships with this group before raising such concerns about people they may have had around since the group's formation."

"Okay, I get it... Or are you having one last-ditch attempt at getting me to pull out and put you in instead?"

"No, Ed. I know you better than that. But I wanted you to be aware that he's a security concern. And secondly, he is likely to irk you."

Ed parked up close to the house's main entrance, and Covey was already parked up waiting. As they approached the house, the main door opened, and an elegantly dressed, slim blonde lady walked out to greet them. "Hi, I'm Charly – Charly Bemelle – but please call me Chick."

"Hi, I'm–"

Charly interrupted Ed mid-flow. "No need, I recognised you as soon as you got out of the car. But I must say, Covey and Creak kept who you are very tight to their chest. I wasn't expecting Edward Thorncroft to be the head of POLO!"

"Well," replied Ed, "I wasn't aware that the head of LSU was a lady. They kept that close to their chest too." As he finished his sentence, he glanced over to Covey disapprovingly.

Covey piped up. "Sorry, Ed. I didn't think that was relevant!"

Ed smiled, and Charly quipped, "I don't think that secret had the same impact as me seeing you turn up! Please, come in."

Entering the house, they made their way to the main living area, and Charly introduced Ed to her second in command.

"This is Demetre Harping. He's been at my side since I started the group, and I'd trust him with my life. I *have* trusted him with my life. We first met when he was in charge of my cancer care."

Ed was focused intently on Demetre and had gone into a trance. "Ed," said Covey, while giving him a gentle shove. "Snap out of it."

"I'm sorry; I do that on occasion," he said in an apologetic tone, while Covey was thinking that 'on occasion' was a stretch!

"I know you," Ed said, continuing to stare at Demetre. "I thought I knew you before Charly introduced us. You had a young oncology registrar by the name of Jennifer Skull working for you. She introduced us at a medical conference some years ago. It was a brief hello, but Jennifer spoke highly of you. Your face and name have stayed with me."

"I'm sorry, Edward, I don't recall having met you, but Jennifer worked for me and, without question, was the best registrar I've had. I recall reading some time ago that she killed herself in prison while awaiting trial for contravening the LPAS laws. The case never mentioned her being part of an organisation fighting LPAS. I thought she'd just got together with a few other doctors to save the lives of children who were in hospital with cancer. I assume, however, she was working for you?"

"She was – and still does, in many ways. Her memory and sacrifice are among a handful of drivers that keep me going. Keep me focused on saving lives, even when the personal cost of doing so is high. Jennifer wasn't caught working for POLO and wasn't linked to POLO by the police. It is this fact that made her arrest and subsequent death much harder. I failed to get Jennifer what she needed, which led to her going it alone."

At this point, Charly jumped in. "This is getting way too depressing, gentlemen. Let's eat. We have much to discuss."

At dinner, they introduced themselves in more detail, with Ed being the exception, as what he did, aside from POLO, was already well known to Charly and Demetre, and Ed wasn't too open at this point to say much about POLO or his personal life.

"So, Charly, you said Demetre was in charge of your cancer care?"

"Yes, and we became good friends during that time."

As the conversation continued, Ed learned that Charly was a geneticist and had met Demetre when a friend recommended him to her as someone she should consider to take charge of her cancer treatment.

"I was scared during my treatment, even though cancer advances made success almost a given, and treatment short. I wasn't frightened by cancer but by the fact that Demetre was treating me illegally. He gave up his own time and took significant risks to ensure that I beat it. So when I decided to set up Life Savers UK (LSU), I asked him to help me get the group up and running. I already knew his views on LPAS. And he had already broken the law to save my life, so the risk of asking him wasn't high."

"I started the group in 2044, and we are now saving a great many lives each month."

"When did you start cancer treatment?" Ed continued to probe.

"March 2040; but LPAS stopped my treatment almost before it had begun. I was initially assured that my treatment would be allowed to progress, given that it would almost certainly beat the cancer within weeks. I remember it well. On day two of my treatment, Demetre sat me down and told me that he was no longer allowed to medicate me and that pain relief would be all he could prescribe. I was devastated. It was almost certainly a death sentence.

"Demetre prescribed pain killers, and I left the clinic. Late that same evening, the doorbell rang, and when I opened it, Demetre was standing there. He told me he had stolen some drugs and that he would continue my treatment at home. He took an enormous risk for me."

Demetre jumped in. "Not really, Charly. It was the early days of LPAS, and they hadn't got their act together. So it was unlikely that I'd be caught."

"Maybe, maybe not," Charly responded. "But all the same, you took action that would have ended your career and liberty if you had been found out."

"I agree with Charly," said Ed. "It was a big call, regardless of how you perceived the risk."

Demetre responded. "I remember walking away from Charly having given her the news that her treatment would stop, and I thought, no, this is crazy. This lady is going to die when we can easily save her. I could not have lived with myself had I not taken the action I did."

Ed warmed to Charly and Demetre, although he still had his guard up. And he knew this would be the case for some time, and that his cautious approach was necessary.

Now in the lounge, the conversation continued. "Your group have way more sophisticated technology than LSU, which leaves me wondering how we've been so lucky, having suffered few setbacks," remarked Charly.

"It didn't start that way for POLO; we've just been lucky to have some excellent technologists in the group who have continued to strengthen security, especially around communications. Likewise, physical security is masterminded by others of equal talent."

"And I understand you have a rule that says only those who need to know someone's identity should know it?"

UNnatural Selection –
Very different ops

"That's right, Charly. But it doesn't always work out that way. Members do get to know others, but as far as we can, we stick to that protocol."

"Not everyone in LSU knows everyone, but we've not had such a rule. I now think we should have."

"Charly, I'm happy to have some of my people help you with security if you wish. There are protocols we have that I would not divulge, but I believe those we can share would be highly beneficial to your group."

Ed was keen to help Charly however he could while ensuring he protected POLO. He was reasonably sure that Charly and her people were legitimate, but caution would be paramount for months, if not years. Linking with other groups was dangerous, even if they were legitimate. Ed reiterated that aside from Charly, Demetre and a couple of other LSU operatives who'd been engaged initially with Covey and Creak, no one else within LSU should be aware of POLO's name. And that for now, only Charly and Demetre should know he was associated with POLO. Furthermore, real names were not to be used when referring to POLO operatives.

He made it clear to Charly that any breach would see an end to their cooperation.

"I understand your concerns, Ed. And I assure you we will not breach your security rules. I'm just so pleased we've managed to hook up. I believe our groups will bring significant benefits to one another."

"Okay, Charly, then we should move forward – cautiously. Covey will select a senior member of our team as your main interface, and I'd ask that you do the same. You and I should plan to meet or at least talk every two weeks, once we have ironed out communications and protocols, if okay with you?"

"That's all good, Ed, and please call me Chick. Everyone else does."

"Okay, Charly, Chick it is." Ed didn't particularly like Charly's nickname; he thought it rude. But she did, and that was what counted.

"From our side, Ed, I'll put forward Hagen Crumbier, one of my closest operators."

Upon hearing the name, Ed couldn't contain himself.

"No, Charly, I'd prefer Demetre – if that's okay with the both of you?"

"Okay... We can do that. Should I be concerned about your tone when I mentioned Hagen?"

"Let's not get into that here, Charly. But I owe you an explanation, which I'd prefer we did one on one?"

"Okay, Ed. One on one is fine." But Charly was a little concerned. Ed hadn't met Hagen, so it was clear that Covey, Creak, or both, had briefed against him. For now, she'd wait to hear what Ed had to say. But she couldn't imagine what the issue was.

As the evening progressed, the four became more relaxed in each other's company. So much so that Ed's bookings at a nearby hotel were cancelled, as he decided they could stay at the rented house, allowing for a much longer evening together. Finally, as the clock in the hallway chimed three times, Charly said she thought they should retire, as she'd arranged breakfast prepared off site, and arriving early morning.

As Ed got into bed, he went over some of what he'd learned.

Charly's team didn't attend accidents. They'd long considered that to be a hazardous undertaking. Ed too had always been acutely aware of the risks associated with plucking people from a road accident, or for that matter a building site after an accident, or other similar situations. But he was driven to do so by the nature of his role as a doctor. He thought that not saving the lives of those involved in road or work accidents was wrong, as all but a tiny percentage of them would almost certainly otherwise die, if not provided with life-saving treatment or drugs.

Charly's group focused on helping people who had bacterial infections, viruses, cancer, heart conditions, et cetera. And that was most likely the reason that Charly's lack of sophisticated technology hadn't brought the house crashing down on her: her group avoided the risky saves. Furthermore, her group performed very few operations, and those that did go ahead were directly linked to a patient already being treated with drugs. Their focus was solely on saving lives using appropriate drugs. And they were saving many thousands, primarily operating outside London.

Ed saw this as a huge plus, as he planned to tap into Charly's network, improve it with skills Charly did not have, and build safe medical houses outside London. In his mind, he was mulling over the idea of absorbing Charly's group into POLO. He'd require Charly's full support, and it would mean prominent roles for both her and Demetre.

However, even if Charly agreed, it wouldn't be quick to affect. A great deal of vetting of the LSU team would have to occur, and many safe operating houses would need to be purchased. And that was just for starters. Ed did, however, see a real upside to such a move.

As for Charly, she retired with her own set of thoughts on the benefits of linking up with POLO. She hadn't, though, considered what was in Ed's mind. She saw the upside of tapping into Ed's group's expertise, allowing her to strengthen LSU and make it more secure. She also retired thinking about Ed's push-back on Hagen, who had been with her for two years. She had decided to have that discussion with Ed before he left. Of course, he was entitled to a view, even if his team had passed on that view. But she had complete confidence in Hagen and was, to be honest, a little put out by Ed's response.

A tap on the bedroom door woke Ed. It was 6 a.m. and having retired at 3 a.m. and slept little, he didn't much feel like getting up, but get up he did. Finally, at 6:45, he arrived downstairs in the dining room. Covey, already at the table sipping coffee, smirked and put her head down as he walked in.

"Okay, Covey. I know, I look dreadful."

"Sorry, Ed, yes, you do!"

"Unlike you, I might add!"

Covey was perfectly turned out, in a lovely grey zip-back tie-neck pencil dress.

"You look amazing, Covey. I, however, look like I feel. Had I slept, three hours would barely have been enough. But I don't think I did, or at least not for long enough to have noticed."

On that note, Charly entered the kitchen in a stunning, mainly blue, floral sheath dress, perfect hair and make-up, and looking as bright as a button.

"I give up!" Ed exclaimed.

"Sorry, Ed?" was Charly's response, looking puzzled.

"Ignore him, Charly. He's upset that we look amazing, and he looks like someone just dragged him through a hedge."

That comment had Charly, then Covey, in fits of laughter, only silenced by the doorbell ringing. Sniggering, Charly said, "I'm sorry, Ed, that was funny! I'll get the door. It'll be the breakfast arriving."

Before Charly returned, Demetre entered the kitchen.

"Aargh! Good. Now I don't feel so bad."

"Sorry, Ed?" Now Demetre was looking confused.

"You don't want to know what Ed's thinking, Demetre," responded Covey with a bright and smiley face.

"Okay, I won't ask."

"Best not," said Ed.

Charly returned to the kitchen with two large boxes and suggested they decamp to the lounge while she sorted out the breakfast. Gulping back a large mug of extra-strong coffee, Ed moved to the lounge with Demetre and Covey. Not too long after, Charly wheeled in a trolley laden with fresh juices, toast, pastries, eggs, bacon, you name it.

"Okay, I'm not playing Mum, so grab a plate and tuck in," she said, grabbing herself a plate.

"Before we settle into this feast, I want to say something before I forget. I've enjoyed our time together and do believe we can form a productive partnership. My cautious approach won't change but spending more time together will help us grow in confidence. I'm hoping I'm not wrong, but I've not warmed to two people as much as you guys in such a short space of time in a while. I hope that's a good omen. I hope my instinct is right."

"Thanks, Ed. You don't mince your words, so I'm pleased by your early read. I feel the same."

A short while after the four of them had sat down to breakfast, Ed's earpiece beeped, meaning one of his external team wanted to talk to him. He got up and left the room on the pretext of visiting the bathroom, clicking on his handset as he exited the lounge.

"Syrinx, it's Honu. We've just clocked two guys on the perimeter, both carrying high-powered binoculars, although they do not appear to be armed."

"Okay, Honu, send me a picture."

The picture of the two interlopers arrived on Ed's phone, and he re-entered the lounge, walked up to Charly and placed his phone beside her plate.

"Yours, I hope?" he said.

"Yes, they work for me, Ed. But it isn't what you think."

"Charly, I'm not thinking what you think I'm thinking. I think you had them wander around to ensure that no one else is on the grounds who shouldn't be, right?"

"Yes, Ed, exactly, but I'm sorry if that concerns you – that wasn't my intention."

"Charly, I'm cautious, security-focused in the extreme. But no, it doesn't concern me. I have the photos because my folks are out there too. However, they're better trained than yours, who seem to have no clue that my people are there, and no clue that they've had their photos taken. It's one of the areas that my folks can support you in."

"I appreciate that, Ed, and in case you're wondering, they didn't see you arrive. I only made the call this morning to have them cover the grounds to ensure all was well."

"I know, Charly. I haven't asked, but I know it's doubtful that your folks were present for more than 30 minutes before my people spotted them. With respect, call them and tell them they can stand down. Wandering around with oversized binoculars is likely to attract attention. Besides, there are six of my people dug in around the grounds. We are in good hands."

"Eight, actually," Covey interjected.

Somewhat worried, Charly picked up her phone and called her people. After a brief conversation, she advised them to stand down.

"You asked if he had anything to report, Charly. Did he?" She shook her head and looked a little discouraged.

"No, Ed, he said it was only the two of them and the birds, and that I shouldn't worry. He said that if anyone else were around, they'd have spotted them! Eight? You can't have eight people out there. And how large a lens was used to take that shot?"

"My folks aren't carrying telephotos. The shot would have been taken using a phone. I'd guess your folks were within spitting distance of mine."

Charly shook her head again, glancing over to Demetre, who was shaking his, too.

"Okay, it's clear we have a lot to learn," she replied, looking a little embarrassed.

"Don't kick yourself, Charly. I'm not knocking your group; they've done amazing things and saved a great many lives. But when all is said and done, you are drug thieves who then distribute them. Your operation hasn't needed the skills mine has. And if we are going to work together, we must help you up your game."

The four returned to a cold breakfast and then went back to the lounge to complete a single page on what to aim for over the coming months.

They completed the work in a few hours, and Covey and Ed were gathering their things, ready to leave.

"Before you go, Ed," said Charly, "can we have a quick word in private?"

"Sure, Charly, no problem."

The two of them went off to another room, and Charly wasted no time.

"Ed, I am concerned, and if I'm honest, I was a little put out by your dismissing Hagen as the interface to your group. I'd like to understand why."

"I'm not ready to provide detail on the backgrounds of my people. However, Creak has a set of skills that have been crucial to our success, and he has concerns about Hagen."

"And what concerns does he have?" said Charly, feeling herself becoming a little emotional.

"For now, Charly, let's say it would be unlikely that any major security unit would employ him."

"Ed, that's not good enough, I'm sorry. I need to know what concerns you about him. He's been with me over two years, and he gets things done. It's why he's at the top table."

"Or maybe not. Maybe if you reflect further, it's his fawning nature that attracts you to him?"

Charly, leaning in, said, "That's insulting, Ed. I don't need, or hire, sycophants."

"Okay, Charly, calm down. I don't mean to insult you. But the reality is, my folks feel he's an insecure individual, and, frankly, of low ability; and that he sucks up just a little too much."

Charly was now incandescent and made clear that she disagreed but would respect Ed's decision.

"This hasn't helped us bond, Charly. I'm sorry about that. I must go with the views of people I would trust with my life. I hope Creak is wrong and that we are over-reacting. But that's our position for now. So please, let's not you and I fall out over this."

"Okay, Ed. We've both said our piece, and something good has come out of this conversation."

"And that would be, Charly?"

"I know if you are thinking it, you'll say it. And I like that quality. So it won't affect us working together, and

I'll respect your wishes to keep Hagen out of the day-to-day interactions, but I would like you to spend some time with him at some point soon."

"I will, Charly, I will. But for now I'd prefer you not to mention who I am. Is that okay?"

"It's not okay. He will feel I am shutting him out, Ed. But I will respect your ask."

Ed and Charly left the room just as Covey was coming down the stairs. Demetre was waiting by the front door to say goodbye. As Covey reached the door, Ed extended his hand to Demetre, saying that he was looking forward to spending more time with him. Then, leaning back, he hugged Charly and said, "We'll talk again soon, Charly. I want you and I to become partners and hope our last conversation doesn't affect that?"

"It won't, Ed," was Charly's reply as she hugged him. "I'm excited. I feel this will be a great partnership, and I accept that my team has all the learning to do. But our footprint, with your help, will enable us to save a great many more lives."

"I agree, Charly, and I'm looking forward to our next in-person session."

As Ed and Covey exited the house, they too said goodbye to each other. They would again be on the same train but would not interact. Ed would not see Covey again for some time.

On the train, Ed ordered coffee and a glass of water and started to go over his thoughts and plans. He was looking forward to working with Charly's team and the rapid expansion it would hopefully support.

However, he wasn't at all happy about the challenging conversation with Charly at the end of their time together and hoped when she calmed down, she would understand his concerns. Ed fired up his computer and sent a secure message to Creak, instructing him to place Hagen Crumbier under tight surveillance, pointing out that he knew that Creak wasn't accusing Hagen of doing anything wrong but that he wanted to learn more about the man before meeting him. Creak responded, "Consider it done."

Ed knew that having such a strong view of someone he hadn't met would have contributed to Charly's anger. But Ed's group had gone from strength to strength because of the abilities of his team. If Creak had concerns, they were grounded in his extensive experience. Ed also knew better than most that the nature of LPAS meant that you could never be sure if someone supported or opposed them, or if they were easy to turn.

Hans was to Ed the stick by which he measured everyone. Someone he knew as well as he knew himself had been willing to turn in a very dear friend. And if Hans could do that, anything from anyone was possible.

UNnatural Selection – Proposing shouldn't be this frightening

Ed arrived at Leonora's apartment, and Leonora got up from the sofa, kissed him and asked if he wanted a drink.

"A very, very large and slightly warmed brandy, please," Ed nervously responded.

Much had happened that had delayed Ed's plans around proposing. He had planned for some time now to pop the question, but that had been dashed by the events leading up to his best friend's death...

And all that followed. Now back on track, Ed was ready to commit and knew in his heart that leaving it any longer would be forever damaging.

"Well, Ed, less than a minute in, and you've made my heart rate go up for all the wrong reasons! Are you building up to bad news?"

"No, yes, no... Argh! I guess you'll be the judge of that, Leonora. I confess I am nervous, for good and bad reasons. And I need to have a serious conversation with you."

Leonora handed him his brandy, and he asked her to sit on the sofa. "Ed, you look so serious." Which made Leonora far more nervous.

"Leonora…" Ed paused: one second, two, three, five, ten…

"Ed, please get on with it. The suspense is killing me!"

Ed took a large gulp of air, slowly releasing it to gain his composure, then said: "Please let me finish before you interrupt."

"Oh, not another one of those conversations, Ed," said Leonora apprehensively.

"The moment I saw you at the gala dinner, I fell in love with you. Oh, I didn't realise it then, but I knew something had changed in me. You took my breath away when you walked up beside me, asking what it was that made me smile. And while we talked at the table, I could feel an ache in my chest as the feeling became stronger. It wasn't angina, as it was strangely pleasant. But I couldn't explain it. I've known ever since that I wanted you around."

Leonora interrupted him: "You want me around, Ed, like a pet!"

"No, Leonora, I don't mean that, you know I don't, sorry, poor choice of words, I'm nervous. I meant, wanted you in my life. I just knew that I'd met an extraordinary woman."

With the briefest of pauses, Ed continued.

"I believe people's lives are a jigsaw puzzle that each of us slowly builds as our life progresses. And for most, the jigsaw is never completed. There are many pieces to the puzzle of life: true love, friendship, happiness, fulfilling career, good health, trust, security, great experiences, laughter, fun – too many to list. But true love is what we all crave most. At least, I believe that to be true. And sadly, true love is the one piece that escapes all but a few who are fortunate enough to find their soul mate."

Leonora was starting to get a little emotional, not sure where this was heading, but hoping it was what she'd waited to hear for so long.

"I've found that all-important piece of the jigsaw in you. With you, my puzzle is complete. Without you, there would be a hole at its centre. I truly believe I have no life without you. When you are not beside me, and my mind is not deluged by the importance of what I am doing, so little time passes between thoughts of you. I miss you every minute we aren't together. That ache I spoke of, I now know, was my heart going supernova."

Leonora was tingling with excitement and already wanted to jump up and hug Ed while simultaneously thinking that this was a soft side to him that she'd not previously experienced. He wasn't usually soppy! However, it was clear that he meant what he was saying, and she was hanging on to his every word.

"On a planet so big, and home to billions of people, what were the odds that you and I should meet? The chances of being born have ridiculously long odds. But finding that one person you are totally in love with is just as rare."

"No one knows more than I that I have left it far too long to tell you how strongly I feel and how I cannot bear to be without you. Yes, I've said it in other ways, but not as I intend to now."

Leonora was starting to fidget.

"I had reasons for not having this conversation earlier, but not the ones you would think; and those reasons are a significant player in my nervousness tonight. But I'll come back to them in a moment."

Dropping onto one knee and producing a large diamond ring, Ed continued. "I'm sorry if what follows isn't inventive or unique – but... will you marry me, Leonora?"

Tears were streaming from Leonora's storm-blue eyes even before Ed got down on one knee.

"Yes, Ed, yes, yes, yes. I've not wanted anything more than for you to ask me for the longest time. After the attempt on Gabriel's life, I thought I had misread our relationship. I was so relieved that you found the one thing to say that brought back my belief in us and my hope for a future together."

Ed got up, and pulling her to her feet, grabbed her tight and kissed her. Then, taking her hand, he placed the ring on her finger, again asking her to sit down, and he sat down beside her.

He was trembling uncontrollably. Leonora placed her hands on his knees to stop them from jerking up and down.

"Leonora, I'm scared, more scared now than I have ever been. I know I should be elated, and I am. But I'm now taking the biggest risk of my life. And I've taken some big risks over the past few years!"

Ed paused for a fleeting moment before he continued.

"I cannot ask you to spend the rest of your life with me, ask you to trust me. Trust that I am completely open and honest with you, as, sadly, I have not been in the past. Even knowing my belated honesty could destroy what we have. You must truly know me, and I am ashamed and wracked with guilt that you believe you do, when you do not."

Ed's chest was rising and falling, faster and faster as his breath became ever more rapid. Sorrow, fear and sadness began welling up inside as he opened his mouth to disclose his life in the shadows. As he did, Leonora placed her hand ever so gently over his mouth, her piercing blue eyes fixed on his. Staring into his eyes and saying nothing for a few seconds, she finally said:

"I could love no one as I love you, Syrinx."

Ed felt his heart had stopped. A mix of emotions exploded like fireworks through his body: fear, shame, guilt, sadness, trailed by joy and surprise, and ending in confusion. Stunned to hear Leonora refer to him by his codename, he tried to speak, but no words came out. The corners of his eyes crinkled and his pupils rapidly dilated. Leonora removed her hand from his mouth as gently as she had placed it there, and his lip quivered as he composed himself to speak; but before he could, Leonora kissed him and said, "Be quiet."

"Ed, a while ago, I had dinner with my old boss, Jill Landsdown. I'm sure you remember her."

Ed most certainly did, having had a run-in with her when they first met.

"It was a private dinner, and Jill – not that she should have – shared some information that LPAS and MI5 had uncovered. Jill said they'd been aware of a group operating in the UK named POLO for some time. She said the group were well organised, well funded, sophisticated. Jill said they had uncovered small snippets of information using very clever technology tools, including what they believed to be several codenames. Codenames they believed belonged to senior members of POLO."

Leonora paused for breath.

"One of the codenames Jill shared with me was Syrinx. I gave it little thought until later that evening, when Jill said they were sure at least one of the codenames belonged to a senior medical professional. I asked if that wasn't obvious, given that many in such organisations would be medically trained. 'So why only one?' I said.

"Jill replied: 'Maybe, it's more than one.' However, from Syrinx, you get the word *syringe*. MI5 concluded that this bold operator was happy for us to recognise this, should their codename ever come to be known. Jill viewed it as a way of flipping them the finger."

Leonora again paused for breath before continuing.

"When Jill pointed out the etymology of the word, I froze momentarily, as a picture flashed into my mind of the red syringe you have tattooed under your arm. I didn't know how, but I instantly knew that you were Syrinx. I would have warned you, had they had more. But it was clear to me that they had no further leads. So I chose not to let you know I was aware you belonged to an anti-LPAS organisation. I felt that one day you might tell me, trust me. And that I should wait for that day."

Ed was tearful, his brain swimming in guilt, ashamed of his deceit upon hearing her words, and humbled by the woman he loved. He was shocked by her revelation.

Her acceptance of his secret life and his deceit towards her was too much. He looked into her eyes, seeing them through his tears. Then, taking a deep breath, he responded.

"I am Syrinx, and POLO is my organisation. I conceived it, I built it, and I run it. And for that I make no apology. We have saved tens of thousands of lives. But notwithstanding the way I have deceived you, which has truly pained me, I've done other things on my journey into illegal life-saving that trouble me deeply. Things for which I can never forgive myself. Things that have changed me at my core in ways I do not like and which I struggle to come to terms with."

The events to which Ed was referring poured into his mind, as if someone had opened the floodgates holding back his sorrow, guilt and shame. Tears exploded down his cheeks. Leonora held his face. The pain Ed felt for having deceived her was etched into his face. She knew these 'other' things must be truly horrible. Looking at him, she said:

"Ed, you, and you alone must exorcise your demons. Only you can balance the good you have done with the bad that was needed to achieve it. I don't need or want the detail. In war, people do bad things, and this is war. I see that now.

"It is a war to end the decay of human values, and one we must win. I see all too clearly now the damage these laws are doing to society, to the human race.

Damage that is as bad as the lives that are needlessly lost." Leonora paused before continuing.

"Ed, you talk in your sleep. I've so often awoken and listened. You toss and turn; tears often glisten in your eyes. Fear, mixed with sadness, clouds your face. You mumble, but nothing ever makes sense. Your face contorts and grimaces with pain.

"I've often cried, watching you suffer in your sleep. Knowing that whatever demons you are battling, it is a battle you are struggling to win. I've wanted so much to ask you to open up to me so I can help you. But I knew it to be a personal battle and that I must watch from the sidelines, hoping that you would one day muster the strength to let me in.

"It was after my conversation with Jill that, for the first time, I knew the pain and sadness I had watched over many nights had their roots in your secret life." Leonora paused one last time.

"Whatever troubles you so deeply, Ed, you must come to terms with it. I know you are a good man, better than any I've met. And a man I want to spend my life with."

Ed held Leonora tight. The conversation hadn't gone as he had expected. The bombshell to be laid at her door – one he had feared could end their relationship at the very point of having told her he wanted to spend his life with her – Leonora had turned it back on him with the revelation that she knew what he did, if not the details of what he had done. As the light outside began to fade, they sat huddled on the sofa, saying nothing more.

UNnatural Selection –
In an instant, life changes

Ed and Leonora had been in the US for several days, holding a series of high-profile meetings, rallies and interviews on prime-time TV. Their mood was upbeat. So far, thousands had turned out, and the vibe at a rally held two days prior was electric.

Leonora had just completed a thundering speech on the decline of human values brought about by the LPAS laws, and on the alternatives governments had to pursue. Considering this was a speech in New York, with an audience that included many United Nations staff and officials, the standing ovation was something to behold.

Leonora left the stage with many trying to get her attention to discuss her views or shake her hand. Ed moved forward, slowed by the sheer size of the crowd all hoping to speak, shake hands, or congratulate her. He pushed through the public towards the stage fence. Lowering his body to duck under the barrier, now only a few feet from her, he noticed a tall, well-dressed lady to his left as she started to level a gun in Leonora's direction.

Ed immediately stood up, his right shoulder catching the barrier as he did, and positioned himself between the woman and Leonora, shouting, "Gun!" Security instantly jumped from the stage, and as Ed got eye contact with Leonora, gunshots eclipsed the boisterous crowd, and Ed went down. Security quickly overpowered the assailant, and more guards jumped off the stage to assist Ed while calling for any medical staff in the room, and an ambulance.

Trembling, Leonora got down beside Ed, knowing she had to compose herself for his sake. It was clear he was seriously injured. Holding his head in her arms, she told him to hold on; help was coming.

"Your speech was inspiring; I'm jealous," Ed murmured in a low, almost inaudible voice. Blood was leaking from his nose and mouth, making it difficult for him to talk. Leonora was panicking and screamed out for help while holding him tightly, repeatedly telling him to hang in there.

"I—struggled for composure as you thundered away. You—are—better at it than I am." Ed's voice was now even weaker, the colour drained from his face. But he showed no sign of pain, which Leonora knew wasn't good.

"Hang on, Ed; help will be here soon," she spluttered, talking through her tears, terrified that he was slipping away.

"I—can't—see—you, Leonora; come—closer."

She was leaning right over the top of Ed and biting her hand to stay composed. "I'm here, Ed. I'm right here."

Ed tried to lift his right arm, and Leonora held it. "It's cold…"

That was all Leonora could make out, his words now almost indecipherable.

Paramedics arrived at Ed's side, pushing security away and asking Leonora to step back as they got to work on Ed, cutting away his shirt and trousers and pulling various articles from their bags. Shots had penetrated Ed's back, upper left leg and right shoulder. He was bleeding heavily and was now dropping in and out of consciousness. More paramedics arrived, along with an emergency doctor, who immediately took charge of stabilising him.

Within a minute of the doctor's arrival, Ed went into cardiac arrest, and a very calm doctor hooked Ed up to a defibrillator, shouting "Clear" before administering the shock. Immediately after shocking him, the doctor started CPR. Thirty chest compressions, followed by two rescue breaths, before recommencing another 30 chest compressions. The doctor continued this cycle several times before Ed began to breathe.

Leonora looked on in horror, biting down on her clenched fist to help her keep control. Her face was red, and tears flowed as if a river had burst its banks. Her body started to shake more uncontrollably, and as it did, Kai pushed her way in beside her and held her tight.

The doctor and medics continued calmly, but with urgency, to work on Ed, restarting his heart twice. Critical but stable, Ed was finally placed on a gurney and wheeled past the shooter and crowd. Lifting him into the ambulance, a medic turned to Leonora. "I am sorry, madam, you can't travel with him. We have work to do."

Leonora was devastated to hear this.

"I have a car. It'll not take us long to get to the hospital," Kai said, pulling Leonora away from the ambulance.

Around 35 minutes later, Leonora and Kai arrived at the hospital and were directed to a waiting room after a nurse updated them, advising them that Ed was in surgery.

They sat in silence for some time, neither able to muster enough control of their emotions for a conversation to take place. Then, Leonora turned to Kai.

"She wanted to kill me, not Ed. So why did he get in the way?" She was still barely in control of her body, which was still shaking.

"Ed did what he had to, Leonora. He would never allow harm to come to you if he could prevent it. Ed knew what he was doing when he stepped between you and that woman. He would not have had it any other way."

"I can't lose him, Kai." Leonora was sobbing uncontrollably, and Kai hugged her tightly.

Kai was feeling sick, and guilt washed over her. She felt she should have been closer to Ed and have stopped the gunman herself, or, at very least, it should have been her between the assailant and Leonora, not Ed. *That's my job*, Kai thought to herself, *to keep Ed safe* – and she'd failed.

A nurse came in to check on them and gave Leonora a sedative to calm her. Finally, after another 25 minutes, Leonora turned to Kai.

"Thank you, Kai. I appreciate you getting me here, and you being here. I haven't known you long, but I can see how much you care for Ed."

"He's an amazing man, a great boss; I'd give my life for him and should have been closer to him," responded Kai.

"Don't beat yourself up, Kai. You're not armed in the US, and you were busy watching Ed's back from the crowd. You could not have seen her from where you were."

"That's the point, Leonora: I should have been better positioned."

"No one, including Ed, would have seen me as a target. I certainly didn't," said Leonora, who was now pacing the room.

"Ed won't accept that, and neither will I. We should have. You are important in Ed's life and an ex-member of LPAS. That should have set alarm bells ringing," Kai responded.

"Ed looked at me fleetingly, Kai, just before the first shot rang out. A look of knowing on his face. He smiled ever so briefly before his face scrunched up with pain," recalled Leonora, now crying again.

Kai took hold of her, and as she did so, the door to the waiting room opened and in walked a doctor in scrubs covered in blood. Leonora could feel her legs buckle and quickly sat down. The doctor recognised her immediately.

"Mr Thorncroft's a fighter. He's out of surgery, but we've had to put him into an induced sleep, so he's on a ventilator."

Leonora gasped for air, letting out a low shriek.

"He's now in our intensive care unit. Give my team 10 minutes, and then I'll take you up to see him."

Leonora plucked up courage, fighting back the tears. "Will he live, Doctor?"

"The next 24 to 72 hours will be critical. I can say little more than that Ed has a fighting chance, but he is critical. He lost a lot of blood and suffered organ damage. We removed two bullets. The bullet to the shoulder hit a bone and exited his body. The bullet to his back caused most of the damage."

"Thank you, Doctor," came the reply from a tearful, visibly shaking Leonora.

"I'll be back in 10 minutes and take you to him." With that, the doctor exited the waiting room, and Kai kissed Leonora on the head, telling her Ed was way too strong to let this be the end of him. As she did, Kai herself became overrun with emotions, trying hard not to cry but unable to stop tears rushing down her face.

"He'd be chuffed, Kai, that the two of us are crying over him," Leonora quipped, now trying to comfort Kai.

Kai smiled, as did Leonora. He'd made it through surgery, and that gave them hope. True to his word, the doctor returned to take Leonora to see Ed.

"Doctor, I'd like my friend to come too. Ed and Kai are very close friends," said Leonora, a pleading look in her eyes.

"Sure thing," responded the doctor.

Leonora and Kai entered the room Ed was in, in ITU. Ahead of them, Ed resembled a cyborg, with wires seemingly entering and exiting his entire body. His head was tilted back, the ventilator keeping him alive.

For a moment, they both froze with the shock of seeing Ed this way, before the doctor said, "I'll give you five minutes, and then you'll need to leave."

Both were looking at Ed in silence. Then Leonora moved forward and gently held his hand, or at least the part of it without tubes, telling him, "You can't leave me, Ed. You promised to marry me, to make me happy for the rest of my life."

"I should go, Leonora, and leave you together." Kai was concerned she was intruding.

"No, Kai, I want you to stay. And Ed would want you to be here too."

Silence fell over the room, except for the low-level beeping from some of the machines and the whooshing sound of the ventilator, which seemingly became louder as time passed. A few minutes later, the doctor returned.

"I am sorry, we need to do some checks on him. We will take good care of him."

Leonora and Kai left the room, returning to the waiting area a floor below. Leonora turned to Kai.

"Ed told me once, on one of those rare occasions he spoke in any detail about his patients, that he had spent hours in surgery patching up a man who had been stabbed multiple times outside a bar in London. Ed said the man was in a real mess when he arrived in the operating room, where Ed then spent three hours working on him. He said he didn't expect him to pull through, but two days later, he was sitting up in bed, sipping tea!

"Ed was chuffed to bits at the man's recovery. He said that's the thing with people: we are all so, so different. You seldom know for sure if or how quickly someone will recover from a traumatic experience.

"But he said the human body could perform amazing feats, and he always told close family that there's always a chance – unless he knew for sure there was none."

"I hear you, Leonora," came the subdued response from Kai.

Kai now, for the first time, checked the messages on her phone. She had 15-plus notes from members of the inner circle. Ed's shooting had hit the global news networks.

"Leonora, I need to step out to speak with members of the inner circle. Are you okay?"

"I'll be fine, thank you, Kai. I've learned in the short time I've been involved in Ed's secret life just how close you all are. Go update them, Kai."

Kai left the room to find a private location to make calls, leaving Leonora alone.

Alone with her thoughts, fear took hold, and Leonora, unable to hold back the tears, was bawling. She knew deep down that Ed's chances were at best poor but was trying desperately not to think negatively. However, a small part of her brain kept bringing negative thoughts to the front of her mind that she was batting back as if playing ping-pong. They welled up in her instincts, telling her that the man she loved was not going to make it. She desperately tried to banish them, fearing that just thinking them would make it so.

She was huddled in the corner of the room when Kai returned. Looking up at Kai, in a clear state of distress,

Leonora called out, "I can't lose him, Kai, I can't. It should be me in there. I didn't want him to do that. Why did he *do* that?"

Kai got down beside her, hugging her close. She didn't say it out loud, but she knew Ed was lucky to be alive. And lucky too that the medics were allowed to work on him, giving him a fighting chance.

A few minutes passed as Leonora regained her composure. Then, looking up at Kai, she said (as if having read Kai's thoughts), "This is what Ed is fighting for: for everyone to have the same life-saving intervention he's getting." She paused momentarily.

"I'm a mess, I know, and you'd think it couldn't possibly be worse, but it could be. I know that all too well. Early in our relationship, I said to Ed, while we talked about LPAS, that sometimes I wished he could see it differently. I was of course defending the law and pushing Ed to see it from a different viewpoint. Do you know what he did?"

Kai shrugged her shoulders while shaking her head.

"He made up a cruel story about my mother having a heart attack and asked me if I would want him to help her by breaking the law.

"I told him that what he had just done was horrible. His reply was brutally honest: 'What I just did was put you inside the mind of a doctor.' He went on: 'Do you know what it is like to have someone break down in front of you, beg you to save their son, daughter, mother, father, sister, brother?' He concluded by telling me, 'No, you don't. But I do.'"

As Leonora recalled Ed's words, the emotion became too much for her. She broke down, sobbing, repeating that he couldn't leave her but fearing that he would. Then, composing herself, she continued:

"I didn't have to beg for his life today. The medical team did all they could for him. They gave him a fighting chance. Maybe because of who he is and the bad press the government would receive if they had not. Or maybe they still had room within their quotas. It doesn't much matter why. They spared me the begging, knowing that it would have fallen on deaf ears. Not because they would not have wanted to save him, but because the law would not have allowed them to." Leonora fell silent one more time, and Kai, still crying, hugged her again before Leonora continued.

"I fear the coming hours, Kai. I don't know what I will do if Ed is not beside me when I wake up in the morning, laughing with me when I laugh and crying when I cry. And I know his work, legal and otherwise, must continue. Ed started me on this journey to fight these laws with his hypothetical story about my mother. It is a journey I want so much to finish with him by my side. But it is a journey I must not walk away from if he cannot be there with me…"